SUPERHEROES SUCK

JAMIE ZAKIAN

Month9Books

ePub ISBN: 978-1-946700-91-9
Mobi ISBN: 978-1-946700-92-6
Trade Paperback ISBN: 978-1-946700-69-8

Published by Month9Books, Raleigh, NC 27609
Cover design by Danielle Doolittle

Month9Books

To my sister, Nikki, who is a super hero in my eyes.

SUPERHEROES SUCK

Shay drummed her fingers on the taxi's vinyl seat as she stared out the window beside her. Flashes of blue lightning lit the tall buildings in the distance, and people ran by the cab in waves. Men with briefcases and women clutching shopping bags pushed and shoved each other in attempts to flee the disturbance a few blocks away.

A boom rattled everything in the car, including the contents of Shay's stomach, and she turned toward her sister. As always, Evie looked super-professional in her power suit and killer heels. Not one strand of hair strayed from her sister's tightly wound bun as the woman typed away on her cell phone's screen. If Evie paid as much attention to her surrounding as she did her appearance, they might not be sitting in the back of a taxi going nowhere during a riotous commotion.

Another crowd of people ran by the taxi. They pointed at the sky while snapping pics of something Shay couldn't see. She let out a huff, but didn't gain a reaction from her sister. A loud throat clearing and a nudge to Evie's arm didn't work either. Evie's infatuation with the statistic reports on her cell phone's screen would go on all night if Shay didn't take drastic measures.

She brought her lips inches from Evie's ear, bit back a smile, and yelled, "You're gonna miss it."

Evie jumped in her seat. The cell phone slipped from her hand and clanked to the floor. "Rude. Are you sixteen or six?"

"This traffic isn't going to budge." Shay picked the fallen cell phone off the sticky floor mat and handed it to Evie. "The superhero spot-it map just dropped a pin on Park and First. The comments say there's a full-on superhero smack down. It's only one block over."

"Right." Evie tossed a twenty into the front seat. "Thanks, sir. We'll walk from here."

Shay waited with her cab door open until Evie nodded at her. Then, she climbed from the car. Evie's perpetual confidence, and the woman's unwavering courage, hadn't transferred into Shay. The panicked screams that echoed off skyscrapers still stung her ears, and the shivers running beneath her skin continued to raise the little hairs on her arms. She ran to Evie's side. When Evie reached out for her, she automatically latched onto her older sister's arm.

"You good?" Evie asked in her momish tone.

"Yeah." Shay yanked her hands off Evie's arm, then pushed her sister away to cover her scaredy-cat behavior. She turned toward the sounds of an explosion, and face-planted into a hysterical woman's chest.

The lady didn't stop her ear-piercing shriek, or slow her mad-dash down the slightly quaking road. Shay jumped to the side to keep from getting mowed over by the frantic woman and banged her knee against the taxi's steel bumper.

Of course, her sister had seen the entire thing. Evie crossed her arms as she looked at Shay with a rather smug expression, and snarky comments brewed within Shay's mind. Before she could unload them, Evie grabbed her by the wrist and pulled her down the crowded street.

Together, they ran past the cars lined up on the boulevard, weaved around the many people who stood stunned in the street, and headed toward the flashes of blue light.

Although Shay would never admit to it, she was happy her sister held her hand tight. A girl could be trampled if she didn't have a big-bad Evie to plow through a crowd. Plus, it helped with the whole scared out of her mind thing.

Elbows struck Shay's chest as she maneuvered through the mob scene. The ground rumbled beneath her shoes and a low growl vibrated the air. She looked up as a streak of fire cut across the sky. Within the flames, two men fought each other. They punched one another inside a speeding ball of fire, right up until the moment they crashed into Liberty Bank.

The bright lights that lit each window in the towering skyscraper flickered out. Chunks of stone and pointed glass rained down onto the sidewalk as a burst of fire blew from the fresh hole in the now dark building.

Every person who'd crammed into the street around Shay either cowered, screamed, or scurried to find shelter. Not Evie. Evie whipped out her cell phone.

"Seriously," Shay yelled, flinching every time a piece of Gemini City's premier financial institution slammed against the pavement beside her.

"I need pics." Evie stood firm in her high heels. You'd never guess giant hunks of skyscraper were crashing to the ground all around her the way she held steady, snapping pictures.

Shay was steady too, though not by choice. Fear had clutched onto her body and rooted her in place. Only her stare moved, bouncing between Evie and the two men who pounded each other's bodies as they plummeted from the hole in the bank fifteen stories above her.

"Watch it," a man shouted.

Somebody gripped Shay by the shoulders and pulled her backward. A car flew through the air right in front of her face, close enough for her to see the shock in her own eyes reflected off the car's shiny fender. The large sedan sailed like a toy across the street, then smashed like a wrecking ball into the coffeehouse.

"Jeez, kid. Don't you know to watch out when the super-freaks are fighting?"

"Yeah, yeah." Shay waved the guy off and hurried back to Evie's side. She peeked at her sister's cell phone, reading its display. *Firestorm using excessive powers, destroyed Liberty Bank. Mr. Amazing showing blatant disregard for human lives by tossing vehicles.*

"This is great, isn't it?" said a woman with a wide smile as she weaved to see beyond the ever-growing spectators. "Just like a movie."

"Great?" Evie barked. "These jerks are wrecking the city."

"Who else is gonna save us from the villains?" The woman flipped Evie off then walked away, just in time for Shay to see Electric-Luxie zap Antiserum.

Electric-Luxie, and all her awesomeness, knocked the supervillain to his back with her thick bolts of lightning, which also split a one-inch fissure down First Avenue.

The people cheered, and the crowd shuffled closer to the three superheroes who stood over the downed villain.

"Ridiculous," Evie said, continuing to work on her incident report.

Super-people brawls had become a common occurrence the last ten years. The bad guys would do something bad, then the good guys would wreck everything to punish them.

The repercussions of super-battles had affected Shay deeply. If she were as old as Evie—if she could remember her parents as anything other than casualties to superhero violence—perhaps she'd be scornful toward the display. But she wasn't. The wonder of witnessing the only five people known to man with super-powered abilities still enthralled her. She hated herself for the excitement she felt, for the awe she held toward what the masses called heroes and villains, but she couldn't help herself. It really was like a movie.

"Don't you wanna watch?" she asked, glancing at Evie.

Evie looked up from her cell phone, for half-a-second, then continued typing. "If I file this report first, I'll be assigned as lead adjustor. A superhero claim this size would net one hell of a commission."

The cheers intensified, the crowd grew thicker, and Shay climbed atop a trash can to get a better view. Beyond the sea of heads, and amid the flaming hunks of broken skyscrapers, Mr. Amazing pulled Electric-Luxie close. The two superheroes gazed into each other's eyes. A hush befell the hundreds of bystanders, even Evie held her breath. Then, they kissed.

A collective gasp rolled over the crowd of onlookers. The intense romance generating between the two superheroes brought a smile to Shay's lips, though she'd blame it on the people's predictability if anyone asked.

"Get down from there," Evie said while typing on her phone's screen. "I'm a government indemnity agent. How's that look?"

Shay jumped to the sidewalk. By the time she looked back at the fire and rubble beside Liberty Bank, the trio of heroes and the battered villain were gone. The people dispersed quickly, leaving police and firefighters to gawk at what could only be described as a war scene.

"What are we going to do tomorrow morning?" said an older man in a fire chief get-up while rubbing his forehead.

Evie stepped closer to the uniformed men and women who'd gathered to stare at the smoldering rubble around them.

"I've already filed an incident report and contacted Emergency Superhero Reparations." Evie pulled her wallet from her purse and flashed her golden badge. "I'm Evie Sinclair, an agent with Gemini City Indemnity."

"A claims adjustor!"

The police swarmed Evie, shaking her hand like she was some kind of rock star, and Shay snickered. This happened every time her sister whipped out that badge. It seemed insurance agents were more popular than superheroes these days.

"Should I send out a press release on the evening news cancelling schools and businesses tomorrow?" asked the police captain, who practically knocked people over to stand before Evie.

"The east-wing of Central Hospital got hit with a fireball," a paramedic cried out.

"Electric-Luxie fried the downtown power grid, again."

"But rush hour," the fire chief yelled. "Day breaks in six hours and there's a mini canyon running down First Avenue."

Voices rose and right on cue, the shoving started. Evie's weary gaze veered away from the supposedly trained emergency response professionals who bickered like children and landed on Shay.

In that moment, Shay could see the exhaustion chip at her sister's flawless veneer. Her heart ached for Evie. Once turning eighteen, Evie became Mom, Dad, and cleanup crew for both Shay and Gemini City. The last ten years of that chore had snuffed the sparkle from her sister's eyes. And the worst part, Shay couldn't help. She didn't have a single clue how to fix this mess, which used to be Downtown. There were sporadic fires, charred hunks of building, and injured people everywhere. It made Shay want to run home and curl under the covers.

Evie hardened her stare then turned back to face the rabble. "No statements to the press. Have the wounded redirected to Southbend Hospital. The ESR will be here within the hour, they'll coordinate debris removal, traffic rerouting, PR, as well as structural and electrical repair."

The way Evie took control, without hesitation, and the fact that strangers twice her age jumped at her commands never failed to impress Shay.

"My flower shop was destroyed," a woman cried out while tugging Evie's arm. "Please, come, add it to the report."

"The coffee shop," said an older man. "Don't forget about the coffee shop."

"Don't worry." Evie backed beside Shay and took a firm hold

on Shay's hand. "I'll include every incident in my report and file it tonight. I just need an officer to escort my sister home."

"Evie," Shay whispered, since the news cameras had zeroed in on them. "I wanna stay, help you."

Since tact was one of Evie's specialties, she turned and shielded Shay from the spying lens. "You have school tomorrow, and an essay to finish on the economic ramifications of extraordinary powers."

"Come, on." Shay almost stomped her foot then remembered ... the cameras. "Home's not safe, you know that."

"You're getting too old to use that excuse. Now, trade shoes with me before you go."

"What?" Shay looked at her ratty sneakers and then at her sister's posh heels. She'd never worn those type of shoes before—the ones that cost more than an average family's weekly food budget—and hadn't ever planned on it.

"Your shoes? That's my consolation prize for action banishment?"

"I am not walking around a superhero incident scene in *Josepha* pumps. Hurry, your police escort is waiting."

Shay eyed the hunky policeman in his crisp blue uniform. The man tipped his hat and a giggle burst from her mouth.

"Here." She handed her sneakers to Evie then grabbed the heels by their thin leather straps. "Text me every hour."

"I will." Evie slipped on the sneakers, kissed Shay on the cheek, and then hurried off into the crowd of frantic people.

Shay knew the drill. Hanging at superhero incident scenes had become a regular event since Evie got promoted to claims adjustor. Still, it never got any easier to leave her sister in the middle of a wreckage. At least something good spawned from this evening's adventure. She got to put on a fabulous pair of shoes and strut out of there with a hottie policeman.

The heels added about four inches to Shay's height and somehow doubled the grit in her spine. She felt unstoppable, until she tried to walk.

Shay hurried across the lobby of her apartment building holding Evie's heels. The glossy floor chilled her bare feet. It was a welcomed sensation after attempting to parade around on the stilts her sister dared to call footwear. Those shoes were beautiful, and completely impractical for everyday use.

In a rush to catch the elevator, she bumped into the cat lady from 2D. That woman could gab an ear off, and smelled a little funky. While avoiding eye contact, Shay quickly apologized and ducked into the elevator.

The door creaked closed, shutting her in the tiny box ... alone. She'd spent a lot of time alone the last three months, and hadn't particularly enjoyed it. Evie was either gunning for another promotion at work, or had a secret boyfriend. Since her sister was no fun, it had to be career-driven.

Shay pulled her cell phone from her pocket, typed *Home alone, again*, and hit send. The elevator rocked to a stop on the top floor.

Before its door could slide all the way open, her bestie, Ollie, popped his head inside.

"I saw you on Channel 3 News," he said, grabbing onto Shay's arm. "Twice."

"I just texted you. How'd you get to my floor so fast?"

Ollie pulled his cell phone from the waistband of his pants, swiped its screen, and then tucked it back in place. "I was on my balcony, saw you roll up in a cop car. Scandalous."

Shay bumped past Ollie and headed for her condo's door. "You know Evie. No one's gonna legal guardian better than her."

"Don't front, you like it."

Of course Shay liked being cared for, protected, but she didn't need it.

"Whatever," she muttered, pushing open her condo's front door.

The television blasted from the brightly lit living room, its glare reflecting off the wall of windows.

"Oh, Shay. Your blatant waste of electricity is shameful." Ollie walked inside, like he owned the place, and plopped onto the sofa. "Half the city is in a blackout, this is just rude."

"We left in a hurry." Shay kicked the door shut behind her, tossed her keys on the kitchen counter, and collapsed on the sofa beside Ollie. "Evie's, like, a glorified ambulance chaser slash aftermath god. There's no time for shutting things off."

"There's an app for that." Ollie dropped the television's remote control he'd been clicking and snatched the satin pumps from Shay's hand.

"Ooh. Where'd you get these? Did Electric-Luxie drop her shoes like Cinderella?"

"No," she snorted. "They're Evie's, we traded kicks."

Ollie held one shoe in his palm, turning it from side to side. "Beautiful. The new *Josepha* ankle-strap sandal pump. Baby goat leather with golden-tinged satin accents. I wanna try 'em on."

"No you don't. They're impossible to walk in."

"Please, girl. I can work heels."

Shay giggled as Ollie squeezed his big feet into the tight shoes. "Don't break them," she said through a snicker. The sides of his wide feet stretched the tiny shoe's straps, and his heel extended far past its back. "Those are probably expensive."

Ollie traipsed around the living room. It looked like he'd mastered heels a long time ago the way his steps glided. Plus, he scored mega bonus points for pulling it off in bright pink tights with a graffiti patterned top.

"You can't put a price on this." He stopped in front of the floor-length window to admire himself. "I feel like a diva galore, but technically they cost one thousand forty-five dollars."

A gasp flew from Shay's mouth before she could stop it. That was far more than one week's worth of groceries.

"No wonder Evie wanted to snag this job tonight. My sister's a shoe addict."

"Aren't we all?" Ollie continued to walk along the windows, striking random poses. "You think Firestorm would like me in these?"

"Firestorm is not gay." Shay held up her hand, as if that could somehow block Ollie's flights of fancy from invading her thought process. There were many, many videos on the internet proving Firestorm's frisky hetero behavior. She was not going to get into this argument again because one blogger posted an unfounded article.

"Yes, he is. Did you see what he was doing when Amaza-Luxie kissed?"

"Hold up." Shay sat tall on the couch, but that didn't help her comprehend Ollie's babble. "Amaza-Luxie?"

"Yeah. You take Mr. Amazing and Electric-Luxie, smooch them together and you get Amaza-Luxie."

"Umm. That's just … No."

Ollie rushed toward the couch in a clank of heels. "But you saw what he did tonight? Firestorm?"

"No. I was watching the kiss, like all the other sane people."

Ollie waved off Shay. "Firestorm knelt over Antiserum. He lifted the villain into his strong, sexy arms and whispered into his ear."

"That did not happen." Shay flopped back against the couch cushions and crossed her arms. "I was there."

"Da' Nile is more than a river, honey." Ollie snatched the remote off the couch. He flipped through channels until finding a superhero recap, an easy feat on a showdown night.

"Look. There it is." He ran up to the large screen and pointed beyond the close-up of a super passionate superhero kiss. Far in the background, cloaked in the shadow of fallen stone, Firestorm crouched over Antiserum on the sidewalk.

"What the—" Shay dashed beside Ollie to join him in gawking at the television. Sure enough, it played out just as Ollie described. "What do you think he's saying to Antiserum?"

"Something like … I'm sorry I left you and drove you evil. I promise if you change your ways, I'll take you back." Ollie clutched his chest, rocking softly on those high heels.

"I'm being for real."

"So am I."

"Anyway." Shay dropped back onto the couch and kicked her feet up on the coffee table. "Did you do that economics essay?"

"Oh crap." Ollie grabbed his sneakers and headed for the front door. "I gotta jet. Catch ya tomorrow."

"Leave the heels," Shay called out, reaching for the remote.

"Yeah. Yeah."

The door squeaked open and then clicked shut. Shay looked over her shoulder at an empty foyer. A heavy silence lingered throughout the condo, despite the commercial blasting through the television's speakers. She always felt this way when Ollie went home—extra hollow. It was his shine. The guy amped up the world's sparkle each time he arrived, then sucked it from the area when he left.

A buzz shook Shay's cell phone. She wrangled it from her jean pocket and unlocked the screen.

Evie: Do your homework! Aren't you glad I checked in :)

"I'm doing my homework," Shay grumbled, using her toes to reach for her backpack. "And yeah. I am glad you checked in."

The scent of bacon drew Shay from sleep. She almost hopped from the bed and bolted out of her room, except Evie would flip her lid if she emerged unprepared for school.

Without bothering to look, she put on the first pair of jeans and whatever shirt touched her hand. A quick stop at the mirror to tie her hair in a bun and she was out her bedroom door.

"Smells good," Shay said. She rounded the long counter that separated the kitchen and living room then sat at one of the tall stools.

Evie turned from the stove. Her *good morning* smile swiftly morphed to a *but really* leer.

"You look …" Evie curved back to her pan of eggs. "Interesting."

Shay flipped through a magazine, nodding to cover the fact she wasn't listening. "How'd it go last night?"

"One-point-two million in damages. Downtown's going to be a mess for at least a week." Evie sat a plate of scrambled eggs and bacon atop the magazine, covering a full-page glossy of Mr. Amazing's chiseled jaw. "I'm looking at a huge payoff if today goes well."

"Yay. More shoes."

"What?" Evie asked, pouring two glasses of orange juice.

"Nothing." Shay moved her plate off Mr. Amazing's face. Mr. Amazing … what an understatement. His light beige skin, jet-black hair, and the virtuous look in his deep brown eyes went far beyond the standard hunk qualities. He was a super hunk. Electric-Luxie was so lucky just to breathe the same air as him.

Shay lifted her fork and its tip dug into her lip, sending pieces of fluffy egg to her lap.

"How do you miss your mouth?" Evie smirked, sitting on the stool beside Shay. "I guess you have a solid excuse to change your outfit now."

"There's nothing wrong with my clothes." Shay wiped bits of egg into her napkin.

"But—"

"Look at your outfit."

Evie looked at her silky sleeveless top and wrinkle-free slacks. "I just got home. These are last night's clothes, and I still look magnificent."

"I gotta go." Shay hopped off the stool and grabbed her backpack. "Don't wanna miss the bus."

"It's still early. You haven't finished your breakfast."

"It's delish." She shoved a heap of now cold eggs into her mouth then crammed in her last piece of bacon. "But the bus is running early." Her words came out in garbles and she swallowed her mouthful of food, then chased it with a gulp of juice. "Because of the detours."

"Right. Sorry about that, it was my idea."

"No worries. It's a good idea. Evie?" When Evie turned to face Shay, Shay's throat sealed closed. She wanted to tell her sister how proud she was of her and how much she admired her, but it sounded cheesy in her head. "Have a good day."

"You too. Why don't you stop by my office after school? We can go out, have a nice dinner."

"Awesome." A quick peek at her cell phone showed three texts from Ollie, all vids of his morning outfit selection. Shay tapped the screen, snickering as she watched his fashion montage, and opened the front door.

"Brush your teeth," Evie called out, stopping Shay in the doorway.

The moment Shay walked from her apartment building and stepped onto the sidewalk, Ollie stomped toward her with his hands on his hips.

"Oh, no. You gotta go change," Ollie said, shaking his finger and his head at her outfit.

"What's wrong with this?" For the first time this morning, Shay actually looked at her clothes. They seemed fine. The fit was proper.

"Red jeans and a bright green shirt, with polka dots! Girl, you look like a crazed elf who just escaped Santa's workshop."

Shay pulled at the bottom of her tee shirt. She had enough problems fitting in at school. The academic crowd hated her for throwing off the grading curve. She had no coordination for sports, and apparently her fashion sense was flawed.

"There's nothing I can do about it now, the bus—"

Air brakes whooshed as a Gemini City bus rolled beside the curb. Its glass door slid open and Shay's stomach dropped. She'd turn around, run back to her condo, and play hooky for the day, but it'd kill her inside to tarnish her perfect attendance record.

"Come on," Ollie said in a groan, climbing onto the bus. "We'll just have to cross our fingers and hope everyone's gone blind."

In the boardroom at Ling Enterprises, Max shifted in a stiff chair. He stared at his reflection on the glossy table in front of him. The city saw a celebrity … a hero when they looked at him, yet he saw a coward. After years of barely surviving beatdowns, he'd finally captured his arch nemesis and he couldn't bring himself to face the guy. He'd actually shown up to one of Simon and Alexie's superhero meetings to avoid the man imprisoned in this building's basement.

"We've received another summons."

Simon's voice cut into Max's thoughts before it traveled out to circle the wide-open boardroom.

"Let me see that." Max leaned onto the table and snatched the paper from Simon's hand. "My name's not even on here. I'm Max Storm, not *Firestorm*. Who'd they mail this to, *Mr. Amazing?*"

He turned the paper over and read the address label. "Nope. It's to you, Simon Ling, but on the summons they put Mr. Amazing. We shouldn't have to go."

"Max is right," Alexie said, which surprised Max more than Simon. "If they don't even have the decency to use our real names, why should we show up? I'd like to issue a summons to the idiot who came up with Electric-Luxie. It's so stupid."

"You should listen to your fake girlfriend," Max said, winking at Simon.

Simon glowered, almost a growl, his fingers curling into a fist.

"I mean Alexie." Max lifted his hands, scooting his chair away from Simon. "You should listen to Alexie."

"Don't start, Max," Alexie said through gritted teeth.

Sitting around a shiny table and pretending to live a perfect life would be the reason Max skipped the daily superhero meetings.

"I lied to a reporter last month, told him I was a gay man to cover for someone, and I only know one gay man."

Alexie crashed her elbows onto the table. "It wasn't a reporter. It was a blogger, and he only had ten followers and a blurry photo."

"I'm not gay." Simon crossed his large arms over top his puffed-up chest. "Ling men can't be gay."

"The one in front of me is," Max mumbled beneath his breath.

"Alexie. Tell him I'm not gay."

"That's enough, Max." Alexie threw a pen across the table, striking Max in the chest. "You know Simon's father is a Ling, which means he can only be half-gay."

Alexie snickered, Max chuckled, and Simon jumped to his feet.

"You guys suck." Simon stomped across the boardroom. The entire building rumbled under each of his heavy steps. He walked from the room, slamming the door shut behind him, and the concrete wall above it cracked right up to the ceiling.

"Do you always have to get him going?" Alexie stood, slowly, her stern gaze locked on Max. "It's getting really expensive to keep fixing this building."

"You should tell Mr. Amazing to control his temper … tantrums." Max hoisted his hands behind his head as he lounged back in his chair.

"Teasing someone about their sexuality is not okay."

"I'm not trying to tease him. I just want him to be honest with himself. He's miserable, hasn't smiled in … ever. If he could burst out of his shell the way he burst out of this room, he'd be much happier."

"That's not for you to decide." Alexie grabbed the summons from the table and headed toward the door.

"Where are you going?"

"To calm Simon down so we can suit up and go to Gemini City Indemnity. We have a new nemesis." Alexie glanced at the paper in her hand. "Evie Sinclair."

Shay trotted down stone steps, practically running away from Gemini City High. Seven hours of school and she received twenty-seven comments on her clothes, all harsh. Not the best of days.

"Shay. Wait up," Ollie yelled above the chatter.

The groups of people hanging on the school's front steps seemed to grow quiet as Shay passed and she ducked her head lower. A few snickers erupted and she picked up the pace to avoid a twenty-eighth comment.

"Your grandma wants her shirt back," some pimply freshman said.

A freshman! The situation just went far beyond humiliation. She may have to reconsider her choice to stay in high school, and jump ahead to college like her guidance counselor suggested. This whole disastrous day was Evie's fault, for letting her leave the apartment dressed like a Christmas-loving freak.

"What's the hurry?" Ollie asked, jogging beside Shay. "We still have thirty minutes until the bus."

"I'm walking."

"We live five blocks over. Is this because of the outfit *faux pas*? It'll blow over the next time Missy Teagle's thong strap shows."

"No." Shay rounded the corner and headed down Liberty Street. "I don't care what *those* people say. I'll probably never see any of them again once we graduate."

The city buzzed around Shay, its pulse beating like a giant heart of metal and glass. Horns honked, children laughed, a vendor called out his daily deal. The hustle and bustle soothed her mind, covering all her worries in its chaos. She slowed her rushed steps, her chest unclenching.

This had been exactly what Shay wanted. She'd put aside a chance to graduate early, and a full ride to MIT, for the normal high school experience. Having to live down a tragic outfit couldn't be any more normal.

Shay stopped on the busy sidewalk and turned to face Ollie. "I'm cool, just meeting Evie at her office. We're going out to dinner."

"Don't you wanna change first?"

"There's no point now. Pretty much everyone saw me."

Ollie tugged at Shay's sleeve. "Who knows, maybe you'll start a trend."

"Yeah. We can call it loser," she said through a grin.

"No. Geek-chic. Let's take down your hair." Ollie shook Shay's bun loose, draping her tangled waves of blond hair over her shoulders. "There. That covers up the top half of this hideous shirt, which we're burning later tonight."

"For real," she said, nodding.

"I'm out. Gotta get a latte before the bus."

Ollie kissed the air directly above Shay's cheek then hurried back up Liberty Street. She continued her stroll, absorbing the warmth only a lively city could produce.

Sunlight gleamed off the many tall buildings, reflecting a rainbow of colors onto the sidewalk. There were people shuffling all around

Shay, but their voices had become muffled. Nothing could pop the impenetrable bubble of bliss created by the sun's rays, which seemed to shine only on her.

She followed a path of sparkly light, right to the big glass doors of her sister's office building. Once she stepped inside, away from the sun's grasp, a chill crept over her. The wide-open lobby of Gemini City Indemnity was extra creepy this afternoon, being emptier than usual.

With a wave to the security guard at the front desk, Shay ducked into the stairwell and took to the concrete steps. She loved it in here. The echoes, solitude, and colorless walls reminded her of childhood.

Since the accident, she spent every day of every summer in this enormous building. The hallways were the hot zones, where the suits hollered. Top floor was no-man's land, home to the evil executives. Of course, cafeteria was base. But this stairwell, it had always been her special hideaway. A place where no one thought to tread, except her.

The fifth-floor door squeaked, as expected, and she strolled into the hall. The rows of cubicles in the center of the floor sat mostly bare. It was strange for three o'clock on a Thursday.

When Shay stepped into Evie's office, her stare stuck to the closed door before Ms. Mayfair, the only secretary who could handle her sister's 'tude, blocked her view.

"Why is Evie's door shut?" Shay asked, bobbing to see beyond Ms. Mayfair's round body. "She always leaves it open, to spy on productivity."

"The president is in there," Ms. Mayfair whispered.

"Mr. Johnson's here!"

"Not of the country, of the company. Mr. Wellington himself."

"Is that bad?" Shay looked over her shoulder, through the glass divider at all the barren desks. "Did everybody get fired?"

"They sent almost everyone home early. There's some VIP clients coming in. Mr. Wellington came to prepare for the meeting with your sister."

"Wow. That's major. Should I make myself scarce?"

"Probably a good idea. It shouldn't take more than an hour, hopefully."

"You know where I'll be." Shay slipped out of Evie's office. The books in her backpack thumped against her spine as she padded back down the hall. Just like the old days, she slipped into the stairwell and sat on the top step.

As she reached for her cell phone, a door opened far below. Footsteps echoed up the stairwell, bouncing off the cramped walls, and Shay scooted to the rail. She stared down the stairwell. A hint of glittery fabric caught her gaze, and drove her heart into her throat.

Shay jolted back from the railing as the footsteps grew louder, and that's when it happened.

Mr. Amazing, Electric-Luxie, and Firestorm rounded the landing. They were in her stairwell, breathing in her discarded air. Although she knew her jaw hung open, for the life of her she could not get it to shut. Her mind screamed *GET PICTURES* but her dumb body didn't budge.

Three superheroes walked past Shay, staring her down, and a rush of excitement flooded her chest. A silky cape brushed her arm and she gasped, darting her eyes away from its owner.

The door behind Shay squeaked open and her entire body, including her lungs, froze. Only once the heavy door slammed to a shut did her cinched airways open. A giggle pushed its way from her chest, choking itself out when Firestorm sat on the top step beside her.

In almost slow motion, Shay looked at the man whose butt was planted on the very step as her own. It took a few seconds for her gaze to part from the ridges of muscles under a tight red jumpsuit, but she finally peeked at the guy's face. It really was him. Freaking Firestorm was sitting right next to her, so close his musky cologne tickled her nose.

"Hey," he said, as if they were best buds.

With the massive lump in Shay's throat, she didn't think it possible but she managed a pathetic, "Hey."

"You umm ..." He slanted forward to better stare at Shay. "Do we know each other?"

"I don't think so." Shay's smile was so big, her words came out in somewhat of a snort and she covered her face. Firestorm was totally hitting on her.

"I'm not hitting on you."

Shay flinched and her head knocked against the railing at her back. Firestorm was totally reading her mind.

"Sorry to bother you," he said, resting his elbows on his knees. "I thought I ... Never mind. So, you hang out in stairwells a lot?"

"Kinda. My sister works here. I'm just waiting for her."

"Your outfit is ..." He rubbed his chin, eyeing Shay up and down. "Different."

Of all the days to meet a superhero. Though, Shay's attire would probably be a mismatched disaster on any day. "Yeah. I lost a bet, or something."

"Really?"

"No." Shay didn't lie, and she wasn't about to start now because an incredibly hot guy batted his eyes at her. "I just made that up, and I have no idea why."

"At least you're honest."

"I'm a complete weirdo," Shay said, lowering her head with shame. She could memorize the atomic number and symbol of every element on the periodic table, yet couldn't master the art of social interactions. "You should hurry, flame away."

His chuckle caused butterflies to whirl in her stomach. She looked at him. Their stares connected, and the butterflies in her tummy upgraded from whirlwind to uncontrollable frenzy status.

Firestorm was a legit superhero, a person movie stars swooned over, but something bigger enamored Shay. Her guard had dropped, on its own. She'd never felt this comfortable with another person.

"Max," he said. Like he needed an introduction.

"I know. Max Storm. Hey. Can I ask you something?"

"Sure. It's only fair, since I interrupted your stairwell chillin' time."

"Last night, what did you say to Antiserum?"

Max's flirty grin twisted to a hard stare, which shriveled Shay's spine.

"Why do you ask?"

She couldn't tell Max she was trying to debunk her bestie's gay theory. It would be crass, and a cover. There were actual reasons she wanted to know what a hero would say to a villain, ones that kept her awake at night.

"Antiserum killed my parents, ten years ago, when he tossed a subway car into our apartment building. I was hurt pretty bad, have a huge scar on my side. I guess … I just hope he suffers as much as the people he's hurt."

"I'm sorry that happened to you, to your family." Max slumped against the wall beside him. "I know what day you're talking about. I'll never forget it. Antiserum took someone from me that day, too."

"Starflux. She was your girlfriend, right?"

Max snickered. It wasn't a happy one, but the sad, broken kind. "Her name was Jenna. Jenna Reagan. We grew up together, in the same group home. Right here in Gemini City."

"And you were both selected for the space program, the youngest cadets ever."

"Well." Max leaned close to Shay. His arm pressed against her own and sparks ignited beneath her skin. "I hacked the supercomputer, added our names on. Don't ever tell anybody."

Max's warm breath flowed over Shay's cheek, shuddering her muscles. She bit into her bottom lip, but it wouldn't stop quivering. An attempt to reply with her body's erratic behavior would only end in embarrassment, so she nodded.

"Twenty people went up in that spaceship to study long-term

effects of living in space, but only four of us came back. We were … different, changed."

Shay knew this story, had read it in every magazine. "A nebula wave from a distant galaxy hit your shuttle, ending the mission a year in. You, Jenna, Simon, and Alexie were the only survivors."

"No. I joined up with Simon and Alexie after I came back. It was me, Jenna, and the Grant brothers who made it through that mission. Lucius and Cyrus."

"Who's Lucius and Cyrus?"

"Antiserum and Dr. Mayhem."

"You knew them, before."

"Yeah. We were good friends, had big plans on how to make the world a better place. Then that nebula wave blasted us. We watched so many die onboard that shuttle, stranded in space."

Max glanced at Shay and a hint of guilt filled his stare. He must be divulging superhero secrets. The tabloids, newspapers, not even vloggers mentioned the villains. Supposedly, their identities were a mystery. Some mystery, one the government probably forced the media to create.

"The four of us were alone up there when our powers started to manifest. After we landed, Lucius and Cyrus got scary. Jenna and I pushed them into a corner. That night, when your parents and Jenna died, it was our first fight and I failed."

Max's hand landed on Shay's knee and he squeezed. "I failed, Jenna, you, and hundreds of others."

Sorrow radiated off Max, practically vibrating the air. Shay always wondered if superheroes stopped to think about the innocent lives they'd taken. To know Max dwelled on it didn't soothe her own anguish. It actually made her feel worse.

"It's not your fault." Shay placed her hand atop Max's, rubbing gently. "I'm sure you tried your hardest. I don't blame you for what happened to me and my parents. It was just fate."

"You don't have to comfort me. I'm a superhero." Max smiled, but it clashed with the sadness in his eyes.

Shay didn't have to comfort him. She wanted to. Max had incredible strength, powers that broke the laws of physics, but he was also a fellow human being who suffered.

Gently, Shay nudged Max's arm with her elbow. "Even a hero needs comfort."

Like a magnet, Max leaned into her and all the oxygen seemed to whoosh from the room. A surge of heat flared inside Shay's chest, burning white hot within seconds. She didn't understand the sensation, hadn't called for it. Max's very presence awakened something deep within her, something foreign. She couldn't identify the tingle in her chest, which meant she couldn't stop it.

The door behind Shay squealed open, crashing against the stairwell wall, and both Shay and Max jumped to their feet.

"Shay? What the ..." Evie's eyes grew wide as she looked at Shay and Max, standing side by side on the top step in the narrow stairwell, and her cheeks burned bright red. "Get over here."

Mr. Amazing and Electric-Luxie started down the stairs as Shay hurried to Evie's side.

"What's this?" Electric-Luxie pointed at Shay, yet kept her gaze on Evie. "A little sister? I bet she'd like to spend the day flying around the city with a superhero."

"Don't even try it." Evie stomped forward. She stopped at the edge of the stairs, staring Electric-Luxie in the eyes. "The summons stands. It's about time you three take responsibility for your actions."

"You're making a huge mistake, Evie Sinclair." Lightning crackled between Electric-Luxie's fingers as she narrowed her stare on Evie.

"I'm not afraid of you, *Electric-Luxie*," Evie said through gritted teeth.

Shay all but cowered in the corner of the small landing, unlike her hardheaded sister. Evie stood firm, completely unfazed by the raging superhero in front of her. It was incredible to witness, and terrifying.

"Come on." Mr. Amazing took Electric-Luxie by the arm, luring her down the steps. "We'll see you in court, Ms. Sinclair."

"Have a good evening, Mr. Ling."

Evie crossed her arms and stared at Max, who remained on the top step.

"I'll see you around sometime, Shay Sinclair," Max said. He ignored Evie's hard glower, grinned at Shay, then trotted down the stairs.

"Okay." A tiny giggle skirted from Shay's mouth, too quick to stop. Her giddy cloud burst when Evie's grumpy face fell into view.

"What were you doing with that man?" Evie latched onto Shay's arm and pulled her from the stairwell.

The heavy door slammed closed behind them once they walked in the hallway and Shay yanked her arm from Evie's clutch. "Nothing. We were just talking."

"It looked like you two were holding hands."

"That's ..." Shay strained to hold a blank expression, since the memory of her palm resting atop Max's hand pushed for a smile to invade her lips. "That didn't happen."

Evie turned toward her office, only to collide into her secretary.

"Sorry, dear," Ms. Mayfair said. She handed Evie her briefcase and long coat. "You were great today."

"Thank you," Evie said softly. She turned to look at Shay and her stare grew cold. "Let's go," she barked.

Evie stormed down the hallway, jabbing the button beside the elevator, and Shay slowly trudged behind. They made it through the elevator ride and out the lobby without exchanging a single word, but when they got into a cab Evie's cork popped.

"I don't want you speaking to that man ever again. He's twice your age."

Up until now, Shay did everything her sister asked. She trusted in Evie, completely. This, however, she couldn't agree with. She refused to penalize a person based on such a trivial classification as one's age.

"I know math was never your strong suit but Max is hardly twice my age. He's only twenty-six."

"Max?" Evie's shout took Shay into a cringe. "Really?" She waved her hand, as if clearing the taxi of some offensive odor. "No. I'm not feeling dinner tonight."

"Good. I'm not hungry anyway." Shay sat back in her seat and closed her eyes. The light touch of Max's fingertips still tingled on her leg, and his voice continued to hum inside her ears.

There had been a connection between her and Max, one she was certain her overactive imagination blew completely out of proportion. The conversation she'd just had with a superhero in a musty stairwell probably played out much differently in real life than in her memory. In fact, it didn't matter what had happened between her and Max. She'd never see him again outside her television.

Shay burst into Ollie's bedroom. Her abrupt entrance must have scared the crap of out him because a little yelp flew from his lips as he spun in his desk chair to face the door.

"I was right," she yelled in Ollie's face. She strolled into his room, shutting the door behind her. "Firestorm is so cis-hetero."

"How do you know?"

"Because." Shay dropped onto Ollie's bed and laid back against his frilly pink pillows. "He touched my leg." One of those girly swoons spewed from her mouth and she pulled Ollie's blanket over her face.

Ollie jumped onto the mattress beside Shay then ripped the blanket from her clutch. "What are you babbling about?"

"Firestorm sat right next to me. We talked, and he laughed at my clothes."

"Well, that part I believe."

"No, for real." Shay sat up, grabbed onto Ollie's shoulders, and shook. She didn't mean to manhandle him, but couldn't help it. The excitement within her teetered its limits of a blow-out.

"They all walked right by me. Mr. Amazing, Electric-Luxie, and … Firestorm. Electric-Luxie's cape touched me. I probably still smell like it." She held her arm under Ollie's nose. "Smell me."

"You're serious." Ollie pushed Shay's arm away from his face. "Details, starting with a breakdown of outfits, hair, posture—"

"He said he wanted to see me again." Shay laid back, gazing up at a poster on the ceiling of the man himself surrounded by bright red flames.

"Who?"

"Max."

"Max?"

"Firestorm," Shay said, pointing at the poster above her.

"Max." The word left Ollie's mouth in a whisper as he sank onto the mattress beside Shay. "How …? What …? You have to start at the very beginning, play-by-play."

Max considered throwing himself out the plate-glass window behind him once Alexie walked into the boardroom. Her expression could strike fear in the heart of Antiserum himself. She was used to getting her way, even before a freak accident in a lightning storm granted her superpowers.

Alexie pushed past Simon, ripped off her cape, and tossed it onto the boardroom table. A low growl trickled from her mouth as she stared at Max. "What were you doing with that girl?"

"Nothing." Max shut the door. There weren't any employees on the upper floors of Ling Enterprises, but reporters lurked in every corner.

Max turned toward the long table, stopped short by the suspicious stares of his allies. "Shay is … we just talked. She's funny."

"So she took a shine to you?" Alexie grinned, much like a cartoon cat about to eat a caged canary.

"No, Lexie." Max charged toward the boardroom table, heading straight to his seat, which forced Simon and Alexie to stagger back. "I know what you're thinking."

"We don't harm the innocent," Simon said to Alexie.

"That Evie Sinclair woman got on my last nerve." Alexie slumped into her chair at the boardroom table in a huff. "We're risking our lives to protect this city from the random freakos out there, and they hit us with a bill."

Simon sat at the table's head. "I've got more than enough money to cover the damages. If the city is in financial trouble, we should help. It's what heroes would do."

"I agree." Alexie sagged lower in her seat, swaying her chair from side to side. "It just … would've been nice if they talked to us about it, in private, instead of taking us straight to court."

Her boots thumped against the marble floor as she sat up straight. "Wait until our publicist gets wind of this."

"Too late," Simon said in a groan. "He already chewed my ear off."

Max turned his chair toward the window. A million lights twinkled throughout the city. Shay was in one of those many buildings below Ling Enterprises. There was something odd about Shay. She emitted a particular vibe, one he hadn't felt in a long time. He needed his laptop, to hack the web and find out everything there was to know about that strange girl.

"Max?"

"We'll go to court tomorrow." Max rose from his chair. "Present ourselves as the true heroes we are and leave our accusers looking like the villains."

Shay rolled over in bed. For the past two hours, she'd tossed and turned despite the pull of exhaustion. She should be sound asleep, dreaming of a kiss from a superhero. Except, that wasn't her. She didn't pine over daredevil hotshots, or any guys for that matter.

The mechanics of the world seemed more attractive than dating. Science held Shay's heart. If anything, she'd rather study Max than make out with him. At least, that was how she felt before she'd actually met the guy.

A tap, tap, tap echoed from across the room and Shay raised her head off the pillows. An orange glow shined through her black curtains, pulsing before it faded out.

Shay hopped out of bed and hurried to the window. Heat scorched her chest, burning stronger with every step. Before she even parted the drapes, she glimpsed Max's face in her mind. Her heart pounded when he was near. It was something she equally loathed and loved.

Once Shay was certain she'd fully cleared the cheesy smile from her lips, she pushed the curtain aside and opened her window.

"You didn't even look," Max said in a whisper. "You just opened the window, blindly."

"I saw your flame, and ... you know." She leaned on the windowsill and looked down at Max's boots, which floated midair fifteen stories above Tenth Avenue. "There's no fire escape at this window."

"Right."

A gust of cool air whistled between the buildings. Max drifted closer to Shay. Their arms touched, and she jolted back from the window.

"Is it weird?" Max asked, hovering outside Shay's open window. "That I'm here?"

"I don't know." Shay sat on the carpet and pulled her nightshirt over her bare knees. "It depends on why you're here."

Max rested his elbows on the window's ledge. Shadows cloaked half his face and starlight shimmered on the other. The contrast of dark and light created an eerie beauty, which added depth to the man tabloids had branded as a simple-minded party guy.

"I never answered your question, from earlier," he said, so low Shay could barely hear his words. "I begged Antiserum to tell me what he did with her, and he told me she'd been recycled."

Shay wanted to reach through the window and hug Max. His words made about as much sense as a penny, but his expression twisted in grief. "I don't under—"

"Everyone thinks Antiserum can poison with a glance, but it's more than that. He can blast a person's soul from their body. And somehow, he learned to harness them. He keeps jars of stolen souls in a secret vault somewhere, so he can absorb them later when he gets weak."

These details had never made the pages of *Superhero Weekly*, nor the newsreels. Shay had watched every clip from the night her parents had died, from every corner of the internet, but she was only trying to catch a glimpse of *their* final moments.

"I don't know what Antiserum does to people, but there's no evidence a person even has a soul. Theologians have spent lifetimes contemplating the human soul's existence. There's no proof."

"I have proof. I saw Antiserum take Jenna's soul. He ripped it right from her body. It floated past me like a cloud of rainbow light. I tried to grab it, but it slipped through my fingers and into his hands."

Max's voice cracked and a glaze coated his far-off stare. "I could feel Jenna, so strong when I touched her soul. The vibrations of her essence seared into my chest, but it didn't hurt. It soothed. I never felt anything like it again, until I saw you in that stairwell."

Shay wrapped her arms around her legs. She needed to pinch herself, to make sure this wasn't a dream, but didn't want Max to see. In a totally sly move, she dug her nail into her thigh.

Nothing happened. Max remained slumped on her windowsill, the noise of city life still streamed into her room, and her insides continued to burn in the most pleasant way.

Max stared at Shay, as if she were a puzzle without its pieces. "Are you different, like us?"

The whirlwind of tingles in Shay's stomach warped to spikes of embarrassment. Max wasn't there to date her. He came to her window in the dead of night to recruit her into his superhero clique.

"No." Shay's tight shoulders unwound, and her hands flopped to the carpet. "There's nothing exceptional about me."

This she knew. Like every kid in Gemini City, she jumped off her bed trying to fly, attempted to throw fire or electricity from her fingertips, punched walls to see if they'd split, only to end with scrapes and bruises.

"That's not true." Max leaned inside the window. "I'm sure you're very exceptional. You seem like a know-it-all. Maybe that's your special power."

A light knock rattled the door and Shay spun from the window. Evie traipsed inside Shay's bedroom, sparking a different, more painful type of blaze in Shay's stomach.

Shay looked back at the window. Curtains danced on the wind, fluttering in front of an empty window. Her relief only lasted seconds. It had been swallowed by a weird sense of disappointment once she'd found Max had gone.

"Whatcha doing?" Evie sat on the floor beside Shay and joined her in gazing out the open window at a dark sky.

Shay didn't want to lie, but she wasn't about to tell the entire truth either. "Couldn't sleep."

"I wish we could see more stars. All the lights block them out." Evie scooted closer to Shay, leaning against her shoulder. "Do you remember when Mom and Dad took us camping?"

"Yeah. You complained the entire time, then a bug flew into your mouth. You ate it and cried for an hour straight."

Evie snickered as she shut the window. "You forgot about the fun parts—the stargazing, the s'mores." She stared out the window for a moment then pulled the curtain closed. "We should go back sometime."

The sadness in Evie's eyes cleared once she looked down at Shay. "Come on, it's late. You've got school tomorrow."

Shay climbed off the floor and hopped into bed. She glanced at the window. Max wouldn't be coming back tonight. Now that he knew she didn't have powers, he may never come back at all.

"Can I go to court with you tomorrow?" The question completely slipped out of Shay's mouth. She hadn't even taken the time to concoct a solid purpose for her presence in court.

"Why?" Evie asked, crossing her arms.

Shay couldn't say how badly she wanted to see Max. To throw a fit and proclaim she'd go anyway wouldn't fly either, so she spouted out the first useable idea that popped into mind.

"This is gonna be history one day. If I'm there, I could take notes and write a report. I bet I'll get an A+ in civics class."

Evie's poker face held strong. Shay couldn't tell if this conversation would go her way, or south.

"Plus." Shay's tone spiked and she fought to dial back the desperation. "I want to be there to support you. I'm really proud of how you're standing up for what you believe in."

The sentiment came out thick but it was true. Although Shay didn't agree with Evie, she was proud of her sister's courage.

"You have no idea how much that means to me. Of course you can go. I was probably going to drag you along anyway. Goodnight, Shay."

"Love you, Evie."

5

Close to one hundred people crammed into the courtroom. Their voices circled the wide-open space, became trapped by the vaulted ceiling, and melded into one big garble.

Shay fidgeted on the hard courtroom bench. She'd scored prime seating in the second row by arriving early with Evie. Her butt had grown numb, but she wasn't getting up and losing her place.

The bench's solid wood armrest dug into Shay's side as she looked behind her. Every one of the many long benches, on both sides of the courthouse, were full of anxious men and woman. Evie stood at the back of the room, beside the open double doors, surrounded by a flock of reporters.

Cameras flashed nonstop, flooding the people in the back rows with white light. The distinguished members of the press shoved each other to get a chance to stick their microphone in Evie's face and ask ridiculous questions. Claims adjustors had become popular after super-people started wrecking everything, but her sister was taking their fame to a new level.

A wave of cheers echoed from afar and the reporters rushed into the hallway, leaving Evie alone with her small group of lawyers. The courtroom that had been filled with chatter only moments ago fell silent. Now, a hush clung to the air.

Every person inside the large courtroom turned to stare at its empty doorway, and the barrage of camera flashes that bounced off the walls outside them, except for Evie. Her sister strolled down the center aisle, head high.

Not one hair straggled from Evie's tightly wrapped bun. The neatly pressed ends of a pinstriped skirt didn't bunch when her sister sat at the table in front of the room. Evie looked magnificent, like a real woman. It stirred up a tiny thread of jealousy inside Shay, which she hated.

The flood of excited hoots grew and camera flashes bathed the courtroom in white. Shay tensed up. The amount of gasps alone told her three superheroes had walked into the room. People on the bench seat next to her, in front of her, and across the aisle from her all turned to soak in the sight. Her body must've missed the social cue to gawk, since she stayed paralyzed.

Footsteps thumped against the wooden floor, louder, stronger. A cape's soft edge brushed against Shay's arm, leaving a trail of prickly heat, and she looked up from her lap.

Firestorm had walked by her, behind Electric-Luxie and Mr. Amazing. The trio marched along with their confident stares dead ahead, and all those nearby shuddered in their wake.

"All rise," a man called out.

Shay tried to climb to her feet, like all the other people, but her muscles felt like jelly. She slumped lower in her seat, hidden behind a shield of bodies. With all eyes on the front of the room, nobody noticed her sitting there in a stupor.

None of this made sense. She was smart, like, IQ off the charts smart. It was obvious her reactions to Max were due to a release of pheromones slamming into her already jacked-up hormones. Simple chemistry. She'd been told knowledge was power. That was clearly a lie. Her brain overflowed with knowledge, yet she couldn't find the power to will her legs to stand.

When everyone returned to their seats, Shay and Evie locked eyes. Her sister looked terrified, which snapped Shay from her fuzzy haze and kicked on her instinct to protect.

Shay loaded all her positivity into a smile and nodded at Evie. That one small gesture brought the steel back to Evie's gaze. Her sister sat tall, like the badass she was, and turned to face the judge upon his tall bench.

"The case before me is very unusual," said the judge, shifting in his large leather chair. "It seems the city has decided to sue Simon Ling a.k.a. Mr. Amazing, Alexie Colt a.k.a. Electric-Luxie, and Max Storm a.k.a. Firestorm for reparations in the sum of one-point-two million dollars."

"Your Honor," Mr. Amazing interrupted, much to the judge's delight. "We are incredibly sorry about the damage done to our great city over the years, and of course we'd be happy to cover the costs. For this and any future losses the city deems necessary."

Applause rang out. The judge almost clapped as well before quickly shaking off his grin and banging the gavel.

"Your Honor?" Evie said unable to mask her shock.

"Ms. Sinclair." A stern expression formed on the judge's wrinkly face as he curved toward Evie. "You are not to address the court unless instructed."

Evie's jaw dropped, which mirrored Shay's expression to a T.

The judge looked back at the trio of superheroes and his smile returned. "I am impressed. The three of you are faced with the most baseless, despicable charges I've ever seen and you come in here showing nothing but grace."

In a huff, the judge turned to stare at Evie. "Would *this* satisfy the city?"

"Judge Mallard," Evie said in that tone she reserved for those about to get a mouthful of sass. "We too are impressed by the valor of the defendant's offer, but this matter is more serious than assigning financial responsibility. In the second part of the brief—"

"Honestly, Ms. Sinclair, I was too appalled by the brief to get beyond the second page. You do realize the three people you're suing are our only defense against the villains who plague our city?"

"Your Honor," said one of Evie's lawyers. "This is highly unprofessional. By neglecting to read the brief, you give us grounds to take this matter to the Supreme Court."

"All right. Give me a second here." The judge opened a file. Each time he turned a page, an annoyed grunt flew from his mouth. He looked up from the pages to stare at Evie, and a sarcastic grin lit his face. "You want to police the superheroes?"

"It goes beyond that, Your Honor," Evie said. "There has to be some type of standards in place. A code of conduct. They need training on how to fight safely and cost-efficiently. If you'll look at exhibit one, you'll see the statistics show—"

"This is absurd, Ms. Sinclair." The judge grumbled, tossing his glasses onto the stack of files in front of him.

"I don't think you know how fighting works," Alexie said, glancing at Evie

The lawyer closest to Evie rose to his feet. "Your honor. This situation has become quite severe. I've been contacted by several senators. They have concerns this type of trouble will spread beyond our city, to their states. I've heard mention of a task force, marshal law."

Whispers swelled throughout the courtroom, and Shay sagged against the armrest of her hard bench seat. She knew what marshal law meant. Soldiers on every corner doing what they wished without explanation, taking away anybody with superpowers no matter good or bad. Max turned to look at Shay, and she glimpsed a twinge of fear in his eyes.

"Now," the lawyer continued, once his pause for dramatic effect wore off. "I don't think any of us want the federal government turning our beloved city upside down. The Superhero Policing Unit we're proposing is to safeguard everyone, especially our super-friends and protectors."

"We'll do it," Max blurted out, and Alexie slapped his chest. "But there's a condition. I know for a fact that Evie Sinclair is biased against superheroes. That makes us fear how impartial she can be. I also know that Ms. Shay Sinclair …"

Max turned. All eyes followed his pointed finger to Shay, and she jolted up in her seat.

"… is favorable toward the plight of the hero. I've composed a dossier on Ms. Shay Sinclair."

Max lifted a file, and Shay almost jumped from her seat to grab it. She had no idea what Max *composed*, or if any of his information was accurate.

"I think you'll find Shay is beyond qualified to oversee a superhero policing unit," said Max as the bailiff passed the file to the judge. "She, and the other Ms. Sinclair will balance each other out. If they both sign off on a rule, we'll follow it."

Evie stood shocked. Only her head moved, to alternate passing dirty looks between Max and Shay.

"This is an impressive profile," said the judge with a gentle nod. "I'll allow this experiment on a trial basis, but, Shay Sinclair."

The judge looked at Shay and her heart jumped into her throat, gagging her.

"You should consider employment with the space program."

"I'm gonna need a copy of that dossier," Evie practically yelled.

After closing the files on his desk, the judge glanced at Evie. "Both parties will receive official instructions on their responsibilities, as well as copies of all documents presented before the court by day's end. You'll all report back here in one month for review."

A giddy grin skirted onto the judge's face as he stole one more glimpse of the superheroes. "It's been both an honor and a pleasure to have you three in my courtroom. Thank you for your continued service to our city and its devoted residences."

The judge glared at Evie then rose to his feet, banging his gavel. "Court adjourned."

Shay jogged down the courthouse steps to catch Evie. The clamor of reporters gave way to the *boos* of superhero supporters, who hissed at them as they pushed through a picket line.

"Evie, slow down," Shay called out, running down the sidewalk after Evie. "You're gonna hurt your feet. I know how hard it is to walk in your shoes."

"You're about to find out how true that really is." Evie stopped short and spun on her high heels. "What was in that file?"

"I don't know, but I doubt it mentioned I'm a junior at Gemini City High."

The suspicion on Evie's face deepened and anger flared within Shay. She was not taking the blame for something she didn't do.

"Don't look at me like that. I'm still trying to figure out what happened back there."

"Did you ..." Evie rubbed her forehead as she took a deep breath. "Are you ... dating?"

"You tell me. I spend every second with you, unless I'm at school or sleeping."

Evie walked toward a small café and sat at a little table just off the bustling sidewalk. "I heard a man's voice coming from your room last night. Firestorm can fly, and your window was open. If you're in a relationship with him, we can talk about it. Figure this out."

Shay sat in the chair across from her sister, waiting for the punchline, but Evie was actually serious. "I don't know him. Never met him before yesterday. I swear."

"This is a disaster." Evie dropped her hand onto the table, her manicured nails clicking against its glass top. "I'm going to have to take this to the Supreme Court, have the judge's ruling overturned."

"What? You'd let the federal government trample all over our city just to keep from working with me?"

"No, to keep you safe. Why do you think I'm doing all this in the first place? Every time I leave you home alone, I'm afraid something's gonna crash through our wall and kill you."

Chills ran along Shay's spine. She feared the same exact thing, but she couldn't tell Evie. It would only add to her sister's totally valid concerns.

"It's no different than following you to superhero incident scenes, which I've been doing for years."

A cyclone of emotions ravaged Evie's face, but the one that stood out most to Shay was doubt. Evie had been her biggest supporter. She couldn't lose her sister's belief, not over something she was confident she'd excel at.

"Please, Evie. I have so many ideas on how to improve safety and reduce structural damage during super-people battles."

For the briefest of seconds, tears welled inside Evie's eyes before she snapped back into rock-solid form. "I planned on asking for your help tonight at dinner. Even had a lab built based on the pictures you showed me from the courses you took last summer. Those superheroes ruin everything."

Shay jumped from her seat and hugged Evie. "Thank you, thank you. You're the best, ever."

"Try to remember that next week—you've seen the type of tyrant I am at work."

Max waited patiently in the back of a limo as Alexie signed magazine covers. Her fake smile would fade, and she'd scream at him once they were alone. He couldn't escape her wrath; she could fly just as fast as him. All he could do was wait patiently.

After a quick wave to the hoard of screaming people, Alexie climbed inside the car and shut the door. Much to Max's surprise, she turned her annoyed stare to Simon.

"What? This is all his doing," Simon said, pointing at Max.

Simon was a jerk. He could've at least taken half the blame for teaching Max the word *dossier*.

"They were gonna sic the feds on us. I had to think of something." Max grabbed a bottle of water from the limo's small bar, opening its lid. "You two never had to submit to government tests. Probes, needles. I'll take my thank you in the form of a gift, preferably a crotch rocket."

Max lifted the water to his lips and Alexie raised her arm. A thin bolt of lightning shot from her palm, crackling the air before striking Max's chest. His body convulsed, and water spilled down the front of his spandex suit.

"D-Dammit, Lexie," Max stuttered, his limbs juddering from the electric zap.

Alexie snickered. "That's what you get. Follow their rules. What's wrong with you? And what was in that file you gave the judge?"

Max couldn't hide the evidence of his misdeeds. The court documents would be released by day's end. "Shay spent the last four summers attending advanced STEM courses at prestigious colleges. I may have elaborated on that aspect of her life, and forgotten to include other small details."

"Like her age," Alexie said in a sneer.

"This might be a good thing," Simon said, scooting away from Alexie. "I'm getting sick of hurting innocent people, destroying a different building every week. I have resources, and we have powers. We could help people across the world. Instead we spend all our time either chasing Lucius and Cyrus or fighting them. If Evie and Shay can help—"

"What can they possibly do?" Alexie slouched down in the limo's leather seat. "They're just regular people."

"You are so special," Ollie yelled, looking up from the court issued documents in his hand.

"Keep it down." Shay closed her bedroom door and sat on the edge of her bed. "I don't want to upset Evie ... any more."

"Shay Sinclair, co-commander of the Superhero Policing Unit."

In hopes of quieting Ollie's loud mouth, Shay turned her back to him and grabbed her cell phone off the nightstand. "I have eighty-seven new messages."

"Full access to classified citizen's files."

"Oh." Shay scrolled down her phone's screen, swiping away texts as more came flooding in. "Forty-two of them are from you."

"Work hands-on with superheroes to integrate a safe streets program!"

"I know what it says. I read it twenty-billion times." Shay snatched the papers from Ollie's hand and placed them gently on her desk.

"How can you be so calm right now? This is the most majorest of all the majors in time."

"I'm just …" Shay couldn't hold back her excitement, not with Ollie's bright smile shining on her. "I'm totally freaking out right now!" She jumped up and down while clutching onto the sides of Ollie's arms.

"I know, me too," Ollie said through a chuckle. "And this isn't even happening to me."

Evie's frown popped into Shay's mind and a pang of guilt wormed its way through her stomach. "But, I'm trying to be chill." She leaned close to Ollie and whispered, "Evie was not very happy."

"I bet," Ollie said softly. "The spotlight's only big enough for her."

"That's not nice, or true. She had a lab built for me to hang in after school. You can't just do that overnight."

Shay's phone continued to buzz, nonstop, and she looked at its display. "I have over forty texts from randoms at school, inviting me to parties at places I didn't even know existed."

"That's awesome. We should go."

"Yeah, right. I have a ton of research to do. There's this new tech that manipulates magnetic fields—"

"Listen to you. Ms. SPU supreme."

Shay was used to her best friend making up words, but this wasn't quirky enough to be an Ollie original. "SPU?"

"It's what the news people are calling your new unit. I'm gonna jet, let you get to your mega-boring research."

Ollie opened Shay's bedroom door then glanced back. The way he looked at her, like she was some kind of god, brought on shivers. For a second, she thought Ollie might snap a pic but he just grinned then left. If her best friend of forever acted this crazy, the rest of the city would be insane by tomorrow.

Shay clicked on her computer and opened a tab. Her face popped onto the screen with the headline, *Youngest Commander-In-Chief Takes City by Storm.* It was a horrible picture of her and a stupid article, filled with half-truths. She glanced at the window and her heart fluttered. In the smooth glass, she caught her own desperate reflection and quickly looked away.

"Childish," Shay muttered, returning to her computer.

Max stood in the empty boardroom. The overhead lights had been dimmed for the night, but the bright shimmers of the city's skyline beamed through the wide window he stared out. He wasn't certain why he'd come to the boardroom. His penthouse suite awaited his arrival one floor above where he stood. He had left-over takeout and beer in his fridge and a DVR full of survival shows, yet he stood alone in the room where most of his reprimands occurred.

"Hey, Max," Simon said, creeping into the room. "Can we talk?"

Simon stepped beside Max, but Max didn't part his gaze from the glimmer of city lights.

"I get a log every night containing everybody's internet usage within this building." Simon glanced at Max, then back out the window. "You accessed the classified citizen file of Shay Sinclair. Hacked into her private MyPage account."

"Simon—"

"Watched videos of her and her friends, over and over again."

"It's not what you think," Max said softly.

"Well. I thought it looked pretty creepy, like you're stalking a sixteen-year-old girl."

"No," Max said in a firm tone. "I wasn't looking at her like that. I was looking for something specific, trying to figure something out."

"Why she's so much like Jenna?"

Max rocked in place. He couldn't stand the name of his lost love coming from another person's mouth.

"I watched some of those videos," Simon said. "I saw it too. It's incredible, the similarities—very strange—but it's not Jenna. That would be impossible."

"But Lucius took her soul."

"And then he devoured it, because that's what evil does. It destroys."

Simon placed his hand on Max's arm. The light touch, and the compassion behind it, weighed Max down like a ton of bricks.

"You have to let Jenna go. Even if Lucius does still have her soul, her body is gone."

"No." Max wrenched his arm from Simon's comforting grip and headed for the door. "Shay can help me find Jenna, I know it."

"Where are you going?"

"To the holding chamber," Max shouted, storming from the room.

Shay peered down the dark hallway, staring at Evie's closed bedroom door. Soft carpet rustled beneath her toes as she crept from her room.

The hall light reflected off a wall full of pictures. Each snapshot depicted a happy family with a mother, father, and two little girls. Their smiles, trapped behind glass, taunted Shay. It was a life she barely remembered with people whose voices she no longer recalled. If it wasn't for Evie's signature grin, she'd never guess that was once her world.

A soft glow shined through the door's cracks and muffled beats of Chillstep thumped louder the closer Shay got to Evie's bedroom. Her sister must be pretty upset. So far, that kind of music only made an appearance on Evie's playlist two times: when Evie's high school boyfriend crushed her heart, and the night after their parents' funeral.

In near silence, Shay rested her cheek against Evie's bedroom door. Any other day, she'd give a quick knock and walk right in, but today felt different. Her older sister became her occupational equal today. That had to sting, even for someone as confident as Evie.

If there was anything Shay hadn't said, she'd say it now, but a million sorrys couldn't erase the day's embarrassment. Within hours, the media had twisted Evie into a vindictive superhero hater and Shay into some kind of prodigy. It wasn't her fault, but apparently guilt trumped reason.

Shay backed away from Evie's door. Her stupid face was probably the last thing Evie wanted to see. In which case, she hoped her sister didn't turn on the TV, or a computer, or pick up a cell phone.

"Oh, God," Shay muttered, turning toward her room.

The thud of Max's boots echoed off gray walls as he hurried along a tight corridor. Lights flickered on overhead as he marched, then blinked out behind him. Ten stories under Ling Enterprises and encased in concrete, no one would hear his boots pound—no one except Lucius Grant.

A yellow shimmer gleamed at the end of the tunnel-like hallway and Max slowed his steps. An unbreakable clear barrier stood between him and the glow of his archenemy's eyes. The small cell that held Lucius had been lined with a special meta-metal the government created, which blocked the man's powers from escaping. Every fiber in Max's being told him he was safe, yet a slight tremor quaked his knees. His friend, his fallen idol, his greatest tormentor, grinned at him from behind solid glass and it hurt more than it enraged.

"Max Storm," Lucius said in a sneer, his voice just as rich through small speakers as it was in real life. "My most promising cadet, and biggest disappointment."

"I think it's hilarious you ended up my pet. Just look at you, trapped in my big glass jar and locked away in my secret vault. Like Jenna. Like all those other innocent people."

"Innocent people." Lucius lunged forward, stopping just before the glass. "You know. When I collect a soul, I can feel if it's tainted by sin. They were all dirty, every single one of them. Even Jenna's supercharged essence tasted sour when I absorbed it."

An evil smirk beamed through thick glass but Max didn't break his hard stare. He couldn't let Lucius see how desperate he was, or he'd never get Jenna back.

"You're exactly where I want you," Max said, resting his arms on the glass. "Buried and powerless. You played right into my hand, Lucius."

"Antiserum," he yelled, banging on the glass.

Max jumped back. He'd be pissed at his own reflexes except Lucius's face, all red and scrunched, warmed his heart.

"I have another cell." Max gestured at the long, dark corridor behind him. "At the far end of this hallway. Your brother, Cyrus, is a good man. The fact he's stuck by your side this long proves it. He doesn't have to sit in that vacant cell, grow old, and die alone like you will. Just tell me where you keep the stolen souls. Tell me how to find Jenna, and I'll give Cyrus a pass."

Lucius shrugged. He crossed his arms, turning his nose up to Max.

"I will find your vault, *Lucius*, and I'll toss your brother in that cell when he shows up to save your ass."

"Maybe, but you'll never find Jenna."

To keep from slipping into a fiery rage, Max turned and walked away. He'd hoped to finally end this conflict with the Grant brothers, wished the friendship they once shared meant something, but wishes weren't real. Max learned that when he watched the woman he loved die.

"Jenna's gone to you. She's mine, all mine."

No matter how fast Max walked, that man's sinister voice followed.

"You're right where I want you, Max. Or maybe, I'm right where I want to be."

The lights clicked off behind Max but the rants grew louder as they echoed off the stone walls. Every word Lucius spoke sliced, and Max couldn't block them out. The shouts laced in hate didn't stop until Max walked onto the elevator and its door closed them away.

He sagged against the wall. Tears filled his eyes, but he used the heat of his flame to burn them to vapors before they could touch his skin.

A buzz filled the tiny space, and Max looked up to see a camera steer toward him.

"Simon," he grumbled. And that dude had the nerve to call *him* a creepy stalker. He lifted his middle finger to the lens then used it to push the top button.

A collective burst of boos and angered yells, from fifteen-stories below a closed window, woke Shay. It wasn't too bad. With her head shoved under three pillows, she could barely hear the symphony of hollers, outcries, and death threats. Then, a man shouted into a bullhorn and she jolted to her feet.

On her way to the window, she formed a solid plan. Open the window wide, scream obscenities out, and slam it closed. That plan blew to bits when she peeked out her curtain.

Mobs of people gathered around her building. They yelled for superhero haters to be arrested, and waved a variety of anti-Evie signs. The poor police officers were losing their battle to keep the crowd from the now barricaded entrance of her building. Chaos, that's what being friendly in stairwells got you.

"Shay." Evie knocked on Shay's door, even though she'd already opened it. "I guess you've seen it then."

"This is wild. How are we going to hail a cab?"

"No more cabs for us, we're on the government's dime now. There's an SPU agent waiting for us in the parking garage. We have our own sedan, equipped with bodyguards."

"SPU agent, how long have you been planning this?"

"Six months." Evie opened Shay's closet. She pulled out a handful of shirts, cringed, and then tossed them over her shoulder. "We need to get you some plain black clothes."

"Anyway." Shay grabbed a bright orange shirt from Evie's grasp. "I like my clothes." She looked down at the blue cartoon bear that waved from the heinous top in her hand. This shirt didn't count, but she loved the rest of her stuff.

"All SPU agents wear black," Evie said, presenting her silky black pantsuit.

"Well then, I guess it's a good thing I'm not an SPU agent. Now, if you'll excuse me, I've been fully capable of dressing myself for the last decade."

"That's a matter of opinion," Evie called out from the doorway. "I believe we just dealt with a grandma Christmas outfit incident."

Shay shut her bedroom door on Evie's smug face. She kicked aside a heap of neon clothes, taking her favorite leopard print leggings off the lamp. Her style was unique, playful, and totally outdated. Not that she cared. The lab waiting for her couldn't judge her wardrobe, but first she had to get past the hundreds of people, cameras, and reporters that would.

"They can all stuff it," Shay yelled, waving her hand toward the window. She wouldn't change herself to please others. Her comfort and identity were far more important than anybody's approval.

After wiggling into her leggings, she put on a blue-fringed skirt and topped it off with a yellow tank.

"Nice and comfy."

The whole time Shay brushed her teeth, she imagined what her lab would look like. If she'd designed it, everyone would be on hover boards. The floors would have LED lights embedded under glass that changed color with a person's mood. There'd be a complete staff of rocket-powered robots, or maybe cyborgs to monitor her experiments while she was away.

Shay rinsed her toothbrush and trotted down the hallway. Her daydreams of tiny robot helpers and floating tables burst when she stepped foot into the living room.

Two men, whose arms probably held more muscle mass than her entire body, blocked the front door. A young woman followed Evie around while shuffling through papers. And big surprise, they all wore black.

"Oh, no," Evie said, lowering her cell phone. "Go change."

"I look fine."

"You look like a blind, senile clown."

A chuckle rang out from one of the gorillas behind Shay. If she didn't need those bodyguards to get past hundreds of protesters who wanted her and Evie's head, she'd assert her authority by creating a to-be-fired list.

"I haven't done my hair yet." Shay twisted her messy hair into a bun then raised her hands at her sides. "There. Super professional."

"I am not getting photographed with you dressed like that. I tell you to wear black and you pick an outfit with every color besides black."

Shay looked at her bright neon clothes, which may have been a tiny push against her sister's totalitarian ways. "It's not every color. I don't have any orange or green."

"Go get something from my closet."

"No." Shay stood tall, which put her at eye level with her big sister even though Evie wore high heels. "I thought we were both supposed to agree on rules."

Shay's smirk came fast. She tried to bite it back, unsuccessfully.

"Really, Shay? Just ... whatever." Evie typed on her cell phone's display as she backed out of the living room, toward the hallway. "It's late, I don't have time for this. Your breakfast is on the counter. We leave in five."

"But, I already brushed."

"Guess you're having mint waffles then."

Shay sat at the counter and dug into her stack of waffles as Evie marched toward the bathroom.

Max clicked off his TV, tossing the remote on a leather sofa. Shay's life had become a spectacle and it was his fault. He felt like a complete ass. To top it off, he'd just made her a target. Cyrus was still out there, cooking up who knew what, and the Sinclair sisters looked like leverage on legs.

He stepped onto his balcony. His suite sat high above the other buildings, deep within the city's heart. He could see the entire West Side, including the ruckus outside Shay's building twelve blocks away.

His jaw clenched and he climbed onto the balcony's railing. The least he could do was make sure Shay got to Ling Enterprises safely. Heat prickled Max's fingertips and he tilted forward, dropping over the balcony's side.

The seconds of freefall blew all thoughts from his mind. Cool air chilled his skin and a blustery fire scorched his insides. When the two sensations collided, flames burst into an orb around him and launched his body upward.

He cut through the air, weaving between skyscrapers. Time seemed to slow when he took flight. In the blur of life passing by, everything became clear. He could see his purpose. The unnatural fire that surrounded him and the strength coursing through his veins reminded him why he got to live when the other cadets onboard the spaceship died. Fate had chosen him as a protector.

In a cyclone of flames, Max landed atop Shay's building. He'd disappointed many people in his twenty-six years, but he wasn't about to let down fate. Flames crackled, fizzling out as he hurried from scorch marks and into the stairwell.

It wasn't until Max stood outside Shay's condo door that he realized the sizzle hadn't faded from his chest. The stairs thoroughly wiped out the rush of flying. He wasn't nervous, pretty chill actually, but his powers fluxed inside his body.

After few deep breaths, he lifted his hand to knock. He didn't get a chance. The door flew open and Shay stumbled back. Like a whirlwind, the fog cleared from his vision and the spikes of power nipping at his flesh dulled to a gentle hum. The mere sight of Shay calmed his nerves, just like it always had when he'd looked at … Jenna.

Before Max could grin at Shay, two dudes dressed like Secret Service agents charged him.

"No, don't," Shay yelled as the men pushed past her, but it was too late. Max had already leveled the first guy with one punch. Since the fist was already out of the bag, he let it fly to the second man's gut. The man's large body sailed down the apartment building hallway. Max turned to face Shay as the guy crashed to the floor beside the elevator.

"Are you okay?" he asked, reaching for Shay's hand. She brushed past him, gawking at the two downed bodies.

"Yeah, but you broke our bodyguards."

"Ah." Max waved toward the guy at his feet, who groaned into the carpet. "These guys are useless. It's like bringing a knife to a bazooka fight."

"They weren't for supervillains. They were for super fanatical protestors who hate us for *suppressing* you and your kind."

"Oh."

"What are you doing here?" asked the other Sinclair sister. Max couldn't remember her name, since he referred to her as Ice Queen in his mind.

"Sorry to bother you, Ms. Sinclair—"

"Evie."

"Right, Evie. Like evil." Max chuckled, and both Shay and Evie crossed their arms. Two sets of annoyed eyes had pinned on him, and it stole the smirk from his lips.

"I wanted to escort you two to Ling Enterprises, make sure you got in safe."

"An escort is unnecessary." Evie kicked the man on the floor aside so she could close her condo door. She straightened her stiff suit jacket and marched down the hallway. "We have a car waiting in the parking garage. And we're not going to Ling Enterprises."

"Where are we going?" Max asked Shay.

"I had an underground facility built," Evie called out, without looking back or breaking her stride toward the elevator. "The address should've been in your instruction packet."

Shay hurried to catch Evie, jumping over the felled man, and Max followed.

"Yeah. I didn't read that packet, too many long words. Was it important?"

Evie let loose a sarcastic chuckle. "No. Not important at all. It's only every detail about the next month of your life."

The elevator dinged. Its door slid open, and a guy in heels stepped into the hallway. "Hey, Shay. I—"

Words were replaced by high-pitched squeals. The guy waved his arms, sagging against the wall.

"Oh my gosh. Oh my. It's you."

"Ollie," Shay said. "This is Max. Max, this is my friend—"

"Oliver," he said, bumping Shay aside.

Max held out his hand and the guy latched on, shaking hard.

"Firestorm! I'm your biggest fan." Ollie leaned close to Max, batting his highly decorated eyes. "Biggest."

"Thanks." Max pried his hand from the slightly invasive grip and jumped into the elevator. Ice Queen seemed a better alternative than fanboy, until her glare bounced off the shiny wall and hit his eye.

"Shay," Evie said in a bark, which broke up the chatter-fest in the hallway.

"Sorry." Shay hurried into the elevator and pressed the bottom button. "Ollie wanted to wish us luck."

Once the door closed, Evie turned to face Max. "What do you want with my little sister?"

"Evie," Shay said in a high-pitched squawk, stepping between them.

"Watch out, Shay." Evie pulled Shay to her side, keeping her frosty stare on Max. "I think this guy is some kind of pervert."

"Pervert," Max shouted, startled by the anger in his own voice.

"No." Shay shook her head, slowly. "That is so wrong, Evie."

"What am I supposed to think? First, I catch you two making out in a stairwell—"

"No," Shay yelled. The red in her cheeks complimented her outfit perfectly. She now had every color of the rainbow.

"Then," Evie went on, pointing her bony finger at Max. "He finds a way to worm you into his life."

That was about all Max could take of the Ice Queen's unfounded accusations. Even though his brain begged to shut up, his mouth opened wide.

"You brought me into your lives. If you hadn't sued us, I would've never went to your office, met Shay in the stairwell, felt that ..."

Evie crept close to Max, butting up against his chest. Her eyes narrowed and her teeth clenched as she peered up at him. "Felt what?"

The elevator door opened with a *ping*, but nobody moved.

"Leave him alone, Evie." Shay grabbed onto Evie's arm, tugging.

Evie backed away from Max. She lifted her palm to his face, as if to dismiss him, and then pranced from the elevator.

Shay squirmed in the backseat of a large black sedan. For the last five blocks, she'd managed to keep her stare off both Evie, who drummed the seat beside her, and Max, who grumbled beneath his breath in the front passenger seat. She couldn't wait to get out of the car. This ride was just as awkward as the one in the elevator, more so since no one spoke.

"Big day, huh?" Shay tossed out, but got no biters. "I got lots of cool ideas."

"Had an underground facility built," Max said, turning in his seat to stare at Evie in the back. "That's quite a feat to pull off in less than twenty-four hours."

"Obviously I had some time to prepare."

"That's strange. To prepare for something you had no idea you could do until yesterday. And costly."

"My board of investors and I were confident the legal system would do what's right for the citizens of our city."

"And who are these investors?"

Evie glanced out her window. "All that information is in your packet."

"Right. Guess I'll just have to ditch the first day of superhero school so I can go home and get my information packet."

"It's not that easy, cowboy." Evie pointed out the front windshield, at a ratty steel building. "Once we drive into that warehouse, you can't go anywhere without a designated SPU agent. And all departures that are non-mission related must be scheduled at least twenty-four hours in advance. It's all in your—"

"Yeah. My information packet. Got it."

Shay leaned into the front, despite Evie's glower. "Don't worry. I can print you out another packet."

A low huff took Max into a slump. "I don't even have my suit with me."

"You guys will probably get new, dull suits. Apparently, all SPU agents wear black."

"You don't." Max eyed Shay from her purple headband to her pink shoes. "You look … colorful."

"Thanks. I think."

Evie grabbed onto Shay's waistband and pulled her back into the seat. A dark shadow fell over the car as they neared the warehouse. The woman driving pressed a button on the dashboard, and a wide bay door slid open.

Shay fidgeted, tapping her foot against the floor mat. She could barely wait to see the high-tech facility her sister spent the last few months secretly constructing.

Brakes squealed, echoing off rusted metal walls, as the car parked inside a completely empty building. The place didn't look very awesome, and she saw no lab equipment of any sort.

The thick bay door slammed shut, blocking out all shreds of sunlight, and Shay hopped from the car.

"Not very impressive," she said, looking around the bare room.

"This is just a front." Evie walked toward a row of shelves against the back wall, her heels clanking against the concrete floor. "Just push on the last shelf and ..."

The metal rack swung open to reveal a shiny steel door with a single button beside it.

"Great," Shay said, with what she considered a trace amount of sass. "Another elevator ride."

"This one will be quicker, but probably just as unpleasant since Max is still here." Evie pressed her thumb against the round button. Its white background lit green, and the door zipped open. "It's fingerprint activated. Only essential personnel are programmed in."

Shay followed Evie and Max inside the elevator. The door slid to a close and her stomach dropped. It could've been the glaring overhead lights, or the tension in this tiny box that flipped her gut in circles. Most likely the speed of the drop was the culprit. At least, that's what she told herself.

The elevator door opened and everyone walked out, but Shay couldn't move. This might be the defining moment of her life. What she did once stepping off the elevator would brand her a winner or a loser. One day, this could be in a history book. Her name would mean something, and she was terrified to find out what.

A loud beep rang out, a red light flashed, and still Shay's stare wouldn't part from the elevator's silver wall. When a foot tapped, she had no choice. People were probably watching, watching her act like a baby.

Shay took a deep breath and turned toward the elevator door. The irritation in Evie's eyes helped level out her nerves, but then Max winked at her and the nerve-meter blew off the chart.

"Come on, Shay," Evie said, holding her hand out to a white room. "Simon and Alexie will be here any minute. They'll need access to the elevator."

"Who?" Shay walked past Evie, stepping onto the steel-grated floor of a round room. The harsh fluorescent lights gleamed off the curved concrete walls. A few desks were situated in the sunken floor that centered the room and a lone, dark hallway sat directly across from the elevator.

"Simon and Alexie," Evie said, staring at Shay as if she were dense. "You know, Mr. Amazing and—"

"Right. My bad." Shay trotted down the small steps and ran her fingers along a shiny desk.

"That's a workstation for the SPU agents," Evie said, strolling around the room's raised walkway. "Touchscreen computers, satellite uplink, and all these walls are remote displays. So our people can track the action from here."

Before Evie could finish her sentence, Shay was typing on the computer's keyboard. She logged into her MyPage account and turned on her favorite Hermitude video, broadcasting it onto every wall in the circular room.

"And a bitchin sound system," Shay said, swaying to the beat.

Max laughed, and Evie tried so hard not to smile her face turned into a squishy pumpkin scowl.

"Lower it," Evie yelled.

"But I can keep it on?"

"Yeah," Evie said, strumming her fingers against her side.

Shay bopped up the steps, following Evie toward the only passageway that broke the round wall of streaming video. Lights blinked on as they walked. They weren't neon or mood changing, but it was still cool.

At the end of the hall, they cut to the right and Shay stopped short. Large steel machines filled a wide-open room. She couldn't speak. Stainless steel wrapped in wires and the gleam of control panels stole her words, until she spotted a woman tightening gold coils around a prism.

"Is that a … neutrino particle accelerator?" Shay asked, in more of a long breath than a phrase.

"Yep."

"Are we working on space travel?" Max asked, gawking at the collection of million-dollar equipment.

"No." Shay waved Max off. "I can use this in practical applications." She walked forward, into a real-deal lab. She had to clasp her fingers together tightly to keep from embracing the particle accelerator.

Evie ushered Shay beyond the glass barrier that shielded the tech she yearned to touch.

"This is an ionic nanobot ignition chamber."

"Shut. Up." Shay dropped to her knees in front of a gold-plated chamber and opened its little door. A green glow shined on the magnetic plates within, drawing her closer. She stuck her head inside the round chamber to inspect every coil, every thin plate. "I can make nanobots?"

"Only in an emergency." Evie shooed Shay away from the machine and closed its door, the bang echoing off the solid ceiling. "Oh, and the long tuby thing in the back—"

Shay jumped to her feet and followed Evie's pointed finger to the back of the room. "Is that a magnetic field generator?"

"It can't be," Max said, circling the machine. "It has three tubes."

"Right," Evie said, patting the machine's control panel. "That's because it's a magnetic, sonic, and X-ray generator."

"Where did you get all this?" Max asked in a near growl. His tone verged scary and burst Shay's new tech bubble.

"Most of it was donated. Colleges and private labs."

"I think I'll wait for my crew by the elevator."

Shay lowered her stare as Max stomped from the lab. Her happiest day was his most miserable. She shouldn't feel guilty; she hardly knew Max, but she did and it sucked.

"What's in the room across the hall?" Shay asked, attempting to cut the tension in the air.

"Sleeping quarters. A training area with simulators, brick slabs on wheels. Stuff like that."

"Evie. This is incredible." Shay's hand swept the room of shining equipment, all of which she planned on kissing later.

"I hope you can make magic with it, because I have no idea what I'm doing."

The doubt in Evie's eyes chipped at the confidence Shay spent all morning building up. She wanted to hug her sister, mostly to comfort herself. Since this was technically work, and Evie was uber-professional, Shay delivered a nice arm pat. "You're gonna make the city safer, maybe the world."

A buzz shook Evie's blazer. She pulled out her cell phone, glanced at its screen, then grinned. "I have to take this. Hetal, your lab assistant, can show you the rest of the equipment."

"I have a lab assistant?"

"Hetal," said a soft voice behind Shay.

Shay turned to find a young woman with a giddy smile and white lab coat draped over her arm.

"It's an honor to work for you, Dr. Sinclair. I heard all about you on the news."

"Hey, Evie," Shay yelled. "This chick just called me Dr. Sinclair."

Evie nodded. She held her thumb up as she continued to gab into her cell phone.

"Here's your lab coat," Hetal said.

Shay only spared a second to stare at the thick blue thread on the crisp, pressed fabric that read *Dr. Sinclair*. She had to get this sucker on her body before someone realized they made a mistake and took it away.

"I'm twenty-four, originally from Pakistan." Hetal stood in her matching lab coat, hands clasped, head high, as though on display in a pageant. "I have a PhD from GCIT in quantum physics with special focus on electromagnetism, and a master's in mechanical engineering."

"Is that an electron microscope?" Shay wandered toward the tall metal machine, covered with twisty wires and stuffed into a corner of the lab.

"Yeah, with holographic interface."

A gasp flew from Shay's lips. She looked beyond the room of treasures at her sister, pacing as she talked into her phone.

"This is the lab of my dreams," Hetal said in a hushed giggle.

"Mine too." It really was. Right down to the coiled beakers, it was everything Shay ever wanted. All those nights she rambled on at dinner about the latest tech, Evie was actually listening.

"Shay," Evie called out, tucking her cell phone into her pocket. "They're here."

"Oh wow," Hetal said, in more of a squeal. She rocked in place, clutching onto her chest. "I can't believe this is happening."

Shay smoothed out the ends of her perfectly fine coat and walked from the lab.

"Wait." Hetal reached for Shay, but didn't move from her spot in the center of the lab. "What do you want me to do?"

"Start taking apart the sonic field generator," Shay said on her way into the hall. "I want to weaponize it."

Max stood beside the elevator. The music had died out, leaving him alone with the white curved walls. He should just go home. Evie and her SPU goon squad couldn't stop him.

As Max reached for the elevator's button, its door slid open and his buddies stepped from the lift. He'd never been happier to see Simon's scowl or Alexie's leer.

"You forgot your suit," Alexie said, tossing a backpack into Max's hands.

"This looks ..." Simon walked down the steps, into the work area that centered the room, and tapped a touchscreen. "... expensive. I thought the idea was to save the city money."

Max trotted down the small steps and stood beside Simon. "*Evil* Sinclair said it was donated by private investors."

"Evil." Alexie chuckled as she dropped into a rolling chair. "That's funny."

"Did you guys read that information packet?"

"I did," Alexie said, swaying from side to side in her chair. "And it didn't say anything about private investors."

"Don't worry." Simon crossed his arms, which only made his already bulging muscles look bigger. "I'm going to put a stop to this bull—"

"Oh good, you're all here," Evie said. She strolled around the walkway of the round room with Shay in tow.

Annoyance clung to Max's mind, but the sight of Shay in a gleaming lab coat brought a smile to his lips. If her hair were darker and eyes brighter, it could be Jenna standing up there.

"There's a lot I want to go over today."

"No, Ms. Sinclair," Simon said.

The Ice Queen cocked her head back. "Evie."

"Your rules aren't working for us." Simon propped his fists on his hips. If the man had been wearing his suit, and there were a bit of wind to billow his cape, he'd look just like his official action figure.

Evie stood up straight, and Simon lifted his chin.

"The standoff begins," Max muttered. He joined Simon in the Evie stare down as Alexie rose from her chair to take her place at Simon's other side.

"I'm the CEO of my family's business, Ms. Sinclair. Ling Enterprises, maybe you've heard of it. The largest global communications conglomerate in the world. Do you like using your cell phone? 'Cause if the network crashes, I'll have to put in twenty-four hours' notice before I can push a few buttons on my computer."

Evie took a deep breath, then forced a smile. "I'm well aware you inherited your father's company last spring. It was in every newspaper. We can have your network uplinked to our operations center."

"Ha!" Simon's grin melted to a hard glower. "You think I'd give you access to my servers? Good one."

"Okay," Shay said, rubbing her forehead. "Ling Enterprises is big, maybe we can move all this stuff over there."

"No way," Evie practically shouted. "Ling Enterprises is far from secret."

"The secret's out," Alexie said. "Reporters followed us here in helicopters. This location will be all over the internet tonight, if it isn't already."

"I can have the sub-basement prepped and all your equipment delivered by night's end." Simon loosened his tight shoulders and delivered one of his lady-killer smiles to Evie. "Plus, I have some pretty swanky corporate suites. Plush carpet, whirlpool tubs, balconies overlooking the city."

"I can't be bought, Simon." Evie leaned against the railing of the raised platform. "But, I can be reasoned with. I want this to work, for you all to be happy. We'll move everything across town. I'll alert the rest of the agents."

Shay headed for the long hallway that led to the lab. "I'm gonna take inventory of the equipment before they haul it away."

Everyone whipped out their cell phones, and Max snuck down the hallway. He crept up behind Shay, who was hunched over a steel table in the lab, and poked her shoulder.

Shay yelped, spun to face Max, and then whacked him on the chest.

"Thank you," he said, backing out of the lab.

"For hitting you?"

"For having our backs." Max walked into the hallway. He peeked over his shoulder, catching a glimpse of Shay's smile before the wall blocked his view.

As Shay stared up at the largest building in Gemini City, a heavy layer of dread settled over her. Ling Enterprises had thousands of glinting windows, which reached into the clouds and spanned an entire city block, but that wasn't what sent sharp vibes to attack her body. There was something under the ground.

A wickedness dwelled somewhere beneath Shay's feet, beneath the pavement. The energy it emitted was strong enough to create an invisible barrier, one that choked her with each step she took toward the wide glass doors of Ling Enterprises.

"What's wrong?" Evie asked. She placed her hand on Shay's shoulder, which slowed the shivers in Shay's bones. "You're pale."

Evie slid her palm along Shay's forehead, initiating her smother-mother mode. Shay pushed Evie's hand away, just in time to spoil a paparazzi from getting an ultra-embarrassing shot.

"I'm fine. Got a little dizzy for a second."

"Let's get inside." Evie took Shay by the arm and led her toward the building's main entrance. "We'll find our suite. You're probably just hungry. It's six o'clock and we haven't eaten since breakfast."

Once inside, the feeling of doom wore off. Ling Enterprises could be any old office building. Any old marble floored, vaulted ceiling, priceless statues in the lobby, office building.

"Think they have room service here?" Shay asked as they walked past an elegant hand-carved stone fountain and toward the elevator.

"It's not a hotel, but we can get delivery. How about Italian?"

When they got to the seventy-sixth floor, the elevator opened to an alcove of floor-length windows.

"Wow." Shay leaned against the window to gawk at the endless sparkle of city lights. "I bet it's even cooler on the hundred-thirteenth floor."

"I don't think we'll get to see the view from the top. I heard that's Simon and Alexie's penthouse."

"There's no way those two are in love with each other," Shay said, walking down the hall.

"What?" Evie pulled a keycard from her pocket and stopped at the last door in the hallway.

"They don't have that … look when they're near each other. It's not at all like the magazines make it seem."

"It's really none of our business." Evie opened the suite's door and the most succulent aroma wafted into the hallway.

"What's that?" Shay followed the wonderful smell to a cart in the foyer of their suite, which put their overpriced condo to shame.

"It smells like," Evie lifted a silver lid, smiling at a seasoned hunk of meat, "roast beef."

Shay lifted a smaller lid and the scent of garlic trailed a puff of steam. "And mashed potatoes."

"That's … so nice. I'm surprised."

"They're superheroes," Shay said with a mouthful of buttermilk biscuit. "They wanna help people."

"I want to help people too." Evie carved into the roast, setting out two slices per china plate. "People like Mom and Dad, who could've lived if someone like me were around."

"I know." Shay loaded up her plate with sides and headed for the huge television in the spacious living room. "Now grab your silver fork and enjoy your gourmet meal."

Evie fell asleep on the leather couch, sitting up, halfway through *Runway Wars*. Now she'll never get to see the tawdry dress that got her favorite contestant voted off.

Gently, Shay guided Evie onto her side and covered her with a satin throw. How her sister could sleep remained a mystery to Shay. Her brain was wired, and a newly designed sonic blaster waited to be tested. Somewhere in this monstrosity of a building, a lab sat with all her fancy new toys.

Shay grabbed the suite's keycard and slipped out the front door. After hitting the elevator button twenty times, she took a step back. Finally, the door slid open and there stood Max, with his cheesy grin.

"Dude," Shay said, narrowing her stare on Max. "Now it's getting stalkerish."

"I was just headed to the lobby. I swear."

"All right." Shay walked inside the elevator, but kept far from Max. "What floor?"

"Umm." So many numbers lit the keypad, including several levels of basement. "Do you know where my lab is?"

"Yeah." Max pressed B3 and the door closed. "Whatcha working on?"

"I adapted the sonic field generator into a sonic burst shooter, even fashioned it to look like a pistol."

"You already made it?"

"Yeah. There are thousands of videos on the internet, from all over the world, of the equipment in that lab. I know how to dismantle each machine, what every part could possibly be used for."

"That's ... impressive."

"I can't take all the credit. My new assistant is a genius, literally. We had the sonic gun welded together in an hour, even tested it on the brick slabs at the other lab before Simon's movers hauled everything away. It's safe on structures. Now, I need a live test subject. I have no clue what it'll do to a person, let alone a super-person."

"You can test it on me."

"No way."

The door opened to the lobby and Max hit the button to close it before anyone could step on. A soft sway rocked the elevator as it continued its downward decent into the basement.

"I'm not afraid," he said, staring into Shay's eyes.

"I am. It could kill you."

Max stepped closer to Shay and every muscle in her body locked stiff. She was getting used to that magnetic jolt, which hovered around him like a cloud, starting to like it in fact. The elevator lurched to a stop and Shay inched away from Max.

"I'll just have to wait and hope a bad guy shows up."

A devious gleam lit Max's eyes, and he blocked the doorway as it opened to a dark concrete hall. "Will your sonic thing go through holes in thick glass?"

"It should. The sound waves will follow any open path, expanding to the space around them. Why?"

"I have the perfect test subject. Come on." Max took Shay by the hand, pulling her from the elevator. "Let's go get your weapon."

69

Shay gripped a small metal case as she followed Max in what could've been circles. All the hallways they walked down looked the same—narrow, dark, and twisty. The only difference was the air. A thickness hung in the air, growing thicker with every turn. At the pace Max walked, she'd never find the route back. After two more elevator rides, one of which was hidden in a wall, they ended up ten stories underground.

Lights flickered on overhead as they walked, casting a yellow glow on the concrete walls. A sense of dread hit Shay, nearly pushing her backward, but she forced her shaky legs to keep moving. They neared a bend and Max stopped short.

"You can't tell anyone about this," he said in a hush.

"About what? I don't even know what's happening. It feels weird down here."

"Don't freak out." Max led Shay down the passage. A light blinked on at the end of the corridor, shining down on a tall man trapped behind a solid, clear wall.

"Who's that?" Shay asked, leaning close to Max.

"Lucius Grant, Antiserum."

Shay yanked her hand from Max's grasp. "He's here! That bastard killed my parents—almost killed me."

"I know, and now you get to shoot him with your sonic ray-gun thingy. Isn't karma awesome?"

"Max. I …"

"Don't be afraid. The cell was specially designed to contain him, and the glass is some kinda ultra-strong plastic. It's unbreakable. He can't hurt you, unless you listen to the crap dribbling out his mouth. So don't."

"But—"

Max latched onto Shay's arm and pulled her down the narrow hallway. If it weren't for him practically dragging her, she never could've made the short trek to the end of the corridor. Invisible waves shoved her back. Walking toward Antiserum was like walking through a wall of quicksand.

"What's this?" a deep voice rumbled through a crackling speaker. "You brought me a gift to apologize for your cowardice?"

"Yeah," Max said through a smile. "I do have a gift for you."

Max nudged Shay's arm but she just gawked at Antiserum. Even though the man had been trapped in a small concrete cell, behind a sheet of unbreakable glass, his dark eyes penetrated every fiber of her being.

"Get the thing," Max whispered.

Shay's grip on the case in her hand tightened. She'd like to arm herself with a weapon, perhaps twenty, but she couldn't move. Her gaze had become locked on Antiserum. His haunting stare, and the slight smirk on his thin lips made her muscles tremble. He couldn't touch her. A solid barrier stood between them, yet he had a hold on her mind.

Max nudged Shay's arm again, harder, which broke the clutch Antiserum had over her and allowed her to take a breath.

"I'm impressed, Max," Antiserum said, without parting his gaze from Shay. "Why did you bring *her* here, gloating?"

"You probably don't remember, since you've done so many despicable things, but you killed *her* parents."

"And?" Antiserum stepped close to the glass. His wide, tall body crowded Shay. It didn't matter that they stood feet apart. The fact she could turn around and walk away didn't make a bit of difference. The way he stared at her, the mixture of confidence and malice in his eyes would follow her for all time.

"That's not enough?" Max yelled. "Destroying an entire family doesn't faze you?"

A cruel laugh flowed from Antiserum's mouth. It streamed from the speakers, blasted into Shay's ears, and traveled through her body to break her courage. She tried to unlatch her case, but her fingers quaked and she missed the latch a few times before finally clicking it open.

"No." Antiserum smirked. "It's perfect. Kismet."

Shay wrapped her hand around the cool steel of her sonic gun. It was heavier than she remembered, clunky and awkward, definitely in need of a reconfiguration.

"Okay," Shay said, pointing the gun at Antiserum. "Let's do this."

"Are you forcing this little girl to shoot me, Max?"

"No," Shay said with a sneer. "It's gonna be my pleasure, douchebag."

Shay pressed the barrel of her gun to a circle of little holes in the glass. She waited for doubt to strike her, for apprehension to weaken her grasp on the gun, but it didn't happen. She wanted to shoot Antiserum. The tiny piece of her that held cruelty had been awakened, and it needed the man to hurt.

Antiserum narrowed his stare on Shay, as if daring her, and she pulled the trigger.

A sonic wave burst from the barrel of her gun. The clear wave rippled the air as it sped toward Antiserum, moving faster than the villain who backed away from it.

The energy wave hit Antiserum in the chest and flung his body against the wall. Long cracks splintered the concrete he'd slammed against. His grunt streamed from the speakers and echoed through the hallway behind Shay as he dropped face down on the floor.

"Nice," Max said. "What's the range on that thing?"

"Is he alive?"

"I'm sure he's fine."

"Are you guys immortal?"

"No. We can die. It'll just take a lot more than that."

Antiserum rolled to his knees, coughing up a wad of blood. His stare beamed pure rage, and he directed it at Shay.

The ground trembled. Shay took a step back from the cell but that was as far as her freaked-out body would go. A loud hum blared in the hallway, growing louder by the second. The sound rattled Shay's insides, wrenched her already twisty stomach.

When Antiserum rose to his feet, the gun slipped from Shay's hand. She hurried to Max's side as the floor's tremble amped up to a full-blown quake.

"What's happening?" she yelled over the growl filling her ears.

"I was gonna ask you that," Max said, pulling Shay close.

She looked at Antiserum. He nodded at her and winked, as though they shared some type of secret. The cracks on the wall behind him grew wider. Chunks of stone rained down to the floor and Antiserum doubled over, gripping his stomach.

A rolling tremor ran through the building, dropping Shay to her knees. She looked up from the floor and Antiserum flew backward through the air. His back slammed flat against the wall. The stone behind him crumbled and a bright flash clouded the world in white.

The rumbling stopped, leaving a silence louder than the violent roar. Shay rubbed her eyes, tried to blink away the glare that hazed her vision.

"He's gone," Max muttered.

Shay gripped onto the wall and pulled herself off the ground. A thump drew her gaze to Antiserum's cell. On the other side of the unblemished glass, hunks of concrete fell from a giant circular hole in the wall.

"I thought you said that gun was structure safe," Max said, in more of a gasp than an accusation.

"It is. My weapon couldn't do something like this." Shay pointed at the perfectly carved hole that now ran through Ling Enterprises and curved upward toward the street. "There's no way we can keep *this* a secret."

"Cyrus. It had to be him."

"Who?"

"Dr. Mayhem," Max said, heading back down the long corridor they came from.

Shay still couldn't get over how pleased Antiserum looked to see her, like he'd found something he'd lost long ago.

"She's been ... recycled." Shay had been speaking to herself, but Max stopped short in the dim hallway.

"What did you just say?"

Shay took off running down the corridor. She wouldn't say it out loud, wouldn't even think the thought pressing against her mind until it had been confirmed. When the passage split two ways, she slid to a stop. Damn her big brain, it had the worst sense of direction. She doubled back, spotting Max in a jog.

"Can you take me to my lab? Please."

Lucius slammed his fists against a rusty metal table, spilling Cyrus's soda.

"Yo, man," Cyrus shouted. "You splashed on my controller."

"How can you just sit there playing video games? Go load up the weapons so we can finish off Ling Enterprises."

"I just busted you out. This is how we regroup—Call of Duty, gummy bears, and soda." Cyrus pointed a stiff finger at Lucius then went back to pressing buttons on his controller.

Rage fell over Lucius like a blanket, except it wasn't comforting. The fury brewing within him throbbed at his temples and threatened to blow his last fuse.

He stomped across the room and drove his fist into the large screen on the wall. Broken glass tumbled around his hand, slicing his skin. The now fuzzy television blinked off. He pulled his fist back from the shattered display, watching little shards of glass pop out of his flesh as it healed.

"There," he said, glancing at Cyrus. "I won the game. Regroup over, let's go."

"What's the hurry?" Cyrus tossed his controller onto the dusty, cracked floor. "We got other things going on."

"They have something of mine and I want it back."

The muscles in Shay's back screamed, but she couldn't move from her hunched position over the long steel workbench in her lab. Not until she finished splicing together the last of the wires she'd stripped. With half the parts from the X-ray generator and most of the electron microscope ruined, this harebrained scheme of hers better work. Those were her two favorite, most useful machines.

"There you are," Evie said, walking into the lab.

The semi-snippy tone of Evie's voice slowed Shay's hands, just a tad.

"I've been looking everywhere for this place. I think we had an earthquake."

"Not exactly." Shay took a second to choose her words. The right combination would explain the situation while leaving her clear of culpability.

"We were attacked."

"What?" Evie shouted. "See, I knew coming here was a bad move."

"It would've happened anyway. They had Antiserum in the basement."

Evie looked around the room of tables Hetal had loaded with dismantled million-dollar high-tech equipment parts. "We *are* in the basement."

"There's other basements, but I might have a bigger problem." Shay looked up from her concoction and into Evie's worried eyes. "I think …"

The thoughts brewing in Shay's mind were too far-fetched to share, but she couldn't leave Evie hanging.

"I think there are two souls inside my body."

"That's, umm—"

"Not possible, right?" Hetal called out from across the room. "Many cultures don't even believe a soul exists."

"The word is subjective." Shay went back to work. The faster she could prove a soul's existence, the quicker she can get back to solving the actual problem of having two. "The biblical concept might not be real, but there is an energy source that drives all living things."

"So what are you doing?" Evie picked up a solid gold conductor and dropped it back onto the metal table. "With all this."

"I'm making an electro-pulse X-ray machine, to take a snapshot of my energy signature. See if anything is different."

"How does this help stop who attacked us?"

"Oh no, it doesn't. It was Dr. Mayhem. Antiserum is his brother, so he busted him out of the secret basement's highly inefficient prison."

"I don't believe in this soul business, and there's absolutely no reason you'd have two. You just want to hang out in here and play with all this equipment instead of work."

Shay wasn't surprised Evie didn't believe her. Evie didn't know what Antiserum's real power was, or what he'd done to Jenna. She'd been fed the media's lies, like everybody else.

"You don't understand—"

"We'll talk more about this later. I need to find Simon." Evie headed toward the hall. She stopped in the lab's wide doorway and glanced at Shay.

"This isn't why you were brought on. You're supposed to find ways to stop destruction, not add more."

"I know. Hetal's working on a—"

An explosion vibrated the floor, rattling all the glass beakers. The silence that followed seemed extra quiet until two more blasts rumbled the air and toppled a rack of test tubes.

Evie took off down the hallway in a sprint and Shay grabbed her redesigned, slimmer sonic gun. The device on Hetal's table looked close enough to the schematic so she grabbed that as well, then ran after Evie.

"Wait," Hetal yelled. "It hasn't been field tested."

"What do you think I'm doing?" Shay's words might've been lost under the shuffle of her feet but it didn't matter. The city was being wrecked, again, and it was her job to stop it.

Shay ran onto the elevator just as its door closed her and Evie inside. "I have weapons."

A ping rang out when Shay flipped a switch at the bottom of her sonic gun. She held it up, having a very proud-mama moment. The LED lights she'd infused within the new glass barrel gave it a real classy touch.

"This works like a real gun, but with a wider range, so don't pull the trigger unless you have a clear shot."

"It looks like something out of a comic book." Evie took the gun and pointed it at the wall, trying her hardest to look hardcore.

"It's cool, right? And it's structure-safe, but it messes people up. Be careful."

Shay powered on the device in her hand, hoping it would work as theorized. Muffled bursts of explosions rocked the elevator, the lights flickering. She held her breath as the panel on the wall lit up with a red *L*.

The elevator door opened and the tall windows in the lobby of Ling Enterprises exploded inward. Alexie sailed backward through the air, right in front of Shay, then crashed against a large statue. Broken stone scattered across the floor as Alexie's body landed on it with a thud.

An icy chill crept into the warm air and Shay stood up straight. A sinister laugh drew her gaze from the motionless superhero on the floor to the hollowed-out window frames in the lobby.

Glass crunched as a tall figure moved through wisps of smoke. She could feel Antiserum, see his smirk clearly in her mind even though a steel mask covered his face. Fallen wires sparked. Their frayed ends flashed when they bounced off Antiserum's thick plastic suit, but he kept walking toward Shay.

"Now, Evie," she yelled, pointing at Antiserum.

Evie raised the sonic gun. She closed her eyes, squealed, and pulled the trigger.

A clear orb shot from the barrel, expanding as it zoomed toward Antiserum. He lifted his hand. A whirlwind of sparkling blue energy swirled in his palm, but before he could twitch a finger, the sonic wave blasted his boots off the marble floor.

Antiserum collided with the crumpled front door of the lobby, yet his body didn't stop propelling through the air. The doorway's bent metal frame broke off when he flew into it and went with him on his way back to the street.

Shay ran to Alexie's side and dropped to her knees beside the fallen superhero. "Wake up, Electric-Luxie. Get up." She latched onto Alexie's ripped suit, shaking. "Evie, do something."

Evie knelt beside Shay. She touched Alexie's neck to feel for a pulse. "She's alive."

That was all Shay needed to hear. Her legs kicked into high gear and she dashed toward the sound of panicked screams, which erupted over the rumbling explosions just outside Ling Enterprises.

Shay jumped through the mangled metal that was once the front entrance of a building and landed on the sidewalk. Her sneakers slid on the glass strewn along the concrete, and hunks of Ling Enterprises crashed down beside her. She looked up, at a bus lodged into the third floor.

"There's my jar."

Antiserum's harsh voice echoed off every building, somehow flowing louder than the terror-filled screams circling around Shay. The streetlights gleamed off Antiserum's shiny red suit as he stomped toward her, with Dr. Mayhem close behind. This was her shot. She could trap them both and end the plague on this city once and for all.

Shay lifted the weapon in her hand. Simon ran in from the side, landing a punch on Dr. Mayhem's masked face, but Antiserum didn't stop his steady march toward her. She had no choice. If she didn't use her weapon now, she'd be a crazed villain's broken jar.

"I'm sorry, Mr. Amazing," she whispered, pressing the weapon's button.

A giant translucent sphere covered the center of Liberty Street. It crackled and rippled in a blue haze as it surrounded Simon and the two villains, locking them inside a solid dome of magnetic field.

Shay stood tall before the forcefield, face-to-face with Antiserum. He punched the smoky barrier and she staggered back a step. Blue flashes spread throughout the curved surface. A low sizzle grew, building into a loud staticy sound of earsplitting proportions. Dr. Mayhem threw Simon against the forcefield and it blinked out, leaving a hollow stillness.

Shay hurried backward, away from the uncontained supervillain. She tripped over a bent streetlamp, and down she went.

Her side hit the ground, hard, and chunks of rock dug into her hip. A shadow fell over Shay and she covered her face.

The whirl of a sonic gun came too late, hitting Shay's ears after an intense force struck her chest and tossed her across the pavement. Her body flailed, helplessly, as she soared through the air alongside Antiserum. She slammed against a building and the flaming cars, screaming people, and piles of rubble faded to black.

Shay floated on the cusp of an endless gray abyss. She couldn't feel her body, but she could smell her mother's perfume. The sweet scent filled her lungs, overpowering the faint stench of burnt rubber. For a second, she was in her old kitchen, baking cookies with her parents. Then, she was pinned beneath a subway car in her living room, crying as a masked man stared down at her. Fingers tore into her flesh, tugging at her insides.

Her own scream pulled her from a haze of nightmares. She sat up straight, despite the throb in her brain, and Evie hugged her so tight she fell back to the ground. Her fuzzy eyes cleared on Evie's tearstained cheeks.

"You're okay," Evie said, assaulting Shay's face with kisses. "Just breathe."

"You shot me," Shay said, her words coming out in a croak.

"I'm so sorry. I didn't think it would kill you."

"Kill me!" Shay tried to climb off the ground, but only got to a sitting position. The world spun around her, and an ache pulsed throughout her chest. She couldn't get up yet. She could barely feel her tingly legs.

"Relax, kiddo." Alexie held up her hand, lightning crackling between her fingers. "You're lucky I'm a defibrillator."

"Simon, Max?" Shay muttered, rolling to her knees.

The sound of cries filtered in over the thump in her temples. She looked up from the cracked pavement below her.

Charred pieces of Ling Enterprises littered the street. Taxi cabs had been overturned, and broken power lines arced as they dangled against buildings.

A rush of frightened cries drew Shay's gaze higher. Men and women were trapped in the bus speared into the front of Ling Enterprises, and they banged on the windows and screamed for help.

"There's people up there." Shay pointed at the bus and Alexie rolled her eyes.

"I'm not really the saving type of superhero. I'm the fighting one."

The media sure did lie about Alexie's wholesome image. Shay didn't know what to say. She just gawked at Alexie.

"All right. I'll rescue the people." Alexie looked up at Ling Enterprises. "At least our building took the hit this time, huh?" With one big leap, she was on the third floor prying open the bus's back door.

"Simon and Max took off, after Antiserum and his sidekick," Evie said, buzzing over Shay like a gnat.

"Help me up."

Once Shay got to her feet, cheers rang out. She flinched, looking over her shoulder. People huddled in a thick crowd at the fringe of the wreckage. They clapped, smiled, called out her name as reporters pushed to the front of the crowd.

"Let's get inside," Evie said, taking Shay by the arm.

"I'm good." Shay pulled away from Evie, glancing at the cameras. "I can do it myself."

Her legs wobbled but kept her upright. Strength returned with each step she took, and the tingle in her toes faded. She bent to grab her forcefield generator and fell to one knee.

"Come on, Jenna. Get up," she mumbled, pushing herself off the ground.

"What'd you just say?" Evie reached for Shay then drew back.

"I didn't say anything." Shay limped into Ling Enterprises, hobbling over broken doorframes. Had she said something? She'd had a thought, which eluded her now, but didn't voice it. At least, she didn't mean to.

"Dr. Sinclair!" Hetal ran out from behind a cracked marble pillar. Her hands were clasped together, so tightly her knuckles had become whiter than her lab coat. "I can't believe the containment field malfunctioned. I'm sorry."

"It's not your fault." Shay thrust the device into Hetal's hands and headed for the elevator. "It needs more juice." She pressed the elevator's down button, almost in sync with the pound of her brain.

"The lift's not working," Hetal said. "We're running on the emergency generators."

"Of course." Shay limped back through the lobby, toward the stairwell.

"Where are you going?" Evie asked, tugging on Shay's ripped lab coat. "You need to sit down, rest."

"I need to get to my lab and finish my X-ray machine. And I don't care if you believe in this *soul business*, just don't tell anyone about it. I don't want Max finding out until there's proof."

Shay pushed open the heavy metal door to the stairwell. She didn't dare look back, couldn't see the hurt her words must have caused Evie. "Come on, Hetal."

Max landed on the roof of the Windsor Hotel. His flames faded to smoke as he stepped beside Simon. "Where'd they go? We were right on their tails."

"I don't know." Simon walked to the roof's edge, looking at his dark building amid the bright skyline. "We should get back."

"I'm not going back. Not until I find Lucius."

"Max. They weren't there for us. They were gunning for Shay."

"That's ridiculous." Max waved Simon off as he paced along the roof's edge.

"Lucius went right to her, called her his jar."

"His jar?" That struck a chord, which set off a domino effect that led to an all-out symphony. "Recycled. Don't you see?"

Before Max could stop himself, he gripped onto the front of Simon's suit. "People are his jars. The city's his vault. It isn't impossible to get Jenna back, because Shay is Jenna."

Simon shoved Max's hands away. "No. Shay is her own person. Whatever Lucius put inside her, it's not Jenna."

"I can set Jenna free, let her be at peace." Max took a firm hold on Simon's cape straps, but the tight grip and the closeness to his dearest friend did nothing to quell the frenzy within his mind.

"Jenna haunts my dreams, every night. I can't close my eyes. Her face is always there, tortured, scared, looking at me for help."

"What are you going to do, carve Shay open to let Jenna's soul free?"

"No." Max released Simon in a shove. The thought had crossed his mind, fleeing as quickly as it slithered in. Simon would see the guilt in his eyes if he didn't hide them, so he lowered his gaze. "I would never."

"You want to get close to Shay? Touch her skin and hope you feel a trace of Jenna's spirit?"

"Stop it." Max walked away, but Simon followed on his heels.

"It's not right, Max. To you or Shay."

Max spun to face Simon, who stumbled back a few paces.

"You have no business judging other people's relationships." Max jabbed Simon on the chest with his finger. "Can you even see anything from inside your closet?"

Simon frowned. The drop of Simon's lips twisted Max's gut.

"I can see the law, and you're breaking it."

"I never even kissed Shay. Not once." Max turned his back on Simon. He had to get off this rooftop, soar away from Simon and his allegations, away from the fact that he *did* yearn to be near Shay.

"Yet," Simon said, and Max jumped off the building's roof.

Shay stared down at her workbench. One wire. All she had to do was connect one wire and her machine would be complete. The truth she already knew would be fact. Irrefutable fact, ready or not.

"Dr. Sinclair?"

Coils squeaked as Shay swiveled her stood to face Hetal. "Just Shay. As much as I love the title of Dr. Sinclair, I'm not a doctor. Dr. Bhatti."

Hetal grinned. "You're the first person to call me that in a professional setting."

"It's cool isn't it?"

"Totally."

The title meant much more to Hetal than Shay, because Hetal had earned it. Shay hoped to feel that pride, one day, without the involvement of a semi-fabricated dossier.

"Whatcha need?"

"What did you see?" Hetal asked, keeping her stare low. "When you died?"

"What?"

"You were gone for one minute forty-nine seconds. I was wondering if you saw anything, for scientific purposes."

"Right." Shay walked to Hetal's workbench and sat across from her. "I did see stuff."

It was stuff Shay had been trying to forget, stuff that gorged open sewn up holes and let the pain she'd buried seep out.

"Flashes, playing board games with my parents, baking, watching movies with Evie. Mostly, it was just a sense of happiness."

"Your own personal Heaven."

"Heaven's not real." Shay couldn't believe in such a place, the scientist in her wouldn't allow it. "It was just neurons, firing off memories to distract the mind from its body dying."

A flustered look swept Hetal's face, her beige cheeks growing hot pink. "Of course."

"My machine's ready." Shay reached over to her workbench and connected the last wire. A high-pitched whirl and three beeps later, a green light blinked on.

Hetal walked beside the workbench Shay had converted into makeshift X-ray machine. She'd used the side of a shelf to suspend the magnetic plates that would snap a pic of her energy. This prototype would royally embarrass her if anybody within the scientific community saw it, but she was proud.

"All the inventions you've crafted are experimental, based in theory." Hetal powered on the X-ray machine's display screen, chuckling when it worked. "How do you know all this, and how do you turn a concept into workable tech so fast?"

"I spent last summer at MIT. This professor with multiple degrees in physics, engineering, and theology personally mentored me. She opened my mind to so many possibilities, taught me to not let doubt or rules hold me back."

"Was that the advanced stem course?" Hetal asked softly.

"Yeah. It was amazing."

"I applied for that." Hetal slumped against the workbench. "Got rejected."

"Sorry." Shay shouldn't mention she'd been invited by the Dean, without actually applying.

Hetal crept closer to Shay. "What's your IQ?"

If the rejection from MIT stung Hetal this badly, she wouldn't like to hear Shay's IQ score. "You probably don't wanna know that."

"It's not over 158, is it?"

Hetal stared at Shay with hopeful eyes, and Shay cringed. Her score was well over 158.

"You definitely don't want to know the answer to that question."

"Oh." Hetal looked at Shay with awe, as if *she* were a superhero. "Are you ready to try your invention, super genius?"

A snicker flew from Shay's mouth. "Ask me after."

"What should I do?"

Shay climbed atop the table, lying under the X-ray machine's long thin panel. "Get behind the lead wall, and cross your fingers."

The soles of Hetal's sneakers squeaked as she hurried across the lab. "What am I crossing my fingers for?"

"One color," Shay said, mostly as a prayer.

"Ready," Hetal called out.

Shay closed her eyes and pressed the button at her side.

The overhead lights flickered as the machine whirred. After a few loud clicks, the machine fell silent. Shay stared at the display wired to the table beneath her, waiting as the image slowly transmitted.

"Is it over?" Hetal yelled from across the lab.

"Yep. It's over." Shay eased off the table, turning away from the display. The outline of her body was filled with blue light and a tiny bit of red, the remnants of a murdered superhero.

"This test is inconclusive," Hetal said, pointing at the screen. "You have no baseline. Everyone could have two or more energy signatures."

"Are you volunteering?"

"Yeah. I'll do it."

Hetal hopped onto the table and Shay grabbed her arm.

"I don't know. It's like getting ten X-rays at the same time."

Hetal laid back on the table, holding a serious expression. "It's for science."

"Okay." Shay saved her image and reset the machine. "Give me a second to get behind the lead then hit that button on your left."

She hurried, as fast as her sore body would move, and leaned against the lead wall. In this instance, she'd love to be proven wrong. She hoped for the best, but foresaw calamity—or worse, catastrophe. Hetal's shoes tapped against the floor, but no hoot followed.

Shay peeked out from behind the lead wall and Hetal shrugged. "Blue?" Shay asked.

"No. Yellow. All yellow."

Max walked into the lab and Shay almost ducked back behind the lead wall but his stare had found her, like always.

"Shay," he said, and Hetal flinched.

Hetal turned from the X-ray machine, took one look at Max, and backed into a shelf.

"Can we talk?" Max asked, staring at Shay. "Alone."

"Oh." Hetal stepped right then left then walked around Max, practically running toward the lab's wide door. "I'm gonna ..." She motioned to the hall with her thumb as she scurried backward from the lab.

Shay snickered. It wasn't that long ago she became dumbstruck at the sight of a superhero. Now, she just babbled random nonsense.

"How was your fight?" Nonsense exhibit number one. "I mean, did you get Lucius and Cyrus?"

"Alexie said you were dead." Max rushed toward Shay, standing only inches from her. "That you would've stayed that way if she hadn't ... I can't believe I just left you there like that, to die."

"It's not your job to look out for me." Shay brushed past Max. She needed to look busy, so she hurried to her X-ray machine to save Hetal's scan.

"Yes it is. I'm supposed to be a hero, protect those who can't protect themselves."

"Please. I've been protecting myself since I was six." Shay powered off her machine. She was running out of unnecessary tasks to perform. Eventually, she'd have to look at Max. It was better to get it over with.

Shay turned toward Max. Fortunately, he stared beyond her, at the wall.

"This was a mistake, bringing you and your sister into our lives." Max's expression twisted, like he'd just bitten into a lemon, and his gaze avoided Shay like the plague. It brought up a distant memory, one she couldn't quite place.

"Did Evie say something to you?"

"Like what?"

Shay studied Max's face, which was not easy since he looked everywhere but her direction. For a second, their eyes connected and an orange-tinged haze clouded her mind.

"You have that look, baby, just like the night you snuck us backstage at The Shed so we could meet the band."

"Jenna!"

Max clutched onto Shay's hand and the fog in her head cleared. She yanked her hand from Max's grasp and pushed him away. Words had come from her mouth, in her own voice, but their meanings didn't connect to anything solid in her mind.

"I'm sorry, Max. I don't know what I just said. Ever since I got hit with the sonic blast, my head's been jumbled."

"Maybe you should sit down."

Max slid his arm around Shay's waist. Tingles accompanied his every touch. It was strange how she felt uncomfortable and completely safe in his embrace at the same time, even stranger that she didn't know which feeling to fear more. She allowed Max to usher her to the lab's small couch. Their legs pressed together as he sat beside her and she scooted away, though not very far.

"Shay. There's something I have to tell you, and it's gonna be a little hard to grasp."

"I'm not Jenna." Shay watched Max's hopeful expression drop, the sparkle leave his eyes.

"But, she's somewhere inside you."

"No. I'm the same me I've always been." Shay traced the scar beneath her shirt with her finger. That mark was a constant reminder of the day her parents died; and now, it would be a souvenir of Antiserum's violation over her body and soul.

Shay took Max's hand, before realizing how inappropriate it might look. It was too late to let go now. His digits were firmly clasped around her own and she'd never be able to pry them off, even if she wanted to.

"I don't know how you can feel Jenna, she's gone. There's only an energy signature left, with no emotions, memories, or feelings."

"You talked about the night we met Razorbill, at The Shed."

Max squeezed Shay's hand so tight her fingers grew numb, and she pulled her arm away.

"I don't know what you're talking about."

"It just happened, like a minute ago."

Shay knew exactly what Max was talking about, but the more she denied it the easier it became to overlook. She understood energy. It was erratic, though it had rules that could explain how one person could theoretically have two different energy signatures. But two actual people sharing one body, one mind … it went beyond breaking the laws of physics. That shattered every scientific belief she held dear.

"Lucius did take something from Jenna and he transferred it into my body, but I don't have her memories. The emotions I feel are my own. It's just energy, not Jenna."

"But you said—"

"I hit my head pretty hard. I might've spouted out some gibberish and you mistook it for something else. It's common in times of stress to associate current situations with similar events of your past."

"No!" Max's shout echoed throughout the wide-open lab, growing louder each time it bounced off a steel wall. "You can't wrap everything in science and put it on a neat little shelf."

He seized Shay by the wrist. His nails dug into her skin as he pulled her arm close to his chest. "Just look into my eyes."

"Stop." Shay jerked back from Max, and his grip on her arm tightened. "Max, you're hurting me."

"What's going on?" Evie yelled as she stomped across the lab.

Max let go of Shay, and she jumped to her feet. "We were just talking," she said, rubbing the indents left by Max's grip.

"New rule." Evie took Shay by the hand while glaring at Max. "You two aren't allowed in the same room together alone."

Evie pulled Shay from the lab and Shay couldn't be more grateful. As a thank you, she let her sister scold her the entire elevator ride upstairs.

Max stayed on that hard couch in the cold lab, cradling his head in his hands. Minutes passed, maybe even hours. He didn't know, didn't care. Outside this lab, a crazy version of his already tragic life waited and he was in no hurry to let it devour the rest of his will.

Boots thumped against the tile, but Max didn't bother to look up. It was Alexie. She was the only person he knew who could manage to sound self-righteous just by walking.

"That was ... pathetic." Alexie sat on the couch beside Max. "And a little scary."

"You and Simon were watching on the video feeds?"

"Yeah, we were." Alexie smacked Max's hands from his face. She placed her finger under his chin and steered his gaze to her. "I popped popcorn and everything, but quickly lost my appetite."

"This isn't a joke." Max pushed Alexie's hand away, ready to match fire for lightning.

"I know." Alexie slouched back against the couch. "I came here to help you."

"By teasing me?"

"No," she said through a chuckle. "By letting you know you're not losing it. When I brought Shay back, she said, 'I will marry you, Max Storm' with her first breath."

"That's the last thing Jenna said to me."

"I know." Alexie's tone and gaze had lost its usual edge of mockery, which allowed her sincerity to show. "And I heard her say that thing about The Shed."

"What does it mean, Lexie? She wasn't like this before."

"I think when Shay died, some things got mixed up. Simon thinks it'll wear off soon."

"Oh does he?" Max looked at the camera overhead. "Mr. Used-to-be-a-Med-Student thinks he's a neurologist because he gave himself superpowers?"

"He also thinks you should stay away from Shay until her concussion clears."

Max lowered his gaze from Alexie's nod. "Simon might be right about that one. I really freaked myself out the way I grabbed her."

"Think about how Shay felt. A little kitten trapped in a lion's claw."

Alexie took a deep breath and her stare drifted up, as if searching the ceiling for the right words. "You're ten years older than Shay. Maybe not in mentality, but in every other way you are her senior. She'll do whatever you tell her, because we're taught to obey our elders."

"That's harsh."

"But it's true. I know you, Max. You're a respectable guy. You wouldn't want a relationship like that."

"I don't." Max jumped up off the couch and stomped out of the lab. Alexie could be so tasteless, crude … and right. Even if he *did* have feelings for Shay, which he didn't, he'd never be happy in an unequal relationship. The child in Shay shined bright. Her always messy hair, lack of makeup, those clothes. The girl had a lot of growing to do, and he didn't want to be the glitch that triggered it.

Max looked up from the floor, at the shiny numbers on Shay's front door. His boots thumped as he staggered back a step.

This was a mistake. He hadn't meant to come here, didn't even remember the elevator ride up seventy-six floors. Almost against his will, he lifted his hand to knock then backed away from the door.

"Idiot," he muttered to himself.

Shay's suite door flew open, and Evie stepped in its threshold.

"Big surprise," she said, curling her fingers into fists. "It's the super-stalker."

"I uh …" Max couldn't explain why he'd come to Shay's front door, because he didn't know, but he did need to do something while he was there.

"I need to apologize. To you. My behavior's been—"

"Appalling, indecent, disturbing."

"Yeah." Max shrank down under the weight of Evie's fierce stare. "And creepy."

"I know about your dead girlfriend's soul." Evie cringed the moment the words flew from her mouth.

"Jenna," Max said softly.

"I'm sorry, that was rude." Evie slouched against her doorway. "I have a boyfriend, and I care about him very much."

"Then, shouldn't you be talking to him right now?"

"It's hard to talk to him. I really like him. I don't care about you so …"

Evie shrugged and Max snickered. "Thanks."

"What I mean to say is I can see how this situation with Shay is hard for you."

"It's gotta be hard for you too. Shay must feel like a daughter to you."

"Yeah." Evie's entire body relaxed, her tightly kept guard coming down half an inch. "Nobody gets it. Because we're sisters, people think it's one big slumber party. But I've watched Shay grow, mature, all by myself. She feels like my kid."

Max stepped closer to Evie, leaning on the opposite side of the doorway. It was nice to have a civilized conversation, even if it was with the Ice Queen. "How old were you when your parents died?"

"Seventeen, but I turned eighteen while Shay was in the hospital and I filed for custody."

"That's horrible. You lost the best parts of your life." Max kept his gaze low. He played a large part in that night's events. He should've caught that subway car midair, should've talked to Lucius instead of hurling fire-encased fists.

"No. I don't think of it that way. Hey. You want to come in, have a beer?"

The question seemed to shock Evie as much as it stunned Max, and it came from her own lips. They hated each other. Evie was smug, self-centered … at least, he'd thought she was.

Max stood up straight. He glanced at the elevator down the hall, then looked inside Shay and Evie's penthouse.

"A beer sounds great."

12

Shay kicked off her blanket. Too extravagant was a thing, and she'd found it. A bed of feathers, with pillows of feathers, and a blanket stuffed with feathers, and it was all wrapped in silk. It made her think of starving children. Her bed of down and silks could feed an entire village if liquidated. With tiny emaciated bellies stuck in her mind, she'd never sleep and the blaring TV in the living room wasn't helping.

She rolled out of bed, thumping her feet as she walked from her room. Her steps slowed once in the suite's small hallway. That wasn't the TV blasting through her wall. It was Max and Evie, giggling.

Not one breath would leave Shay's body as she slinked along the wall on tipped-toes. Their words echoed down the dark hallway, crystal clear, and she froze in place. This hit a new level of low. Lurking in shadows, listening to harmless chitchat about a burned down movie theater was grade A creeper behavior.

Her loser instinct kicked into overdrive. Just as she backed away from the hall's end, the talking stopped. Two, three seconds passed with no sound but a crinkle of leather.

Part of Shay wanted to jump back in bed and pull those fancy covers over her head, but the part that needed to peek into the living room won out.

Shay crept to the end of the hallway and peered into the living room. One glimpse of Evie's arms around Max's neck, their lips pressed together, was all she needed to throw up a little in her mouth. She hurried to her room, choking down gulps of air. As softly as possible, she closed her bedroom door then slumped against the wall.

A warm streak ran down her cheek, cooling her way too hot skin. She wiped it away and looked at her fingers.

Tears?

Relief cut through her misery. It had been a long time since she cried. She'd feared her tears had run dry. The sting of betrayal swiftly returned, followed by a bout of stupidity.

Shay climbed back in her soft bed and sunk into the smooth pillows. A soul ached inside her body, but it wasn't her own. It left an odd feeling, one of self-pity and compassion.

Science and logic had abandoned her. Another person's soul wrenched in agony within her, and she actually felt the burn. It shouldn't be possible. Jenna's consciousness shouldn't have carried over into Shay, just the energy.

Shay pulled the blanket to her chin. The false comfort these elegant linens provided worked this time. Silky sheets tingled her skin. The fluffy pillows swallowed her thoughts, and wiped away the image of Max's hand on her sister's cheek. The last bits of sadness she clung to slipped away, adrift under sleep's gentle call.

"The door's opening," Simon said, peeking over his laptop at Alexie.

Alexie crawled across the couch. She snuggled beside Simon, turning the computer in his lap so she could get a glimpse. "How long's it been?"

"Max went into Shay's suite over an hour ago."

"That's so—" Alexie gasped, gripping onto the sides of the laptop's thin display. "He's with the other Sinclair!"

Simon watched in sheer disbelief as Max hugged Evie in the suite's doorway. "Unbelievable."

"This guy." Alexie sat up straight, pounding her fist into her palm. "You want me to drag Max's ass up here?"

"No." Simon closed the lid of his laptop. "It's late. We'll lay into him tomorrow."

Alexie shrugged. She picked her fallen magazine off the floor and continued flipping through its pages. "It's gonna be funny when those two sisters start pulling each other's hair out. My money's on Shay, she's more of a scrapper."

"What is Max thinking? First it's Shay then it's Evie."

"Don't forget Jenna's soul," Alexie said. "Jenna is definitely alive inside Shay. I heard it myself."

"That troubles me the most." Simon placed his laptop on the coffee table. "I didn't know Jenna that well, but I've seen the old space program's footage of her. She was strong, determined. If her consciousness is awake inside Shay, it'll find a way out. It's just a matter of time."

"What would happen to Shay?"

Simon had only gotten through two years of medical school before his … incident, but the professors hadn't explained a soul. He didn't know what a soul was, what would happen to a person if two resided in one body. Nobody could know such a thing, except the man who ate souls for breakfast—Antiserum.

"From what I've seen in movies, there can only be one driver behind a wheel. I don't know how strong Shay's mind is, but she could get lost. Forever."

"We cannot let Max find out about this." The magazine tumbled from Alexie's hand, fluttering to the floor. "He's completely irrational when it comes to Jenna."

"We need to find a way to get Jenna's soul out of Shay, without hurting Shay."

If only they knew someone who could pull a soul from a body, someone rational.

"We were a great team, those few months. Us, Max, Jenna, and the Grant brothers."

Alexie snickered, more of a snort. "The Liberty Squad."

"That's right. That's what we used to call ourselves," Simon said with a grin.

"You want to bring Lucius back into the fold?"

"We complimented each other perfectly, when we worked together."

Alexie stared at Simon as if he'd grown two heads. "We can't work together. Lucius always has to shine brighter than everyone else."

"Maybe he's done with that."

A low huff flowed from Alexie's mouth. She placed her hand on Simon's knee. "I miss them too, but—"

"Good. Then you won't mind going undercover to feel Lucius and Cyrus out."

"What?"

"Really, all you have to do is sway Lucius back to our side and Cyrus will follow."

"You can forget all that."

Alexie scooted to the sofa's edge. Any minute, she'd leave the room, perhaps the building.

"Just hear me out." Simon poured a splash of brandy into two glasses and handed one to Alexie.

A steady beep ripped Shay from a deep slumber. She opened her eyes, sunlight beamed to her brain, and she buried her face in a pillow. The beep ringing out from her nightstand didn't stop. Either someone had set an alarm, or her cell phone was blowing up.

Without looking, Shay reached for her nightstand. She slapped her palm against its cool metal top until a buzz vibrated her fingers. It had been her cell phone, and it really was blowing up with texts.

Shay lifted her head from the pillows and looked at her phone. There were 115 messages, and rising.

"WTF," she muttered, scrolling on her screen.

Most of the texts were from Ollie, begging her to get him into some party at the lake. The other messages were invites to a party at the lake.

A knock shook Shay's bedroom door. "Shay," Evie said, wiggling the locked knob. "Are you up?"

Just the sound of Evie's voice twisted Shay's stomach. She could rip her sister's hair out right now, hence the locked door. That solid piece of wood between them should keep Shay from freaking out, for something she wasn't supposed to see, with a man she shouldn't care so much about.

"Be out in a minute," Shay yelled, in a bit of a bark.

"Why is the door locked? Open up."

"I'm getting dressed." Shay laid back against the pillows, typing a quick message to Ollie. Only after Evie's feet clumped away did she crawl from bed.

A killer outfit was essential today. Not the usual gaudy kid stuff, just a plain black tank and blue jeans. Sexy yet casual. Now, to brush her teeth and get out the front door without too much Evie.

In record time, Shay freshened up. After a few practice *what, I'm laidback* faces in the mirror, she walked down the hallway.

"Good morning," Evie said over a steaming mug of coffee.

"If you say so."

"What?" Evie's smile warped into a frown as she reached for a box of pancake batter.

"Nothing." Shay grabbed her lab coat and headed for the door. "No breakfast for me, I'm going to the lab. Lots to do, probably be busy all day."

"Oh." Evie looked lost as she clutched the pancake batter box and stared at the empty griddle. "Okay. I'll be busy all afternoon too. Why don't we meet back here around five, have dinner?"

"Whatever," Shay mumbled to herself. "Sounds great," she said, rushing out the suite.

A mansion sat in the north-end of Gemini City. Acres of green grass surrounded the massive stone manor. There were fifteen bedrooms, with king-sized beds fitted in the finest cotton, three swimming pools … a hot tub. Lucius and his brother had grown up on that estate. It was their home, and they couldn't get within a hundred-mile radius of it without Max attacking.

Like most misunderstood men who'd been labeled a villain, Lucius had to construct a secret lair in the only abandoned building inside the city limits—an asylum.

Lucius picked a double-edged knife off a dusty table and hurled it across the room. The blade coasted right in front of Cyrus's nose before sticking into the door Cyrus was trying to sneak out of.

"Where are you going, little brother?"

Cyrus pulled the knife from the door's frame, tossing it to the floor. "Lunch, with my girlfriend."

"That tart."

"Hey. That *tart* is the only one who's ever backed Storm and his sidekicks into a corner."

Lucius couldn't deny that. His brother's not so fake anymore relationship had become quite fruitful to their ventures.

"The tart is useful. I'll give you that much. Perhaps she could be even more useful, once you're done with her of course."

"What'd you mean?"

"Allow me to present." Lucius held his hand out to the open doorway beside him and another, exact replica of himself walked into the room. "Mimic."

The dark stare, smooth motions, right down to Lucius's own signature smirk were spot-on. It was like looking in a mirror, except Lucius knew who really hid behind the illusion.

Cyrus rushed in front of Mimic. His jaw hinged open as he scanned the perfect rendition of Lucius. "What is this?"

"Not what, who," Mimic said in Lucius's deep voice.

With one finger, Mimic tapped Cyrus on his bare wrist. Before Cyrus could draw back a fist, Mimic's form morphed from that of Lucius to the spitting image of Cyrus.

"What the ..." Cyrus backed away from the imitation of himself and grabbed Lucius by the arm. "You found someone else with superpowers."

"No. I gave someone else superpowers, using your invention."

"How? Who is that?"

"Wouldn't you like to know?" Mimic said, transforming into a tall blonde woman.

"I had to devour three souls to power the machine myself, since you failed to devise a power source. The machine recreated a nebula burst, just like you hypothesized."

Lucius stood in front of Mimic, admiring the choice of form. "I had no idea the test subject would develop such a resourceful ability."

Cyrus crept closer to Mimic, circled it, examined every inch of the body it had chosen to wear. "I think a person's individual genetic code determines what type of ability they'll have."

"How do you mean?" Lucius asked, already working up a selection process in his mind.

"For instance, before the … incident, I used to be really good at getting into people's minds, persuading them—"

"And now you can actually get into a person's mind, make them see things, do things."

"Right. I'll bet," Cyrus gestured at Mimic, "this person had a form of echopraxia, where a person can't help but copy another's movements."

"Interesting." Lucius turned away from Mimic, looking at Cyrus. "What do you think your girlfriend will be, when I upgrade her?"

A hint of rage flashed across Cyrus's face. "Lucius—"

"Antiserum!"

Cyrus closed his eyes and took a deep breath. "Brother. You got lucky this time, really lucky. Ninety-percent of the people you put in that machine will die."

"It's a good thing your relationship isn't real then, huh?" Lucius waved his hand toward the door, and it swung open. "Go. Enjoy your lunch, and meet me at the lake afterward. We're going to a party."

Shay lounged against a soft leather seat in the back of a corporate sedan. The perks of rolling with a billionaire were awesome. She had private cars on demand, equipped with drivers who didn't ask questions. It was pretty scary how easily she could adapt to this type of lavish treatment.

As the car slowed, parking in front of her apartment building, she rolled down her window. Like a breath of fresh air, Ollie's smile rushed in. Shay hadn't realized how much she'd missed Ollie until glimpsing him strut toward her in a hot pink jumpsuit with matching boa.

"Car service." Ollie stopped on the sidewalk to eye the shiny black sedan. "Well, well. Don't mind if I do."

The moment Ollie slid into the backseat, Shay threw her arms around his neck and hugged tight.

"Whoa!" Ollie hugged back then wiggled out from her embrace. "I missed you too, girl. It's been wild. I've become somewhat of a celebrity, as your bestie and most trusted advisor of course."

"Of course." Shay ran her hand through the strand of Ollie's pink feathers. "You look great."

"Right." Ollie flung aside his boa, modeling his skintight jumpsuit quite well in the cramped car. "Pink is a fabulous color on me. It brings out my cool brown tones."

He stopped admiring himself long enough to take in Shay and his head tilted to one side. "You look ..." His finger tapped his chin as he studied her from head to toe. "Different. Like some kinda sexy, confident scientist."

"That's 'cause I am a sexy, confident scientist," Shay said, rocking an attitude that matched her media-driven charade.

"Dang." Ollie leaned back against his door. "Did you have sex?"

"No." Shay snorted, but only a little. Snorts didn't match her outfit. "But I did die."

"What?" Ollie stripped off his boa then dug into his purse, pulling out handfuls of makeup. "Hold up. I wanna put some sparkle on your face while you tell me everything that's been going down."

Max stood on the seventy-sixth floor of Ling Enterprises, staring at a closed door. He would knock if he wasn't afraid of who'd answer. It was Shay that drove him to this door, but he owed Evie some kind of explanation for what went down the night before.

"What are you doing?"

Max turned from the door to find Alexie leaning against the wall.

"Nothing," he said, straining to keep a cool face. "I was just ... looking for Shay."

"For Shay or Evie?" Alexie folded her arms in front of her chest, smirking.

"You and Simon need to get a life." Max walked past Alexie, bumping his shoulder against her arm as he strolled by. "Instead of spying on mine."

"You are my life. In case you've forgotten, we're supposed to be a team. The *three* of us."

That took the stomp right out of Max's steps. He looked back at Alexie, and she grabbed onto his hand.

"Max, talk to me. What are you thinking?"

Every muscle in Max's body wilted under Alexie's gentle stare. Alexie and Simon were more than teammates, bigger than family. It'd be stupid to push them away now, when he needed them most.

"I'm scared, Lexie. I know I can bring Jenna out, but the cost. There's a gleam in Shay's eyes. In the moments when Jenna spoke to me, that gleam disappeared. Two souls can't share one body."

Max slouched against the window, staring out at the bustling city below. He yearned to be one of those people, traipsing along the sidewalks. How great it would be to have average concerns, ones that only seemed like life and death.

"I've wanted to find Jenna's soul and set it free for so long, but now I can get Jenna back. I'm scared I'll do it, that I'll destroy Shay to have Jenna by my side once again. I'm scared I'll turn into Lucius, sacrifice the innocent for my own happiness."

"Don't you see? That's exactly what Lucius wants, to turn you to his side. Why else would he put Jenna's soul inside a child? He knows if you traded the life of an innocent for Jenna's, you'd never be the same. Never be able to look at yourself again, like him."

Max leaned toward Alexie, letting his weight fall against her shoulder.

"Besides," she said, glancing at Max. "You don't want to go around wearing an iron mask and demanding people call you *Firestorm*, do you?"

A chuckle flowed from Max's mouth, taking about five-pounds of stress with it. "Don't worry, that'll never happen."

"We'll do whatever it takes to get Jenna's soul out of Shay's body, safely." Alexie took Max's hand and held tight. "If we have to go along with somebody's far-fetched idea, so be it. We're heroes, it's what we do."

People swarmed Shay the second she climbed from her car. Their voices, and constant barrage of questions, barely registered over the beat of speakers just beyond the grassy hill beside Shay. A full-fledged party raged at the lake below the gentle slope, but she couldn't get to it. What seemed to be the entire populace of Gemini City High crowded around her, stopping her short halfway down the hill.

Ollie was pulled from her grasp. She couldn't see a hint of his bright pink boa beyond the sea of faces. The people around her looked familiar, but she didn't know anyone's name. It was like being at school, except everyone was dancing and shoving test tubes of pink and blue liquid in her hands.

"Shay Sinclair?"

Shay downed two drinks, one of each color, as a small group of varsity-jacket-wearing dudes pushed the crowd from her space.

"I'm so glad you made it," said the guy in the center, taking Shay by the arm.

Shay's usual instinct to cower down and slink away from the "cool people" didn't kick on. Instead, she ogled the tall piece of gorgeous who clutched onto her arm. His blond hair was way shinier and much thicker than her own, and his blue eyes seemed to sparkle in the sunlight.

The guy was way too hot for her, but she wasn't letting go of his arm. Especially not now, since walking had become iffy after slamming those drinks. Plus, she was pretty sure the guy was captain of G.C. High's football team, Ted or Tom. It was a major score.

"This is lit," Shay said as they strolled through crowds of dancing bodies, moving closer to the DJ table at the lake's edge.

"Let's get you a drink."

Mr. Way-Too-Hot glided his hand to the arch of Shay's back. The soft stroke of his fingertips clouded her already hazy mind, but she wasn't exactly *there* yet. She needed a bit more fuzz in her brain to fully forget the previous night's events.

"I like the blue ones," she said, pointing at a guy with a handful of test tubes.

"Gotcha." He snatched two drinks and handed one to Shay.

"Thanks." She twisted the tube in her fingers, taking a sip. Her gaze stuck to the dimples that followed Mr. Way-Too-Hot's smile. Normally, she'd feel stupid staring at the guy; but for some reason, her head was extra loopy at the moment.

A flock of sophomores rushed toward Shay on her right, and bubbly freshmen crowded her on the left. The shouting and pushing started up again. Questions about superheroes flew through the air, which grew thicker as the crowd pushed in around Shay.

"I think your fans want you to say something," Mr. Way-Too-Hot said, grabbing a mic from the DJ.

Shay slammed her drink, teetering on her toes. The most pleasant buzz vibrated her entire body. Its hum drowned out all her gloomy thoughts. In fact, she could no longer recall a single thing that bothered her.

The music cut off, which let the crowd's excited voices ring out loud and clear. Shay took the mic and climbed atop the DJ table. Hands raised toward her. Most were holding little tubey drinks, and she took one.

"Hey," Shay said, tapping the mic. "You guys wanna know something about superheroes?"

A hush fell over the crowd, clicks of cameras the only sound.

"Superheroes suck," Shay yelled, lifting her tube in the air.

Cheers erupted and Shay drank down her blue awesomeness, which was what she'd be calling this drink from now on.

The DJ cranked up the music. Sharp hits of dubstep blasted throughout the small field once again and everybody resumed dancing. Mr. Way-Too-Hot helped Shay off the table since it wasn't easy climbing down while swaying to the beat.

Shay sunk against the cliché hot guy's chest, draping her arms around his neck. "You ever *been* with a superhero scientist?"

Mr. Way-Too-Hot clutched onto Shay's hips and pulled her closer. "No."

"Do you want to?" Shay rose to the tips of her toes. Their lips connected and explosions rang out. It wasn't love at first kiss explosions. The gazebo beside the lake actually freaking blew up.

Screams rang out as shards of flaming wood shot through the crowd. Everybody ran for the hillside. The rush of the crowd crashed against Shay like a wave. She was carried into a mob of pushing arms, a wall of bodies crushing her chest. Bursts of black fire surged on all sides, pushing the crowd in against her even tighter. A rumble shook the ground, and the flame's heat replaced all trace of oxygen.

Just as the press of hard chests threatened to suffocate Shay, someone grabbed her by the arm and pulled her through the crowd. Cool air struck Shay like a slap, stinging her sweaty skin as she was dragged away from the people who ran toward the parking lot at the hill's crest. The blur that clouded her vision cleared, and hot pink feathers smacked her face.

"Ollie?" She swatted the boa aside, which allowed her to glimpse Ollie's grin.

"Having fun?" Ollie pulled Shay behind a tree in a small patch of woods.

"I was. What's going on?"

"Antiserum." Ollie pointed at a cloaked figure, who threw balls of black fire throughout the field of people fleeing the lake's edge.

"Crap." Shay ducked back behind the wide tree. "I think he's looking for me."

"We gotta get out of here. Come on."

Ollie took Shay by the hand and pulled her deeper into the tight trees beside them. A wild churn nipped at her stomach, which slowed her steps. The trees began to spin, and that churn in her belly warped into a straight-up burn.

"Wait." Shay yanked her hand free from Ollie's clutch, stopping to gasp for breath. "I can't. I need a minute."

"We have to keep going."

Shay waved Ollie off. "There's something wrong with me. I'm seriously impaired for running right now."

"No. You're seriously drunk right now. Come on. We're almost there."

Ollie tugged Shay's arm and the heat in her stomach rose into her chest.

"Oh no." She leaned over and about a pint of blue awesomeness spewed from her mouth, landing on her sneakers. The trees whirled around her even faster and she dropped to her knees.

"Ollie?"

Shay looked behind her but Ollie was gone. There were only trees in the field around her. Their colorful leaves waved in the cool breeze, a cool breeze that failed to chill the fire that blazed in her stomach.

"Not again." Her hands hit the dirt and another round of not so awesome anymore blue drink came up.

"What in the world?"

Shay looked up from the puke-pile below her. At first, her heart fluttered at the sight of Alexie's sparkly blue jumpsuit. A superhero had come to her aid, right when she needed one most. Then she saw Alexie's scowl.

"Blue awesomeness," Shay said through pants. "Too much. I had too much."

"Yeah. I don't know what that means." Alexie inched away from

Shay. She looked through the trees, at the screaming people running from the lake's side. "I'm gonna get your sister."

"No!" Shay reached for Alexie, only able to swat the fringe of her cape. "I do not want to see *her* right now."

"Did something happen?" Alexie knelt beside Shay and brushed clumps of matted hair from her face. "Between you and Evie?"

"Umm yeah. Evie totally hooked up with Max last night."

"In front of you?"

"No." Shay plopped down on the grass. She pulled her knees to her chest, took one look at her vomit covered shoes, and stretched her legs back out. "They thought I was asleep, which might be worse."

"Why?" Alexie sat next to Shay, as if groups of teens weren't being attacked by a supervillain only yards away. "Are you and Max a thing?"

Shay looked at Alexie, way too fast, and a bout of the spins hit her once again. "You know we're not a thing, but it feels like he belongs to me."

"That's the second soul inside you talking." Alexie hopped to her feet then held her hand out in front of Shay. "Up, drunkie. I'm taking you home."

Standing wasn't as hard as Shay expected, especially with a superhero doing most of the work. The walk back to the car might be a different story.

"Hold on tight," Alexie said, wrapping Shay in a bear hug.

"What? We're flying?" Shay tried to squirm away, but Alexie had one hella grip.

"My teleportation power is in the shop."

"No way. I'm not gonna be the girl who throws up on Electric-Luxie midair."

"Then you better close your eyes, and your mouth."

Before Shay could speak, her feet were off the ground. She held onto Alexie tight as they soared through the air. Far below her dangling feet, she glimpsed Max and Simon corner Antiserum at the lake's edge before tall buildings blocked her view.

"I should be helping them," Shay muttered.

Alexie landed on the roof of Ling Enterprise, slowly letting go of Shay.

"Yeah, you should've been," she said, taking off in a crackle of lightning.

Evie pushed through flocks of screaming people. She stared down a small slope that led to the lake and scanned the crowd of frightened faces.

Shay would never leave her lab for this. The pop-up rave at Midtown Lake looked passé. Granted, supervillains had blown the sound system to charred pieces, but still. There weren't hors d'oeuvres or gift bags being passed around. The news, police scanners, and Ollie's texts must be a mistake.

She turned, only to collide with hard plastic. A solid, black chest plate ... she'd just walked into a solid, black chest plate and only one type of person wore those: a supervillain.

Although her brain begged to stay ignorant, she looked up at the man in front of her. Shock turned Evie's muscles to stone as she stared at the shapeless fabric mask of Dr. Mayhem. She opened her mouth to scream, but only a gasp trickled out.

Dr. Mayhem lifted his arm. His gloved hand reached for Evie, and still her stupid legs wouldn't budge.

The rough tip of a glove glided along Evie's cheek and she closed her eyes. Deep booms of fireballs, terror-filled cries, and the tiny voice in her head that shouted for her to run all fell under the thump of her heart's beat.

In a gust of heated air, the dark presence around Evie lifted. She opened her eyes. Dr. Mayhem's cloak fluttered as he walked down the hill, away from her. The tightness in her chest loosened. Air rushed back into her lungs, bringing with it enough sense to remember the weapon in her purse.

Evie reached inside her purse. The cold metal of Shay's sonic gun grazed her palm. She grabbed onto its handle and lifted the weapon, holding it close to her chest.

Through crowds of people, she glimpsed Dr. Mayhem creep behind Simon and Max. He stretched his arms out, holding his palms overtop their heads.

Simon and Max turned away from Antiserum, and then started hurling fists at each other. Dr. Mayhem stepped beside Antiserum. It looked like the two villains were chuckling as they watched Simon and Max punch the crap out of one another, but Evie couldn't tell. All she could hear were the frantic screams of annoyingly inebriated teenagers.

The heels of Evie's shoes sunk into damp earth as she hurried down the grassy hillside. She pushed and shoved to keep from being trampled by the wave of people who ran away from the supervillains she rushed toward.

Once she reached the bottom of the hill, beyond the mobs of terrified people, the villains were gone. Just an empty fire-singed field remained, with two superheroes rolling in the grass and beating each other to a pulp.

Evie ran beside Simon, who pinned Max in a chokehold, and kicked them both in their sides.

"Snap out of it," she yelled, but they didn't so much as glance her way.

Simon picked Max off the ground, lifted him high above his head, then slammed his back against a bench seat.

Wood and metal shot out as Simon drove Max into the gravel. A wall of flames built before Max's palms. He pushed his hands out and a wave of flames flung Simon backward.

The fringe of Max's fire blast knocked Evie to her knees. They weren't going to stop. Whatever Dr. Mayhem did to them, it wouldn't end until one or both of them died.

Evie lifted the sonic blaster. A pang of dread hit her stomach as she pointed the gun at Max and Simon. This weapon killed Shay, but she had to do something.

"Stop," Alexie yelled. Her voice rumbled the air like thunder, and thick bolts of blue lightning struck the ground as she landed beside Evie. "What are these two fools doing?"

Evie ducked as a ball of flames, which had been intended for Simon, soared overhead. She ran behind Alexie, using the woman as a superhero shield.

"Dr. Mayhem put the whammy on them. They won't stop."

"And you thought it'd be a good idea to shoot them with the highly lethal weapon that killed your sister?"

"They're superheroes. I figured they could take the blast."

Alexie let out a huff and stepped closer to the bloody men, who slowed in the exchange of blows but showed no signs of stopping. A hiss sizzled above the slap of fists as tiny arms of electricity danced between her fingertips.

She pointed at Simon and Max. Blue lightning streamed from her fingertip. The wide bolt struck the men wrestling on the ground, and launched their bodies through the air.

As Alexie spun to face Evie, Simon and Max plunged into the lake. "Whammy fixed."

"Did you find Shay?" Evie glanced around the near empty field, ignoring the small groups of crying, non-Shay girls.

"Yeah." Alexie quickly turned away from Evie, looking at Max as he crawled from the lake. "Shay was in the lab this whole time. Some girl was running around the party pretending to be her."

"That's what I thought. Shay wouldn't be caught dead at a tacky event like this."

Max sparked a whirlwind of flames around his body, and Evie shielded her face from its heat. The fire sputtered out and he adjusted his now dry suit.

"Thanks, Lexie," he said, helping Simon from the lake.

"Why did you attack Simon?" Evie asked Max. She dropped the gun into her purse and grabbed her cell phone to record his answer.

"I thought I was attacking Lucius."

"Me too." Simon pushed his dislocated shoulder back into place, groaning when the bone popped into its socket. "We need to find a way to block Cyrus from our minds."

"I'll get Shay on top of that." Evie pulled up her contacts list and Alexie placed her hand atop the phone's screen.

"Let me. I used to date Cyrus, I know a little something about how his mind works."

Lightning flashed and the wind bellowed as Alexie shot off the ground. Evie cupped her eyes to block the sun's rays, watching Alexie fly between gleaming skyscrapers.

"She dated Dr. Mayhem?"

"Before he went dark," Max said.

Simon smoothed back his wet hair, then wrung lake water from his cape. "I still think Cyrus brainwashed her."

"None of this is in my files." Evie rubbed her forehead, but the spike of annoyance lingered. She had an entire server's worth of information on superheroes, and one page of general data on Antiserum and Dr. Mayhem. Whatever details were on that page had eluded her, and the more she thought about the villains the foggier her brain became.

"I don't even know what Antiserum and Dr. Mayhem look like without their masks."

"Yeah." Simon frowned, glancing at Max. "A few years ago, Cyrus broadcasted his brainwaves throughout the city. It seemed to have erased their identities from everybody's minds."

"What?" Fury clutched onto Evie. It was one thing to wreck her city, but violating her mind crossed every moral line.

"The only reason it didn't affect us is because we flew up," Max pointed at the puffy clouds above them, "over the signal. I pelted Cyrus with fireballs while Alexie fried the broadcast tower."

"I feel robbed." Evie wrapped her arms around herself, but it provided very little comfort. "No wonder you guys don't want me around. I can't help. I don't even know anything about … Lucius and Cyrus?"

"I'll see if I can dig up some stuff for you," Simon said.

Like Alexie, he rocketed off the ground and flew toward Ling Enterprises, leaving Evie alone with Max. She silently prayed Max would jet off toward the sky as well, but he stayed in front of her with his gaze low.

"How'd you know we were here?" he asked, glancing at the now wrecked gazebos and wooden benches beside the lake.

"I was on a date at the restaurant across the street and heard it on the police scanner."

"Do you need a lift back?" Max grinned as he pointed at the sky.

"No thanks. I only fly on planes, and my driver's waiting." To run from this awkward conversation would be crass, so Evie slowly backed away.

"About last night—"

"That was a mistake." Evie's tone verged on the rude side, and she dialed it down a notch. "I mean. We should just forget about that, never mention it again."

"Yeah." Max rubbed the back of his neck, shrugging. "That's … what I was thinking, also. Plus, you have a boyfriend."

"Who I like very much, but don't mention him either. I haven't told Shay about him yet. The timing … and you."

"I get it."

"Good." Evie picked up the backward pace, stumbling on the hill's slope. "I'll see you later."

"You sure you're good to get back?"

"Yep." With a wave, Evie turned from what she considered her biggest near hookup mistake to date. She did have a boyfriend, and she really was starting to love him, but he wasn't the person who caused guilt to eat away at her insides. Fitz was an easy-going man. He'd most likely forgive her misdeed. But if Shay found out what happened on the suite's couch last night, she'd lose her little sister forever.

14

Shay sat at a workstation in the lab, holding her head in her hands. Even after a shower, comfy clothes, non-puke shoes, and about a gallon of coffee, her brain still whirled and pounded. She had no idea what had happened at the lake. Ollie wouldn't talk to her. He accused her of ditching him at the party to make-out with a jock in the woods. The last text he sent to her said they needed to take a break. Then he blocked her, from calling and on social media.

She didn't understand. She'd been with Ollie in the woods, not a jock.

"Hey," Alexie said, sitting on the stool across from Shay. "You look rough."

"I feel rough. Why do people drink? It's only fun for the first ten minutes."

Alexie snickered. "It's different when you're older. That's why there's a drinking age."

"Right."

"Listen." Alexie slapped her palm on the shiny table, not only rattling the scatter of motherboards lying atop it but Shay's brain as well. "Evie should be back soon. I told her you were here, in the lab this whole time, and that some girl was impersonating you."

"But, everyone was snapping pics. My face will probably be on the five o'clock news, and the cover of *Superhero Weekly*."

"With the way you were dressed, and the clown makeup painted on your face, Evie will never believe it was you."

"Thanks for looking out, after I got puke on your suit." Shay tried to force a smile, but the shame inside her wouldn't allow it.

"I've had worse on my suit." Alexie rose from the stool and headed for the door. "Oh, I almost forgot." She stopped in the lab's wide doorway, looking back at Shay.

"We need a device to block Dr. Mayhem from our minds. He uses some kind of mental projection, beams his thoughts into people's brains. I'm sure you'll figure something out."

Shay dropped her head onto the table. The cool metal felt like bliss against her heated forehead. Right now, she couldn't muster up a substantial thought let alone create a gadget to block others.

"Hetal," Shay yelled. Her voice bounced off the table in front of her face and punched her in the brain harder than a superhero hit. A groan carried her upright. She swayed on the stool, its legs tapping the concrete floor as it rocked.

"I converted the power source on the forcefield generator." Hetal maneuvered around disassembled machines while struggling to carry a thick steel tube. "But, it's bigger now."

The heavy pipe, which was supposed to be a slim forcefield generator one could carry into battle, thumped against the table. Shay massaged her achy temples. She only took quick peeks at the monstrosity atop her workbench, a workbench she'd planned on resting her head upon all night. Anything more than a glance at the failed experiment could cause her to break out into a cranky-girl hissy fit.

"This is not practical," Shay said, pushing the clunky long tube to the edge of her table. She could just see herself now, falling flat on her face while running into a battle with this thing.

"I know." Hetal slumped onto the stool beside Shay. "But unless you make this thing nuclear powered, there's not much more I can do."

"I'll just ... make it work. There's something more important we need to deal with."

"Your TV debut?"

"What?"

"I saw you on the news, slamming shots and yelling about how superheroes suck."

Shay cringed. Dinner with Evie was going to be fun.

"Crap." Shay looked at the clock on the wall, saw she was five minutes late for dinner, and jumped to her feet. "I'll be back in an hour."

Halfway to the door, Shay remembered why she'd yelled for Hetal and doubled back to the workbench. "We need to construct a device that can block brainwaves. Something small; pocket-sized, but strong enough to cover a fifty-foot radius."

"Oh, is that it?" Hetal shook her head. "I know very little about neuroscience."

"Me neither. I'll do some research while I'm gone." Shay walked to the lab's door. She stopped in its threshold and glanced back at Hetal.

The woman's tiny frame looked even smaller while alone in the spacious lab, her brown skin smoother against the bright gleam of stainless steel. It didn't seem right to Shay, for her to run off while Hetal was holed up in a cold room, alone, working.

"Get some grub, take a few hours to chill."

"This *is* how I chill."

"Smart girl," Shay said, walking into the hallway. Lab chilling was far better than lake partying. If only she'd known that earlier, her head wouldn't be all fuzzy and gut twisty.

Shay stepped into the elevator, holding her stomach as the lift shot up seventy-six floors.

"You had one job," Lucius shouted. He paced on the cracked floor of the asylum's old dayroom in attempt to vent his anger. It wasn't working. "Get the girl, bring the girl to Cyrus. It's not like I asked you to hack Shay's cell phone, sift through hundreds of ridiculous messages, organize an attack. No, I did all that."

Mimic flashed through shapes—an old black woman, a scrawny kid dressed in pink, Lucius complete with steel mask, before transforming into the curvy blonde woman it loved parading around in so much.

"I'm sorry. Shay started puking then Electric-Luxie showed up. I got scared and ran."

Lucius raised his hand, his hooked fingers hovering at Mimic's throat. "Scared and ran?"

"I don't have any other powers except shapeshifting. It's not like I get the person's abilities when I shift into them, just their form. Hits break me. Fire and lightning kill me."

"That's not the only thing that'll kill you." Lucius grabbed Mimic by the throat and squeezed.

"It thinks because it looks like a hot chick we won't hurt it," Cyrus said, stepping beside Lucius. "But really, a fluke is just a fluke."

"An under-cooked supervillain," Lucius said in a sneer. "Maybe I should toss it back in the machine, let it finish baking."

"That wouldn't work. Another dose of radiation from my machine, and this mutation of a person will die."

"I can do better." Mimic gagged while squirming to get out of

Lucius's tight grip. "Please."

Lucius narrowed his eyes. For the life of him, he couldn't fathom how something could be so beneficial yet useless at the same time. He released his clutch and Mimic fell to the floor, coughing.

"I saw you." Lucius turned to face Cyrus and his smile dropped. "At the lake."

"I saw you too," Cyrus said as he unpacked a new flat screen television.

"With that woman."

"Don't start, Lucius."

"Antiserum!" He crashed his fist against a table, cracking it down the center. "My name is Antiserum."

"Why?" Cyrus stood tall. "Because Lucius Grant wouldn't do things like this?"

"You do things like this with me."

"I'm a loyal fool. What's your excuse?"

Lucius walked toward the shiny new television and brought back his foot to kick its screen.

"I paid for that with your debit card," Cyrus called out.

"Ahh!" Lucius stormed from the room, punching broken windows on his way out.

After ten minutes of moving food around a plate, Shay set down her fork.

"Too spicy?" Evie asked, sipping a glass of wine.

"I'm not that hungry." The rice had done wonders for her stomach but the chicken; spicy was an understatement, more like fiery chunks of razor blade.

"You've been quiet. I thought you'd jump on a chance to rub the dual soul thing in my face. Is something bothering you?"

"What would be bothering me, Evie?" Shay looked at Evie, unable to control her harsh glares.

"You were up last night?" Evie asked into her lap. "Heard something?"

"What would I have heard?" Shay hopped to her feet but that didn't quash the jitter in her legs. "You, hoing it up with the first boy who showed interest in me?"

"Max is not a boy." Evie threw her napkin onto the table as she rose from her seat. "He's a grown man, who's too old for you."

"Then by all means, help yourself."

"I don't want *Max*." Evie crossed her arms. "He's smug and cocky, and he's not really that good looking. Very scrawny."

"I don't care if you want Max, because I never *wanted* him in the first place." Shay's hip bumped the chair as she hurried toward the door. It crashed against the tile floor and she flinched with her hand on the knob.

"It was … really hurtful for you to do that with Max in the same apartment as me, whether you thought I was asleep or not."

Shay opened the suite's front door and marched into the hallway. She walked past the elevator, to the end of the hall, and into the stairwell.

It was far shorter to go up than down, so Shay headed to the roof. A breath of fresh air and a glimpse of city lights would wipe her palette clean, replace the image of an Evie/Max kiss from her mind.

"Want Max," she grumbled to herself as she stomped up the last set of stairs. She didn't want Max, never had, but her stupid body needed to be near him. Even now, when she'd like to slug Max, she wished for his company. Max was no doubt wishing for her way hotter, age appropriate sister.

Her groan was eclipsed by the heavy steel door's squeak as she pushed it open. She stepped outside, onto the roof of Ling Enterprises, and took in a lungful of crisp night air.

"Shay?"

Shay yelped, jumping in place as Max stepped from the shadows.

"Seriously?" She could've went down a floor and hopped an elevator to the lobby, but she came to the very spot the man she was dying and dreading to see just so happened to be.

"What are you doing up here?" Max asked.

"I ... needed some air. What are *you* doing?" Shay kept her gaze on the speckles of city lights as she walked away from Max, toward the building's edge.

"Chilly," Max said, slowly walking closer to Shay.

"What, out here?"

"Your tone. Shay—"

Max's hand brushed Shay's arm, and she jerked away from his touch.

"Why did you have sex with my sister?"

For a second, Max just stared at Shay. It'd be funny, a stumped superhero, if the subject matter didn't sicken her.

"Things happened," Max said, looking like *he* might cry. "But we didn't have sex. I swear."

"That's not what it sounded like." Shay's bottom lip quivered. She bit down on it, hoping the pain would stop its shudder.

"You were awake?" Max covered his face, kneeling at Shay's feet. "I don't know what to say."

"How about sorry I'm such a playa."

"I'm not," Max said to the ground below him.

A gasp flew from Shay's lips, knocking her back a step. "You're not sorry?"

Max looked up, into Shay's eyes. Pain filled his stare. The sight of such a strong man broken by agony pierced Shay's chest, but she couldn't allow herself to feel it. Her heart had already been ripped to tatters when he and Evie betrayed her.

"I am incredibly sorry, and I'm not a player." Max stood up and took Shay's hand. "I only did that with Evie to try and convince myself I wasn't …"

A gust of wind blew Max's cologne into Shay's lungs. She closed her eyes, feeling the spark of his body as he leaned closer to her.

The intensity could swallow her whole. Just the idea of being swept up by this rush, falling toward no ground, stirred the instinct to run screaming.

Shay yanked her hand from Max's grasp and backed toward the stairwell door.

"Don't touch me, it's wrong." A tear skated down her cheek and she didn't know why. When a wall of waterworks clouded her vision, she ran into the stairwell.

15

Shay hit a red button on the wall, which closed the thick glass door of her lab. It was a beautiful sight, solid glass sealing her in. Evie, Max, not even Hetal could get to her through this sturdy barrier of people-blocking heaven.

"Why'd you shut the door?" Hetal asked, crawling out from behind the remains of a once beautiful electron microscope.

"I thought you went home."

"Home? There isn't a laboratory at my home." With an armful of circuitry, Hetal wobbled toward an already overloaded workstation.

"You're working so hard. It makes me feel bad. Are they even paying you?"

Hetal released the cluster of motherboards, transistors, and wire harnesses onto the table beside Shay. "Of course, very well. Are you all right? You look like you've been crying."

Shay turned her back to Hetal, wiping her eyes. "Allergies or something."

"You want to talk about it?"

"About my allergies?" Shay sat on a metal stool and slumped onto the workbench.

"About Max."

His name brought a shiver, one that rippled beneath Shay's flesh. She lowered her head into the fold of her arm. For some reason, it seemed easier to talk to the shiny table than Hetal.

"Honestly, I have no idea if I even like the guy or not. But there's this little part of me that burns when he's not around and scorches when he is. It feels different from the other parts of me; foreign, but I like it, a lot. I'm afraid. I could fall into that burn, get lost."

Shay peeked at Hetal, who studied her like a Millennium Prize Problem. Not a surprise. She sounded like a conundrum and felt like a crazy person.

"It makes sense," Hetal said, staring off into a corner.

"It does?"

"Yeah. I mean, everybody knows the Jenna and Max story. Two teens run away, hop aboard a spaceship and jet to the stars. Everyone dies in space but their love keeps them alive, only to have her die a few months after they return. Love like that doesn't just fade. It transcends, surpasses a point beyond where the laws of physics can reach."

Shay sat up straight, gawking at Hetal. "I can't believe you're saying this. You're a scientist."

"With scientific proof of life after death. Jenna's consciousness still exists. Her feelings, spirit, maybe even her memories are alive inside you, fighting with your own essence."

"So I'm not crazy, just two different people?"

"How old were you, when this soul implantation took place?"

"Is that what we're calling it?"

Hetal nodded. She grabbed a loose piece of paper and scribbled notes.

"You're working up a case report?" Shay cried out. She reached for the paper, and Hetal moved it away.

"Yeah. This is going to score me the Nobel. Can we experiment on you?"

"I don't know, maybe."

After a few minutes of frantic writing, Hetal looked up at Shay. "Do you remember your life before Jenna?"

"Sort of. Stupid things. My dollhouse, the color of our old kitchen walls, sitting on the couch with my parents and Evie. I was six when the accident happened, when my parents died and Antiserum ... did that to me."

Shay couldn't be upset. Her pain from the injuries she'd sustained had faded. The memories of that night—of her own parents—were long gone. If she allowed herself to feel violated, she'd become Antiserum's victim and she refused to be anyone's victim.

"Right, so nobody would be able to judge behavior changes?"

"Wait." Shay choked up. She couldn't say it. The thought she'd been ignoring since this second soul had been revealed didn't want to become actual words.

"I didn't mean anything." Hetal kept her stare low, her scribbles slowing to a halt.

"You think I won't be me anymore once the soul's removed."

"I am not implying that."

"I'm still me." Shay slapped her hand on the table. The sting traveled through her palm; *her* palm, not Jenna's. "A soul shoved inside you can't change who you are. Can it?"

Hetal lifted her shoulders into a shrug. "I ... umm. I don't think so. Evie."

"Evie might know if I was different then, she—"

"No. Evie." Hetal dropped her pen and pointed at the closed lab door.

Shay turned on her stool. Evie waved at her from the other side of the glass wall that sealed the lab off from the hallway. At least twenty layers of anger melted at the sight of her sister's frown. Stupid, that's what she was for fighting with Evie over a guy neither one of them would nab in the end.

Shay's sneakers slid on glossy tile as she hurried across the lab to open its door.

Alexie sat on an empty bench in Midtown Park alongside a deserted jogger's trail. She leaned back against the splintered wood and gazed up at the moon through thick trees. It was warm for fall, but nobody should be strolling down this desolate path. At least, not a good guy.

She had to go along with Simon's plan, and somehow coerce Lucius into giving up his perpetual pursuit for world domination. Things were getting out of hand with Max, and after what happened at the lake earlier, she had no choice. Besides, it was good to keep an enemy close, made it easier to stab them in the back.

A cool chill slithered into the night air and a bitter taste crept into Alexie's mouth.

"Lucius," she said, without moving a muscle.

Lucius strolled in front of Alexie, full costume, and hoisted his hands to his hips. The sharp edges on his body armor reflected the sliver of moonlight that broke through the trees, and his hooded cloak cast a shadow over the fierce expression on his metal mask.

"Is that absurd helmet necessary?"

"Look who's talking." Lucius pointed at Alexie's suit. "Think you have enough sparkles on your cape?"

Alexie twirled her fingers around the end of her silky cape, gesturing at the empty seat beside her.

"I was surprised to receive your call." Lucius pulled off his helmet, pushed back strands of black hair off his forehead, and then sat beside

Alexie. "You knew the device I gave you could only reach me once. Your super-buddies are fine, the world isn't ending. What could you possibly want from little ol' me?"

"Max won't follow in your footsteps, no matter how hard you push him. He'd die to protect that girl, or any girl, Jenna's soul or not."

"So what?" Lucius dropped his helmet into his lap, holding a blank stare on Alexie.

"I know you still care about Max, somewhere deep inside that hollow cavity you call a heart. You might want him to suffer, but you'd freak out if he actually died."

Lucius chuckled as he picked a stray thread off his red cloak. "You haven't changed a bit, still thinking you know everything."

"Why don't you just do the decent thing, set Jenna's soul free? If only for the fact that she was your crewmate on the space mission that changed both your lives."

"I don't owe Jenna anything, or Max." Lucius jumped to his feet. He stood in front of Alexie, bending to sneer in her face. "If it wasn't for me and Cyrus, they both would've died up there. They betrayed me, turned their backs when I needed them. I will devour both their souls."

The words trembled as Lucius spoke them, but it wasn't cruelty. It was hurt that quaked his voice. Lucius regretted his role in Jenna's death, and missed his friends. Alexie could tell by the look of sorrow in his eyes. There was a chance she could reunite them all. It was a very, very slim chance, but she had to take it.

"No you won't," she said plainly. "Or you would've done it by now."

Lucius snickered and his tight shoulders loosened.

"Tell you what," he said, backing away from Alexie a few steps. "Since I'm fair, I'll take a trade. I'll fix the Jenna problem and leave this Shay girl alone, in exchange for you."

Alexie jolted back, the park bench creaking under her weight. "What?"

"Join me, willingly, and it's done."

"Join you in what?"

"In making a better world."

Lucius waved his hand and a portal of near blinding light opened beside him. "I'll be in touch."

Light flashed and a gust of hot air blew Alexie's hair back. She covered her eyes, turning from the bright white glow. Once the whistle of wind died out and darkness returned, she looked back to find an empty park.

Shay snuggled beside Evie on the couch in their suite, beneath a soft fleece throw. This moment, when her head rested on a bony shoulder as fashion models pranced on the TV screen meant everything. Boys, labs, displaced souls all took a back burner to family.

A quick jerk shook Evie's body, which was acting as Shay's pillow. Soon Evie would start snoring, then drooling.

Shay scooted over on the long couch, sinking into the cushions at its other end. A soft red light pulsed on the ceiling, and the most gentle hum tickled her ears. Her eyes grew heavy, but the crimson glow that flooded her vision kept them open. The blinking red light swirled, the hum grew louder, and her stomach burned.

There was no air. Shay couldn't breathe, not while staring at the spin of flashing lights, with the blast of a high-pitched screech in her ears.

"I can't believe that worked," said a man.

His rough voice snapped Shay from a red-tinged haze. She gasped to catch her breath, getting a lungful of exhaust-laced air. A horn honked and she jumped to the side, her bare feet slapping concrete.

She was on the sidewalk out front of Ling Enterprises, in her Barry the Bear jammies, and she wasn't alone. Dr. Mayhem stood in front of her, so close she could see his breaths puffing out the sparkly fabric on his solid black mask.

"Your mind's easy to get into, girl," he said, grabbing Shay by the arm.

Antiserum stepped from the shadows, the streetlight glinting off his iron mask. "You just became a bargaining chip."

Shay screamed for help. She pulled against Dr. Mayhem's clutch, but the few people who strolled along the sidewalk seemed blind to her presence.

"They see what I want them to see." Dr. Mayhem wrapped his arm around Shay and flew away. The icy wind stung her cheeks as they soared toward the dark sky.

"Stop," she yelled, banging her fist on Dr. Mayhem's hard chest plate.

"I'll drop you," he said in a growl.

Dr. Mayhem released his grip on Shay. She plunged downward between skyscrapers, racing toward the traffic-filled street, and Dr. Mayhem scooped her into his arms again.

This time, she didn't hurl punches at the supervillain who sped across the city with her in one hand. She wrapped her arms around his neck and held on for dear life.

"You're tired," he whispered into Shay's ear and she yawned. "You're going to sleep for one hour, dream of Max."

Shay's eyelids grew heavy, closing her into dreams of Max holding her in *his* strong arms.

A rumble vibrated the windows, and jolted Evie from sleep. She reached for Shay, grabbing only air. Her heart thumped. Something was wrong. Evie couldn't explain how she knew—perhaps instinct, or the fact she'd become keen to the distinct feel of danger—but she could sense something was terribly wrong with Shay.

Evie turned on lights in the empty suite as she walked toward Shay's room, but the brightness didn't chase off the dreadful vibes clinging to the air.

She opened Shay's bedroom door and ... nothing. Rumpled sheets occupied the bed, clothes were strewn across the floor, but no Shay.

"The lab. She must be working."

Evie dialed Shay's cell phone and a ring sounded from the coffee table.

"Dammit," she grumbled, trying the lab's landline.

"Dr. Bhatti," said Hetal, her voice streamed through Evie's speaker.

"It's Evie. Is Shay down there?"

"No. I haven't seen her since she left with you. Is everything okay?"

"I'll get back to you on that one." Evie ended the call, paced around the kitchen a few times, then dialed Simon.

"Hel—"

"Shay's missing!"

"Evie? What happened?"

"I woke up, and Shay was gone." Evie's hand trembled, the phone tapping against her ear. "Something's not right, I have a really bad feeling."

"Okay. Just hold on, let me log into the security system."

Evie strummed her fingers on the kitchen's granite countertop. Two seconds might have passed, it could've been two hours for all she knew.

"All right," Simon said above the soft click of a keyboard in the background. "Shay walked out of your suite ten minutes ago, in her pajamas, and got onto the elevator."

Another two seconds of torturous silence passed, which Evie couldn't handle. "Then what?"

"Hold on I'm fast forwarding. Shay got off at the lobby and walked out the front door."

"In her pajamas?"

"And bare feet. Oh no."

Evie clutched onto her phone tighter. "What?" Her grip turned crushing, and the case of her flimsy cell phone creaked. "You can't say *oh no* and then nothing."

"Lucius and Cyrus took her."

"No." The ability to take in air left Evie. It was like an invisible hand reached inside her body and squeezed her chest. "Please don't say that. Please."

"Stay put, I'll be right down."

The line went dead and Evie stared at the cell phone's screen, as if willing it to reveal Shay's location. Her legs shook, so fiercely it brought her to the floor. A shuddering breath finally burst from her lungs. Now that her airways were clear, a flood of cries felt free to pour from her mouth.

A distant shout stirred Shay from a dream of Max's lips brushing against her cheek. She rolled onto her side, forcing her eyes to open. Gray stones blurred into view, a large wall of cracked gray stones. Shay sat up and the back of her head clunked against solid metal.

"Perfect," said a deep voice, directly behind Shay.

Fear ran through her body, inciting every muscle and both her fingers and her bare toes to shake. She could feel bars at her back, see no means to escape the tiny cell surrounding her, and that voice. That wicked voice still ringing in her ears was no stranger.

"Antiserum." Shay sat tall in the dark room, despite the terror brewing in her stomach.

"My, my, how the tables have turned. Do you remember being on the opposite side of the cage? What it felt like? I bet my experience will be a lot better than yours."

The man behind Shay was scary, but she'd taken enough crap from scary people these last few days. She hardened her expression and turned on her knees to face the man on the other side of her iron bars.

It shocked her to see Antiserum without his mask, to see Lucius's confident face. Aside from the standard villain outfit, complete with an armor chest plate and red cape, he didn't look like a bad guy. Lucius looked like any other man, especially when he wasn't trying to wear an evil and ominous glower. His dark eyes now held a gentle edge, and it gave her the strength to yell at him.

"What do you want?"

"Excuse me?"

"Do you want Jenna's soul? Do you want my soul? Do you just want me dead? What is it you really want? *Lucius.*" Her lips pushed for a smile, but she held them straight.

Lucius lunged toward Shay, his fists up, and stopped right in front of her cell's bars. "You'll find out what I want in about twenty minutes, after I power up my brother's machine. You like experiments don't you, Dr. Sinclair?"

His laughter bounced off the damp walls, even after he walked away. The dim lights in the hallway cut out once Lucius shut the solid metal door.

In a wide room of cobwebs and small cells, Shay sat alone in total darkness. She pulled her knees to her chest. Every little sound boomed, but none louder than her own breath. Something furry ran across her toes. She kicked her feet, might have screamed a little while scurrying backward on the dirt-covered floor. Her elbow slammed against a jagged stone wall and sharp barbs of pain spread throughout her arm.

She had to get out of this cell, get help. Someone needed to help her.

"Calm down," said a voice, much like her own, from somewhere in the darkness.

"Who's there?" Shay called out, curling her fingers into fists.

"Please. Like you don't know."

"Jenna?"

An orange glow ignited right in front of Shay's face, encircling a teenage girl. Even if Shay hadn't seen pictures, watched old news footage, she'd know it was Jenna. Not for the shine of solar rays, which clung to the girl's body like a glove, but from the warmth of her very presence.

"How is this … how are you here, in my cell?"

"You tell me, you're the hotshot scientist."

Shay blinked, twice, but Jenna still sat in front her looking bored.

"You're a figment of my imagination. I must have lost my mind. I'm not talking to you. Go away, figment."

Jenna snickered. She flicked her fingers and a tiny ball of energy sailed through the air, then zapped Shay in the chest.

"Can a figment do that?"

Shay rubbed her chest but the sting didn't dull. "Maybe. That hurt."

"Sissy." Jenna jumped to her feet and clutched onto the cell's rusty bars.

"Get us out of here. If you're not a figment, you can do that."

Jenna slouched back against the bars. "Maybe I am a figment. I've been trying to get your attention since you were knee-high to a Smurf, and I just blasted the shit out of Lucius. He didn't even flinch."

"That's great." Shay tossed her hands up before they fell back to her lap. "I'm crazy."

"I don't think you're crazy."

"Of course *you* don't, you're my imagination."

Jenna knelt in front of Shay. "I'm not your imagination. I got out for a second. You let me out."

"What do you mean?"

"In the lab, with Max. I whispered in your ear, begged you to let me out and you did. Now you can see me and I feel different, stronger."

Shay slanted to the side, leaning away from Jenna, and Jenna followed.

"Let me out, Shay."

"No." Shay would shove Jenna from her face, but she was terrified to touch the maybe figment/possible ghost. "You're already out, just, go away."

"You know what I mean." Jenna grabbed Shay's hand, squeezing. "I know you remember doing it, I saw you type it in your journal. Let ... me ... out."

Heat surged from Jenna's touch. Shay tried to pull back but Jenna's grip tightened.

"I'll save us. Don't you wanna see Evie again?"

"Stop." Shay pulled herself from Jenna's near crushing grip, and her hand whacked against the pointy stone wall. "If I let you out, you'll never let me back in. I'm not a superhero. What if I get lost?"

Jenna smiled. She draped one arm around Shay's shoulder. "You've been my only friend for the last ten years, and you don't even know it. I've gone everywhere with you, seen what you've seen, felt your happiness and sorrow. I love you, stupid. I'd never let you get lost."

Boots thumped in the distance, closer, louder, then the door to the room squealed open.

"Do it now, Shay," Jenna yelled, grabbing onto the sides of Shay's arms.

Shay cowered down, but couldn't escape the dread weighing on her shoulders. "I'm scared."

"You should be," Lucius said, unlocking the gate to Shay's cell.

Evie paced in front of a cluttered workbench, her steps echoing throughout the lab. She had no clue how Shay could love this place. It was cold, sterile. Even though crap littered every corner, a hollowness clung to the wide-open space.

"Try to relax," Simon said from the doorway. "Max and Lexie should check in any—"

"We're here." Alexie stepped inside the lab while Max lingered in the doorway beside Simon. "We circled the city twice, but we don't know what to look for."

"She's dead." Evie covered her mouth before any other irrational thoughts could slip out.

"What's wrong with you?" Max stomped in front of Evie. "Pull yourself together, or get out."

"Max," Simon yelled.

"No." Evie forced her shaky hands to steady and stood tall. "Max is right. I need to get it together."

Catastrophe had always been Evie's thing. She was no stranger to blood, had seen countless bodies—including her parents—but if the smallest scrape blemished her sister's skin, she lost the ability to do anything except sob and panic profusely. Well not this time.

Evie looked at Hetal, whose face lit up with a mixture of terror and excitement. "What would Shay do right now?"

Hetal hopped off her stool, inching closer to Evie and Alexie. "I've always wanted to be a part of an actual superhero strategy convo."

The giddy smile on Hetal's lips only lasted seconds. Then a serious expression gripped her face. "Let me think." She tapped her chin as she looked around the lab.

"Dr. Sinclair theorized that people with superpowers emit a different energy frequency than others. Maybe, if we had access to a satellite, I could design a program to track that energy. There's only two other people with superpowers. It should lead us right to them."

"I have three satellites," Simon said, heading to the nearest computer.

Max turned on the monitor beside Simon and took a seat at the long desk of computers. "I know code." He glanced at Hetal between rampant keystrokes. "You work up the sequence on this energy frequency. I'll write the program."

Evie glanced at Alexie, only to receive a scowl.

"What?" Alexie snapped. "I'm not a computer geek or a lab nerd."

"Yeah, me neither." Evie sat on a stool at Shay's workbench, fidgeting with strands of colorful wires. "I guess we just wait then."

Alexie dragged a stool to the workbench, sitting beside Evie. "Shay's not dead."

"I know. I don't know why I said that. I'm an idiot."

"It's okay to be afraid."

Alexie rubbed Evie's shoulder, gently, the way a friend would. Except, they weren't friends. They were co-workers, and it was Alexie's job to deliver comfort and hope.

"She's all I have." Tears followed Evie's words, and a lump rose in her throat to cut off her voice.

"We'll get her back. I promise."

A promise from a superhero, it might've meant something a few hours ago when her sister was safe in her clutches.

Lucius practically crushed Shay's arm with his large hand as he pushed her down a narrow hallway. Cracked tiles scraped the bottoms of her feet, slicing the soft skin between her toes. The ice-cold floor sent shivers into every limb, at least that's what she chose to blame it on. Not fear. The monster behind her would probably smell fear and enjoy its scent too much.

Shay struggled to see down the dark hall behind her, looking for

Jenna. Lucius shoved her forward and she fell against the wall.

"Quite stalling." Lucius grabbed Shay's other arm, dragging her down the hallway. "It'll all be over soon."

"What will?"

"I'm taking care of a problem for a friend, but I'm doing it my way."

A low hum crackled through the air, growing louder with every forced step. She'd beg but it wouldn't help; and reason, that concept didn't dwell here—wherever here was. By the looks of the broken floors, cracked walls, and cobweb-covered stretchers, she'd guess they stumbled into Satan's personal hospital.

"Don't worry." Lucius stopped beside a steel door and grinned at Shay. "I have a good feeling about this procedure."

He slammed Shay's side against the door, which flung the metal slab wide open. A tall man turned from a large metal chamber, dodging a burst of steam.

"I don't know, brother," said the man.

Shay stared at the guy beside the strange, gold machine. His dark hair, light eyes, cleft chin seemed so familiar.

"I know you," she said, pointing at the guy whose name she could almost remember.

"Let's do it," the man said to Lucius as he turned back toward the machine.

Shay wiggled against the grip squeezing her arms. "What are you—"

Lucius shoved Shay deeper into a small room of cluttered workbenches, and Jenna stepped out of the machine's wire-lined chamber.

"You don't wanna go in there," Jenna said, gesturing at the thin doorway behind her. "It's not comfy."

"Help."

"No one's coming to help," Lucius said in a sneer.

"I can't help," Jenna said. "Not unless you let me out."

Shay stomped her bare foot, shook her head. "No."

Lucius pulled Shay close to his side. "You'll thank me for this one day."

"You're gonna die, Shay." Jenna ran in front of Shay, staring into her eyes. "We'll both disappear forever if you don't let me out."

"I can't. You'll never let me come back."

Lucius released his tight clutch on Shay's arm and glanced around the room. "Who are you talking to?"

"I swear." Jenna took Shay by the hand, locking their fingers together. "As soon as I save us, I'll let you back."

"Get inside the chamber." Lucius pushed Shay toward the machine, separating her grip on Jenna.

Sparks showered from the machine's entrance, nipping at Shay's arms. A control panel's gauges lit up with percentages, a high-pitched whirl filled the room, and her knees quaked.

"Okay." Shay yanked her arm from Lucius's clutch and seized onto Jenna's hand. "I let you out."

Once the ripping tug in her chest dulled to a soft ache and the haze cleared, a giggle skirted from her lips. It was the tingle. Her fingertips, ears, even her bloodied bare feet prickled with life.

Jenna stared at the two men who crept toward her. Seeing their dumb faces and apish stances reminded her of old times, and it brought a smile to her lips.

"Cyrus, Lucius. It's been a while."

Lucius grabbed Jenna by the throat and she rammed her knee into his nuts. She stepped aside as he dropped to his side on the ground. Cyrus swung his wide fist at her face, and she ducked it quite easily.

"You always lead with a right hook."

"Jenna?" Cyrus circled Jenna, his fists clenched. "Is that you in there?"

Jenna grabbed a pipe from the floor.

"Wait," Cyrus shouted, lifting his hands. "Let me help you. Put the pipe down and maybe we can figure out how to get you to stay, permanently."

Jenna's shoulders loosened, her arm lowering. Cyrus smiled, walking toward her and she swung the pipe at the side of his head. She didn't want help from a man who stood back and watched his brother kill people.

As Cyrus thumped to the ground beside Lucius, Jenna sprinted out the door. Her shoulder hit the wall, shooting prickles down her arm. Pain, even pain felt awesome.

Jenna ran as fast as Shay's beanpole body would allow, which wasn't very.

"Screw this."

With a skip and a jump, Jenna ... fell flat to her face.

"I can't fly!"

She slammed her fists against the hard floor and pushed herself to her feet. "Whatevs. I'm enjoying this too much anyway."

After climbing rickety stairs and running down endless hallways, she found more dark and twisty hallways. Jenna took a step, catching her reflection in a window. The stringy golden hair and dull brown eyes shocked her still. Then she remembered, not her body.

Since she wouldn't have to deal with scratches and scrapes later, she drove her elbow through the window. Shards of glass rained down, carving thin red lines on her arm.

The sting circulated through her body, igniting every nerve in the most delicious way. It was a sensation Shay could never appreciate, having lived inside skin all her life.

A cool breeze grazed Jenna's cheek and she stuck her head outside, inhaling deeply. Dead fish and salt water filled her lungs. The stench clung to her nose, ruining any chance to get a whiff of sweet city air.

"I will get one," she said in a grumble as she leapt from the window. Her bare feet slapped pavement, tiny pebbles ripping her tender skin.

Without looking back, Jenna ran. Her legs throbbed, feet slick with blood, but she ran past wooden docks and empty streets. Villains could've lurked on every corner and she wouldn't have seen it. Her gaze was locked on the tall, wide building that gleamed brighter than all the others it towered over.

Shay's voice screamed in Jenna's mind. Shay was frightened. She wanted to escape the cold gray place where Jenna lived, wanted to come back to the colorful world that Jenna now walked in, but Jenna wasn't ready to swap places yet.

"I will let you back. Just … shut up." Jenna stopped in the middle of the street, looking at herself in a car's window. An escaped mental patient. That's what she saw when glimpsing this hideous reflection, ugly pink pajamas to boot.

"Aw, hell no. We'll get arrested running around like this." Jenna glanced around then reached for the car's handle. After a quick prayer, she pulled and it opened.

Like the ghost she was, Jenna slipped inside the car. "Yes, Shay. I am gonna steal this car." She felt underneath the seat, found a wad of gum, but no car keys.

"Tell me how to hotwire a car?" she asked Shay, who now haunted the rearview mirror.

The Shay in the mirror shook her head, and Jenna groaned.

"Very nice, real hero like." In a last ditch effort, Jenna flipped down the sun visor and keys tumbled into her lap. "Ha. Looks like I don't need your help."

Shay shouted protests within Jenna's mind, but Jenna ignored them and started the car. "Be quiet. I have to drive."

Max pushed past Evie, ran out the lobby of Ling Enterprises, and stopped on the sidewalk. His knees bent, eyes on the sky. Just as flames ignited beneath his boots, tires screeched and a car skid to a stop beside him.

He jumped back from the curb as the car's door flung open. A scratched up, bloody Shay climbed from the driver's seat and both relief and rage flooded his chest.

"Shay," Evie cried out.

Shay didn't flinch. Her gaze had zeroed in on Max and never left. Then, like a moment ripped straight out of his dreams, she ran into his arms. Her fingers glided through his hair, quaking his knees.

"I missed you, baby," she said, in a throaty whisper that didn't belong to Shay.

"Jenn—"

Her lips covered Max's mouth, stealing his words. The second she kissed him, he knew. It was definitely Jenna. He held her tight and strong hands pried him away.

"Dude," Alexie yelled as Simon pushed Max against a wall.

Evie marched up to Max and slapped him across the cheek, which earned her a hard shove from Shay; or rather, from Jenna.

"Hey," Shay shouted in Evie's face. "Watch it, bossy-butt. That's my man." She hit Simon until he let Max go then cuddled under Max's arm.

"What the hell are you doing?" Evie shrieked.

"This isn't Shay," Max said. Lights flashed, and the clicks of cameras bounced off the buildings. "We should get inside." He tried to push Shay... Jenna away, but she clung to his arm with both hands. Once inside Ling Enterprises, she went in for another kiss.

"Have you lost your mind?" Evie yelled at Shay, pulling her away from Max.

"That's not Shay," Max said again, mostly to himself.

"What?"

"Yeah." Shay jerked her hand free from Evie's clutch, then pushed Evie. "So back off, bossy-butt, or I'll solarslap you."

"Oh shit," Alexie muttered. Her jaw hung open as she stood beside

Evie to gawk at Shay's body moving and talking under Jenna's will.

"Hey, Sparkles," Shay said through an enormous grin.

Alexie gasped. "It is Jenna."

Shay hip-checked Evie aside, then shooed everyone from her way. She walked toward Max, and he backed away from her.

"Don't," Max said, hold his arm out stiff.

"It's okay, baby. Shay still owes me for saving her life. She won't mind."

"Ew." Evie stepped in between them, but looked at neither one. "Shay … Jenna … whoever you are, you're about to get put on lockdown if you don't chill."

"Evie." Max placed his hand on Evie's shoulder, gently. "Can I have a minute with her? Please."

Part of him wished Evie would say no, or perhaps slap him again, but she didn't. She just walked to the other side of the lobby, beside a stunned Simon and Alexie, with her stare low.

"Come on, baby. Take me to our room. I got a beatdown and need some TLC."

"Jenna." Max pulled her toward a corner, and everybody in the lobby slowly followed. "The girl you're in is only sixteen."

"So what. I'm seventeen."

"But, I'm twenty-six. Look at me. It's been ten years."

"I don't care how old you are, stupid."

She reached for Max's hand, and he moved away. The sharpest ache stemmed from her touch, crippling his will. He thought it'd feel great to have Jenna back again, but to see her spirit—glimpse her shine trapped within another person's eyes—only ripped, tore, sliced at his soul.

"I care," Max said softly. "And the girl you're in, she wouldn't think it's right. I'm sorry. I can't."

Max turned his back before he could see the heartbreak on anybody's face. It took every ounce of strength not to look back. It was a good thing. If he had looked back, he would've ran to Jenna.

He would have scooped her into his arms and flew off with her. Instead, he took to the skies alone.

Jenna hurried to the window, watching Max jet off in a whirlwind of flames. Shay's eyes glared at her in the glass and she shot back from the window.

"He ditched me."

"Umm." Alexie patted Jenna on the arm, lightly. "He doesn't want to be with you because, you know, you're dead."

"But I'm here."

"That's not you, Jenna. We buried you a long time ago."

Evie marched forward with that bossy-butt look that Jenna had always hated.

"Get out of my sister, you bitch."

"Ooh." Jenna took a step toward Evie, bumping the woman's shoulder. "*Nasty.* Shay hates you. You do know that, right?"

"Liar!" Evie lifted her hand to slap Jenna and Alexie carted her away, but that didn't stop the woman's mouth from spewing.

"Some heroes you all are. You'll sacrifice a sixteen-year-old girl to hang with a buddy."

Jenna stood in the middle of the lobby, dripping blood from her fingertips, watching Evie throw a fit while being ushered away. It wasn't exactly the homecoming she'd envisioned. Shay's voice thundered in her ears, growing louder by the second, and she gripped her temples.

"Please, just a little bit longer."

"Shay ... I mean, Jenna." Simon reached for Jenna's hand then drew his arm back. "Why don't we get those cuts bandaged?"

Jenna's gaze dropped to the little red pools at her feet. The dark blood tumbling from her stolen meat suit smeared across the bright floor, blocking its shine.

"There's nothing left for me here, is there?"

"I'm sorry, Jenna."

The look in Simon's eyes, the tone of his voice. It oozed pity. A flesh and bone body wasn't as fun as Jenna remembered, especially not a plain one like this. Her aches weren't even healing, they were actually getting worse.

Jenna limped toward the open elevator. She hurried past Simon, stepped inside the elevator, and hit the button for the top floor. The door slid shut, closing off Simon and his shouts.

Her reflection shined on every surface, surrounding her. Instead of glimpsing her own lost eyes, she saw Shay's face. That girl was going to be angry. Shay would never trust her again, not that it mattered.

"I'm almost done. Just one more thing."

With a *ding*, the elevator door opened and Jenna hobbled out on her cut feet. A frosty stairwell and three doors later, she was on the rooftop staring at Max's back.

"I knew you'd be up here."

Max turned toward her but he wouldn't look at her face. She couldn't blame him. Ten years and a different body stood between them. All that time suspended in a gray fog, she hadn't realized life went on for the people she left behind.

"Jenna, I—"

"No, don't." Jenna crept closer to Max, gazing at him in the moonlight. Lines creased his forehead, a dark stubble claiming his chin. He really did look older, kind of ... sexier.

"I understand why it's hard for you. I know you've been looking for me, for my soul."

His eyes glazed over and she choked up. She blinked back her own tears, straining to keep her voice steady.

"I want you to let me go. We were the greatest loves of each other's lives, and that's enough for me. I'm happy. I want you to be happy too."

A tear fell from Max's eye, splashing the back of Jenna's hand. He opened his mouth but before he could speak, she laid her lips atop his.

This time, he kissed back. Slow and soft, he kissed her. It was the way he always had, the memory she'd been clinging to while alone in the dark. Jenna wrapped her arms around Max's neck and held him tight one last time.

"I love you, baby," she whispered into his ear. "See you on the other side."

She closed her eyes and drifted away from his words, his touch, and fell back into an empty gray world of shadows and echoes.

Leather crinkled as Evie sat up on the couch in her suite. She'd locked herself in here, alone, to weep in privacy. She should've taken this soul business more serious, should've listened to Shay when she tried to explain it. Now Shay was gone, and she had no idea how to get her sister back.

After blowing her nose, Evie tossed a soggy tissue across the living room and then downed an entire glass of wine. Half a bottle of this ridiculously smooth Bordeaux and her tears still flowed. The remedy must lie at the bottom of the bottle. In which case, Evie had some more drinking to do.

As she reached for the wine, the suite's front door was kicked open. Max rushed inside the living room carrying Shay, and Evie jumped to her feet.

"She just collapsed," Max said, verging hysteria.

"Put her on the couch." Evie flung the blanket aside and Max laid Shay on the leather cushions.

"What happened?" She bumped Max from her way, running a hand along Shay's forehead. "Where's Simon? Alexie?"

"I don't know. We were on the roof—"

"You, and the horn-dog soul inside my sister's body were on the roof, alone?" Evie pushed crumpled tissues aside in search of her cell phone.

"She found me up there. We were … talking and she passed out."

"Talking?" Evie's eyes left the cell phone's screen long enough to roll then she continued typing her message.

"Who are you calling?"

"I'm texting Simon. I'd feel safer being with you if he were here."

"I'm not gonna hurt you."

Evie snickered. "I know, but I might hurt you."

"That's not fair, Evie. You have no idea how hard it's been for me."

"Fair." Evie tossed her cell phone onto an armchair and it bounced off the cushion, clattering to the floor.

"My parents dying wasn't fair. Shay having another person's soul shoved inside her body when she was six wasn't fair. If you're looking for fair, you came to the wrong place."

Evie could slap Max for being naïve, but the look of defeat in his eyes sucked the fun right out of that notion. Before he could say a word, or conjure up another expression that made her want to hug him, she knelt beside Shay.

"Will it be … *Jenna* when she wakes up?"

"I don't know." Max sat on the arm of the couch, staring at Shay.

"But you want it to be Jenna?"

Max buried his face in his hands, his shoulders trembling. "I don't know."

18

Voices broke through a gray fog, bringing with them the throb of pain. There wasn't a single place on her body that didn't ache. Her head pounded, feet burned, but the worst was her chest. A sharp stab pierced her heart. This pain didn't belong to her, it wasn't of her body or soul. Jenna let Shay back, but left behind the deepest pit of sadness.

"Jenna?"

Max's eyes blurred into view. He looked at Shay with such hope and fear. It split Shay's broken heart open even wider. She sat up, happy to find herself on the couch in her suite's living room. There were a lot of people gathered around her, but not one of them was the person she'd been seeking. None of them were Jenna.

"No. It's just me, Shay."

Evie hugged Shay. "I knew you'd find your way back."

"I'm sorry, Evie." Shay pried Evie's hands from her neck so she could get a glimpse of her sister's perfect smile. "I don't hate you. I've never hated you."

"I know."

"Do you remember everything?" Simon asked.

Shay looked at Max. She didn't just remember. She had felt Jenna's anguish, experienced the intensity between the ghost girl and Max.

"Yeah. It was like watching myself in a black and white movie."

"Do you know where you were? Where their lair is?"

"Yes. I was in an abandoned hospital, near the docks."

"The old asylum," Alexie said, heading for the door.

Simon patted Shay on the arm then rushed out the suite's kicked-open front door after Alexie.

Max stood in front of Shay, fidgeting with the bottom of his shirt. "Shay—"

"Come on, Max," Alexie yelled from the hallway.

"I'm really glad you're back," Max said, hurrying out of the room.

"Be careful." Shay turned toward the front door, but Max was already gone.

The emptiness of the room hung thick, dragging her back into the couch cushions. She shouldn't miss Max, or Jenna. She'd just met Max and only recently discovered Jenna's soul residing inside her body, yet a strong pull drew her to them both.

Evie took Shay's hand and the void in her chest filled with love. Shay drew Evie close. She hugged her sister so tight Evie's back cracked a little.

"What did Dr. Mayhem and Antiserum do to you?" Evie asked. She wriggled from Shay's embrace, inspecting the fresh bandages along Shay's arm.

"Nothing. This was mostly from Jenna. I don't think she's used to non-healing skin."

"*Jenna*. She's a maniac."

Evie's nose crinkled, lips bunching, and a snicker flew from Shay's mouth. She really did owe Jenna everything. Jenna promised to bring her back to her sister and here she was, sitting beside Evie.

"Jenna saved me. She beat the crap out of two supervillains, with no powers, and made your face turn fifty shades of red. I know you don't think so, but she really is a *super* hero."

Evie squeezed onto the couch beside Shay and crawled under the blanket. "Has she been popping in and out of your body this whole time? Because that would explain the dark makeup phase last fall."

"No. I never actually felt her until … I got hit with the sonic blast."

"You mean, until I killed you."

Shay grabbed Evie's hand. She wanted to tell her sister it was okay, that it wasn't her fault, but it would be lies. Something happened to her that night, the night she died. The places she went and people she spoke with grew fainter as the days passed, but the knowledge she'd grazed something significant would never leave her mind.

"I crossed a veil," Shay said, even though Evie could never really understand what that meant. "It unlocked a door in my mind, allowed me to see what's been there the entire time."

Evie leaned back on the couch and narrowed her stare on Shay. "How do I even know you're you right now?"

"You sucked your thumb until you were sixteen."

"Hey!" Evie smacked Shay's arm then glanced around the empty suite. "That's a secret."

"A secret only I know." Shay rested her head on Evie's shoulder. "I'm sure you knew right off the bat it wasn't me."

"Oh, yeah. You ran up and kissed Max, all dramatic, just like in every generic teen flick."

"Anyway." She'd never do something that vapid. "That's just so …"

"I know," Evie said, with a dead-serious expression.

"All right." Shay snuggled closer to Evie. She pulled the soft blanket up to her scratched cheek and nudged the TV's remote with her toe. "Put on *Runway Wars*. I want to see if the snotty girl gets the boot."

Lucius crept into a corner of the dayroom, squishing Cyrus against the wall. His stare followed Max and the *hero* squad as they walked right past him.

"I don't even want to move," he whispered to Cyrus.

"Why?" Cyrus pushed Lucius aside and walked across the room. "They can't see us." He waved his hand in front of Simon's face then stuck up two middle fingers, chuckling.

"This is great." Lucius tailed the trio of so-called heroes deeper into the asylum, grinning at Cyrus. "We should stay invisible."

"Can't do, brother. Sixty minutes, tops, or you really will be staying like this. Forever."

Cyrus tilted to the side, staring at Alexie's butt as her cape swung. "Think she still digs me?"

"You had your chance," Lucius said in a growl.

"I don't think they're here," Max said.

Lucius secretly followed his adversaries down a hallway, which would lead them back to the dayroom. He cut in front of Cyrus, so *he* could walk behind Alexie. "She needs a darker, stronger man."

"Don't even think about it."

"I'm already thinking about it." Lucius reached out to trace the blue streaks in Alexie's black hair.

"Hey." Cyrus crashed his hand against the wall, blocking the tight corridor and stopping Lucius in his tracks. He stared daggers, but Lucius didn't back down.

"We should go," Simon's voice echoed down the hallway, "this could be a decoy. They could be at our place right now."

Max and his super-buddies stomped their polished boots, and

broke windows somewhere down the hallway, as Lucius stood tall in front of his little brother.

"You have a new woman, and I promise you'll like her much better once I'm done with her."

Cyrus grabbed Lucius by the cloak straps and slammed his back against the wall. "Stay away from my women, all of them."

Lucius laughed but he wasn't amused, at least not by the anger in his brother's eyes. His fist clenched. If Cyrus didn't let go of his cloak soon, he'd have to swing.

"It's too late, plans are already in motion."

The watch on Cyrus's wrist beeped, and he released his grip on Lucius. Little chirps filled the hall as Cyrus pressed buttons on his watch. A low hum bounced off the walls, vibrating the air as an electric-laced breeze rushed down the hallway.

"We're visible again."

"I'm not a monster." Lucius clutched onto his brother's shoulder, holding firm. "I can tell you like this new girl. There has to be a way to test people, see if they can withstand the blast."

"Maybe." Cyrus shrugged away from Lucius, his gaze wandering off. "Each of us, even Simon and Alexie, have an additional strand in our DNA sequence, which allowed for successful mutation."

"Exactly," Lucius said, trying not to use his scheming voice. "You go whip up a test and I'll bring her to you. If she isn't a candidate, I'll let her go."

"Yeah, all right." Cyrus glanced back at Lucius as he walked away. "But let me know before she gets here, so I can put my mask on. I don't want to blow it with her."

Geniuses were beyond gullible. Mention scientific tests and they forget all about plots to steal ex-girlfriends.

Lucius leaned against the dusty wall in the dark corridor, gazing out a cracked window. Through fractured glass, he stared at the moon as it hovered beside Ling Enterprises. Twenty-four hours ago, he'd given a wayward superhero a proposition in the park. It was time for him to get an answer.

"Alexie," Lucius said in a whisper. He flung his cloak over his shoulder and walked down the hallway.

The world's problems hung over Alexie's head … her world anyway. She leaned against the elevator wall, beside Simon, as the lift shot up 113 floors to their penthouse. Shay could live a normal life, with one soul. Lucius and Cyrus would stop destroying Gemini City. All she had to do was be the bad guy.

"Max insisted on spending the night at Shay's suite," Simon said. "Swore he'd stay in the living room."

The elevator door opened to their penthouse and Alexie made a beeline for her room.

"Is something wrong?" Simon asked, unclipping his cape.

Alexie couldn't tell Simon she was scared to go along with his plan to sway the Grant brothers back to their side. She didn't want him to know she was afraid of becoming an actual villain if she pretended to be one. A real hero didn't wonder what it'd be like to do whatever they pleased and take whatever they wanted. She shouldn't have those thoughts either. She definitely shouldn't voice them.

"No. I'm just tired." Without a glance back, Alexie hurried into her room and locked the door.

A faint glow shined through her wide windows. The city lights bathed her carpet in a yellow tinge, and lit the room like a tiny desk lamp.

If she returned to the asylum, alone, Lucius would appear. Then, she could convince him she wanted to be evil—so she could convince him to be good—but her legs wouldn't move.

Simon had been her best friend since college. He really wanted this to work. Deep inside, she'd also like to have Lucius and Cyrus rejoin their group, in a non-villainous way.

"Thinking about me?"

Alexie yelped. She stared into the shadows of her room and Lucius crept into the soft light that beamed through her window.

"How'd you get in here?" she asked, as quietly as one could growl.

"I told you I'd be in touch," Lucius said in a whisper. "Do you have an answer for me?"

"Why would I? You kidnapped Shay."

"I took Shay to fix the Jenna soul problem, as a sign of good faith. She fought back. I didn't want to hurt her, which is why I let her go." Lucius stepped toward Alexie and she crept away from him, pressing her back against the cool window behind her.

"You blowing me off has nothing to do with Shay. You've always been a frightened little girl."

Lucius reached for Alexie's cheek and she slapped his hand away, giving him an electric-charged shove.

"I'm not afraid of you." Lightning arced between her fingertips, but she forced it to subside. Simon was in the next room. The walls in this penthouse were thick, though not thick enough to mask the crackle of pure energy.

Lucius chuckled as he rubbed the spot where she had zapped him. "No, you're not afraid of me. You're afraid of yourself."

His dark eyes locked on Alexie, a slight smile lingering on his lips. "I've seen inside your soul. It's wicked, deliciously wicked."

The tone of Lucius's silky voice hummed in Alexie's head. Two seconds. It would only take two seconds to throw Lucius through her window, but her clenched fists wouldn't unlock.

"It must be difficult for you." Lucius slid his hand into Alexie's hair, his gentle touch igniting sparks beneath her skin. "Dealing with those two golden boys all day."

He moved closer to Alexie and their chests pressed against each other.

"They're not like us. They can't think realistically, don't have what it takes to actually change the world. Let me show you what it means to be a hero."

Lucius ducked, bringing his lips inches from Alexie's mouth. Warm breath tickled her lips, sending shivers to nip at her spine.

"If you kiss me, I'll fry your ass to a crisp."

Lucius backed away from Alexie, taking the air with him.

"When you finally decide to come around, I might not want you anymore." He pushed open the window, smirked, and jumped out, leaving Alexie alone with the cool breeze.

19

Shay sat upright on the couch with a start. A scream had pulled her from a dreamless sleep. It was her name, shouted by a strange voice. She'd heard the fear-stricken call clearly; but now, in the stillness of a sun-lit room, she wasn't sure.

The couch cushion beside Shay was bare, with only throw pillows in the place where Evie should be. She jumped up off the empty couch, and a snore drew her stare to the loveseat.

"Max?" Shay muttered.

Max's head rolled to the side and a strand of his hair fell over his closed eyes. She backed out of the living room. Max's safe arms looked too inviting to stare at and not crawl into, hence her steady flee away from him.

A gust of air whistled as Shay stepped into the hallway. The scent of exhaust lingered on a chilled breeze, lifting the hairs on her arms. She hurried down the hallway, bursting through Evie's bedroom door.

Curtains danced in front of an open window, and the sound of far-off street traffic was the only noise in the empty room. A spike of panic hit the bottom of Shay's stomach. There was no cause for alarm. The room looked fine, yet a full-blown freak-out loomed on her horizon.

"Evie," Shay yelled. She stumbled from Evie's bedroom, crashing against the wall.

Max ran into the hallway. The bathroom door between him and Shay opened, and Evie stepped out.

"What's wrong?" Evie asked, looking at Shay then Max.

"I, umm …" Shay didn't know what to say. *I'm a big sissy* would fit, but she wasn't about to let that fly from her mouth.

Max walked down the hallway to join Evie in staring at Shay. "Did something happen?"

"No." Shay's tight body unwound and she slumped against the wall.

"I couldn't find you," she said to Evie, instantly feeling stupid. The only explanation she could think of for her irrational behavior was …

"The window's open."

"Sorry." Evie rubbed Shay's shoulder on her way into her bedroom. "I was watching the sunrise." She shut the window then pulled the curtains closed. "It's been a while since I've gotten up early enough to do that."

"But, you're always up before the sun."

Evie ignored Shay and pointed at Max. "When did you get here, and how'd you get in? Oh right, the front door's been kicked open. Some operation you guys are running around here."

Now Max squirmed, much to Shay's enjoyment. It was nice to *not* be the one in the hot seat with a dumb look on their face for a change.

"We struck out last night," Max said. "I thought someone should be here, to protect you both."

"By snoring?" Shay asked in a snicker.

"I'm a light sleeper. I heard you squawk like a chicken." Max poked Shay on the arm and she giggled, then whacked his hand away.

"All right." Evie shooed Max from her bedroom doorway. He walked backward down the hall, and she kept shuffling him toward the front door. "Don't you have someplace to be?"

"Nope." Max sidestepped Evie. He strolled into the living room and sat on the arm of the couch.

Shay stood at the hallway's edge, waiting for that little vein to pulse on Evie's temple, for hilarious insults to be shouted at Max, but her sister just shrank down.

"This is ... interesting," Shay said, in a way that would strongly suggest otherwise. "But I need to shower, get to the lab."

"The lab," Evie called out as she fumbled with the espresso machine. "I'll go with you."

"Why? You hate the lab."

"I have a slow day and it'll be nice, like old times. Except now, I'll follow you to work."

"Sounds like fun," Max said. He sunk into the couch cushions, making himself quite comfortable. "I'll go too."

Shay stared at Max just chilling in her living room, then looked at Evie bumbling around the kitchen. That little anger vein was probably pulsing in her own temple right now.

"I don't need a bunch of babysitters."

"That's not what this is," Max said.

"Of course not," Evie muttered.

They both rambled nonsense through fake grins, waving their hands around way too much. It'd be comical, if it weren't *her* life.

"Whatever." Shay walked away from the blah-blah-we-just-wanna-hang-blah, and shut herself inside the nice and quiet bathroom.

It was sweet they cared; annoying, but sweet. She didn't need them though. When she got into her lab, she was going to make so many weapons.

Rusty hinges squealed as Lucius pushed open a heavy door. The lab his brother had set-up in the abandoned asylum's basement impressed him. It paled in comparison to the sterile, pristine laboratory they had at the Grant manor, but Cyrus had tried his hardest with the rusted workbenches, fried wires, and piles of antiquated machinery they had to work with.

Lucius stepped into the room and Cyrus turned away, pulling his mask over his head.

"You don't need it. Your girl's feisty, I had to sedate her."

"If you hurt her—"

"Relax. Damn, little brother. If I didn't know better, I'd think you were in love with this woman." Lucius yanked the mask off Cyrus's face to gauge his brother's expression. Blank, just like a man who manipulated minds should be.

He tossed the hood at Cyrus. "Don't worry. I'll let you be the one to hurt her."

That chipped his brother's icy stare, just a tad. He could push harder, force Cyrus into a telekinetic fury, but he needed most of the junk in this room.

"Have you finished your test?"

"Yeah." Cyrus grabbed a test tube and a mouth swab off the steel table beside him. "I just need a DNA sample."

Lucius held out his hand and Cyrus stormed past him.

"I'll do it," Cyrus said, stopping in the doorway. "Where is she?"

"In the same place you put Shay."

Cyrus let out a low growl then hurried into the hallway.

"It's okay," Lucius called out as he rushed after Cyrus. "I spray-painted *Shay was here* real big on the wall, so she wouldn't feel lonely."

"Cute."

The spite that trembled his brother's voice kept Lucius back a few steps. Cyrus would only take so much. If Lucius pressed the wrong buttons, his brother would get into his mind and make him see his own flesh melt off. Again.

Cyrus headed deeper into the asylum. The thud of his boots echoed off the cracked walls, rumbling through the narrow hallways of cobweb-covered medical equipment. He stopped in front of a dented steel door, glancing at Lucius.

"I got this," he said through gritted teeth.

It was clearly meant to be a warning, one Lucius would heed. He backed away from Cyrus, slowly. His steps didn't reverse out of fear for Cyrus's powers. He wanted to respect his brother's wishes. Cyrus had given up everything for him, even his own belief in right and wrong. The least Lucius could do was give Cyrus the illusion of control, on rare occasions.

Cyrus pulled his shiny cloth mask over his face, opened the solid metal door at the hall's end, and walked into the holding room.

Lucius made it halfway down the hall before the talons of curiosity dug into his side. In near silence, he crept toward the holding room's doorway and peeked inside. Cyrus knelt in the dirt, caressing the unconscious woman's hand through the bars. The mask hid his brother's face, but those gentle touches gave away the truth. Love had infected his brother's heart. It would be a complication for sure, though nothing was eternal. Except for power, of course.

Shay pushed past Max and bumped Evie from her way to get off the elevator first. It had been a weird morning. Evie hadn't even made breakfast, for the first time in memory. Shay needed to get inside the lab, her sanctuary, her sanity, her place of true bliss. One whiff of machine oil, a glimpse of scattered circuit boards, and her frazzled nerves would level out to chilled vibes.

A smile popped onto her lips as she rounded the corner. The

scent of fresh electronics filled her lungs, and Hetal's face blocked her view of the lab.

"I knew they'd save you," Hetal said, hugging Shay.

"Not us." Max strolled into the lab, unhindered by a smothering embrace. "All that work we did and Shay walked up to the front door. Good thing too, it would've taken forever to search all those locations."

"What work?" Shay asked. She squeezed past Hetal, who still crowded her, and scanned the lab to ensure everything was as she left it. "What locations?"

"You're going to love this." Hetal took Shay by the hand and pulled her toward the computers. "We constructed a program based on your theory."

Shay stared at a map of Gemini City on the computer screen, which had clusters of blinking red dots all over it. "My theory?"

"Yeah. How individuals with superpowers emit a distinctive energy signature."

"You found a way to track them?" Little lights flashed, entrancing Shay's stare with its barrage of red glimmer. There were so many of them, spread throughout the city.

"Wait." Evie pointed at the computer's screen. "Are you saying all these blips are people who have the potential to gain superpowers?"

Hetal leaned back in her seat, staring at Evie in confusion. "Don't you remember? Last night you said you were going to assemble a task force, bring them all in to interview and see if they displayed powers of any kind."

"Right." Evie pulled out her cell phone. "Didn't get much sleep, must've slipped my mind. At least I started typing the email." She glanced at the computer screen then at Hetal. "Can you send me a list with addresses?"

"Sure." Hetal reached past Max, smirking when her arm brushed against his, and typed on the keyboard. "There you go."

Evie grinned. She stared at her cell phone, her legs shuffling backward toward the door. "I'll catch you later, Shay. I really want to get on top of this."

"Okay. Text me about ..." Shay glanced at the doorway, but Evie was gone. "Lunch."

Her stomach grumbled and she grabbed it, but the mini roar kept howling.

"Hungry?" Hetal asked in a snicker.

"Yeah. Evie didn't make breakfast." It felt silly to say, since she was fully capable of dumping cereal into a bowl. She just never had to do that before.

"Me too." Hetal took off her lab coat and draped it over a chair. "I'll grab us something from the diner down the block." She picked up her backpack and headed for the door. "Any requests?"

"Pancakes," Shay and Max called out, almost in sync.

"Got it."

Shay looked at Max, hoping he'd be the next to leave. The way he lounged on her couch, like he belonged, replaced the attraction she held toward him with layers of irritation. His need to hang around only tortured her mind. He had to know that. It had to bother him too, especially after that kiss.

"I remember everything that happened last night."

Max lowered his gaze to the shiny floor. "Me too."

The distraught look on Max's face pulled Shay's body toward him, but her brain kept her legs rooted in place, which put her in a somewhat defunct robot sway.

"I'm sorry," Shay muttered to her shoes.

"Why are you sorry?"

"I never felt a love that intense before. Didn't even know it could exist. I'm sorry you both lost that."

"You could feel Jenna?" Max's voice cracked and he cleared his throat. "What she was feeling?"

Even now, after Jenna had gone silent, the crushing weight of their love pressed against her chest. It stained her own soul, would follow her as long as she drew breath. She couldn't tell Max that. He already had sad puppy dog eyes. If his misery grew any deeper, she'd likely throw her arms around him. That would finish her. Once she held onto him, she'd never want to let go.

"I should be apologizing to you." Max rose to his feet. "I feel all skeevy, kissing you without your permission."

The air vibrated as Max moved toward Shay. She would run, but her legs wobbled too badly. She'd end up face down on the metal floor.

"When you collapsed in my arms," Max said, in a near whisper. "I wasn't thinking about Jenna."

Shay's breath, the light tremor in her muscles, even her precious thoughts stopped. Only tingles flowed throughout her body, and they traveled at a speed that threatened to rip her skin apart if Max so much as touched her.

Max stood directly in front of Shay and stared into her eyes. "I was thinking about you."

The electric vibe between them surged. Shay backed away from Max, almost feeling the break in connection over the waves of shivers.

"Max, I …" Shay swallowed, hard, since her throat decided now was the perfect time to run dry. "I don't think about you in that way." The statement was spoken to him, though meant for herself. If she repeated it enough times in her mind it had to become true.

"You don't, or won't?"

Shay didn't move, didn't dare look at Max. The whole, if I don't see you this isn't happening thing might work. It was childish, but the only logical approach.

"I understand," Max said. He returned to the small couch, which allowed cool air to rush over Shay. "I'm too old. It's gross, I'm totally gross."

"Yeah you are." Shay held a straight face, for all of two seconds before a chuckle burst from her mouth.

Screams echoed down the halls of the asylum. They weren't the terror-filled kind that Lucius had come to enjoy, more of the 'I'll rip your evil heart out' variety.

Cyrus snickered as a slew of obscenities flowed into the room, trailed by a loud crash. "For such a sweet girl, she has a filthy mouth. I had no idea."

"I don't know whether to high-five you or start digging your grave." Lucius stomped across the steel-grated floor and slammed the lab's door shut, but the solid steel door only muffled that woman's infuriating racket.

"Are the results in yet?" His fists clenched as a faint shrill pierced his ears. "I'm hoping it's negative, so I can dump her ass in the harbor."

"You'd put her back where you got her from if it were negative, which it's not."

"Really?" Lucius rushed to Cyrus's workstation. He leaned over the long table and peeked at the computer. The lines on its screen

167

told him nothing but his brother's stare, teeming with fire, was a different story.

"And you're smiling. Does this mean you want to supercharge your girlfriend now?"

"I'm starting to like the idea," Cyrus said through a grin. "She's a lot stronger than I thought, in spirit. Maybe she'll get enhanced strength, give Simon a run for his money."

"You can't tell, with all your squiggly lines?"

Cyrus rubbed his chin as he stared at the monitor. "No. I might be able to later on, after a few more conversions—"

"Conversions. I like that."

"I know you're just placating me." Cyrus stepped around the workstation, puffing out his chest as he stood tall in front of Lucius. "You don't want any tests because you plan on putting everybody in that machine. You want the weak to die and the special to twist into something unnatural like us."

"I want those who are worthy to be given the best advantages. What's wrong with that?"

"Free will." Cyrus glanced at the machine behind him. "You're not God. It's not up to you who lives and dies, or how they live. This is real evil. If we do this, there's no coming back."

"Back?" Rage flooded Lucius's chest, growing and churning inside him. "Back to what? Max and his super-squad of boy scouts? If that's what you want, brother, I'm sure they'll welcome you with open arms."

He turned from Cyrus, resisted the urge to drive his fist through everything in sight. "Go. Crawl to Max and beg for his mercy."

"That's not what I want."

Lucius couldn't stop his muscles from coiling tighter. Cyrus was all he had, the last piece of good he had left in his life to keep him human.

A hand landed on his shoulder, his brother's hand. The grip was soft, gentle, yet strong enough to relax Lucius's tight muscles. That touch, the affection, left a warm sensation in his chest, one he'd long forgotten.

"I want to change the world with you, brother," Cyrus said in true sincerity. "But I want to give people a choice, and not murder thousands of innocents just because they're different from us."

"That's noble." Lucius turned back toward Cyrus, grasping onto the sides of his arms. "And brilliant. We don't have to release the test. We'll just let the public know about the machine, tell them they have a fifty-fifty chance to become super-powered or die. Allow the choice to be their own."

"That's not exactly what—"

"No. It's perfect. The majority of sheeple will go for it, regardless of the consequences. They'll all die, the chosen few will live, and we'll become the misunderstood saviors of humanity. The new superheroes who eradicated disease and ended suffering."

"It's not a fifty-fifty chance. Only ten percent will survive the blast."

"Earth is severely overpopulated. Don't second guess your genius."

Lucius walked toward the lab's door, leaving Cyrus wide-eyed beside his machine. "The entire world will be a better place when only people with superpowers live in it. Now get that power source worked out. I can't use souls to run that machine any longer. We shouldn't utilize evil means to liberate the people, not if we're trying to be heroes. Right?"

Cyrus groaned, a sour look crossing his face. "Where are you going?"

"Upstairs to strangle Mimic. The fluke won't stop blowing up my phone."

"Is it male or female, originally? Lucius?"

Lucius opened the heavy steel door, which let the shouts of Cyrus's wretched woman into the room.

"It's a chick," he said, walking from the lab.

"This is where I was," Shay said to Max and Hetal, between chews. She pointed the bacon in her hand at the map on her computer screen, leaving a greasy smear overtop the group of red dots that blinked at the asylum. "There's indicator marks at this location. They must still be there."

"We looked, but that place is a maze," Max said.

"Did you find the machine?"

Max closed his empty Styrofoam carton, which once held a tall stack of pancakes, and tossed it into the trash bin at the end of the long computer desk. "What machine?"

"Down the hall from the dungeon-like cells, in the mad scientist lab."

"Like this one," Hetal said with a smile.

"No." Shay actually took offense to that comment. Her lab was sanitary, ultra-shiny, and absolutely perfect. "Like the creaky metal floors, frayed wires arcing, bad lighting kind."

"I didn't see any of that."

Hetal put down her coffee and grabbed a tablet. "What did this machine look like?"

"Why?" Shay swiveled her chair to face Hetal. "You gonna do a search in the mad scientist directory?"

"Umm, yeah."

Shay dropped her grin. So that's what they taught at college, how to get all the good connections.

"But really," Hetal said, typing on the display in her lap. "All tech is based off each other, it's just modified to suit the user's needs. If I can find the general design, maybe we can figure out what they're up to."

"Is that why they took you?" Max asked. "To fix their machine?"

"No." Shay rubbed the sides of her arms as a chill crept in to ice her skin. "I think they were going to put me in the machine."

Hetal raised her hand, waved it around at the wrist.

"This isn't school," Shay said, turning her attention back to Hetal. "Was it square?"

"Round, like the nanobot chamber but way bigger. It was liquid cooled with wide magnetic plates on the inside and thin ones around the outside."

"That's ..." Hetal shook her head, eyes wide. "I've never heard of anything like that."

Shay turned her chair toward Max. "What are they up to?"

"How should I know?"

Shay had to look away from the cute crinkle of Max's nose, or she'd never be able to continue drilling the man. "You knew them, before the powers. You guys were friends, right?"

Max shifted in his chair. "That was a long time ago."

"Yeah, but, people don't really change. Their core beliefs stay the same, it's a person's approach toward the world that alters."

Max smirked as he stared into a corner of the room. "Lucius always talked about making the world a better place. He dreamt of a future free from viruses and disease. A world where people had no reason to hate each other, because everyone was equal. And Cyrus. The guy's an actual rocket scientist, but when it came to his brother ... he just follows Lucius, blindly."

"No way!" Shay jumped up from her chair, which sent it rolling across the glossy floor to crash into a table.

"What?" Max asked, rising to his feet.

"I'm going first," Hetal said. "After beta testing, obviously."

Max's stare alternated between Shay and Hetal, a lost look in his eyes. "What?"

Shay couldn't believe Max hadn't figured it out. It couldn't be more clear what Lucius and Cyrus were up to. "They're—"

"Shay," Simon called out from the lab's entrance. He spotted her behind the wall of computers then hurried across the lab.

"Have you seen Evie?" he asked, stepping beside Shay while typing on his cell phone.

"She went to assemble some task force."

"No." Simon tucked his phone into his pocket. "The captain of the task force just contacted me. She never checked in."

Shay gripped her stomach, which had started to churn. Twenty different scenarios ran through her mind, all of them ending with Evie in a ditch—and they didn't even have ditches in the city.

"She left over two hours ago," was all her brain could whip up, besides *Oh my God, Oh my God* and that wouldn't help.

"Why don't you give her a call?" Simon said. "She didn't answer mine."

"I'm sure she's fine," Hetal added. "It's not like Evie has a superhero's soul inside her body too. Right?"

"No." Shay shoved aside tablets and empty Styrofoam cartons, and grabbed her cell phone. The words *nobody wants Evie* almost flew from her mouth, except it wouldn't be true. She wanted Evie, right now.

With a shaky finger, she tapped the picture of her sister's frowny face. After two rings, Shay was sure she'd never see Evie again. Three and she almost ran from the room to shout her sister's name from the rooftop. When the forth ring broke off and Evie said, "Hello." Shay didn't know what to do.

"Evie?" she sputtered.

"Hey. I'm in a meeting right now. Can I call you back in twenty?"

"Sure, I—"

"It's not important, is it?"

"No. I—"

"Okay. Talk to you in a bit."

Shay flinched when a click replaced Evie's voice. She looked up from the rudeness that just erupted from her phone's speaker, caught

Simon's leery expression, and shrugged. "Evie's at a meeting."

"What kind of meeting?"

Max rubbed his chin. "Evie seemed off today. Don't you think?"

"And what was up with her outfit," Hetal said. "Sweats and sneaks, does Evie jog?"

"I don't know." Shay lifted her hands, pushing through the crowd that now swarmed her. "I have to go make weapons. I'll sound the alarm if I hear something."

She hurried to her workbench but the annoyance lingered. They all posed valid questions and she should know the answers, yet she didn't. Other than the breakfast mishap, she hadn't noticed anything different. She hadn't even noticed Evie was wearing sneakers, which she refused to believe until she saw it with her own eyes.

Visuals of Evie in a silky jogger suit streamed through her mind and she pushed them aside, chuckling. There was no time for fantasies. She had a great idea for a containment field grenade, structure safe of course.

A cool breeze rolled off the harbor. The salty air curled around Alexie, blowing strands of hair in front of her eyes. Every blue streak that fell into view tinted the world in a somber shade. Not that the asylum in front of her needed anything extra to add to its creepy ambience. The building's crumbling walls, its barred windows hiding dark shadows in broad daylight, reeked of evil … and dead fish, which basically smelled the same.

A sharp crack rang out, echoing over the harbor's gentle waves, and a layer of frost crept along the water's surface.

Alexie didn't have to look over her shoulder to know Lucius

stood behind her. A heavy weight pressed against her chest, and hope drained in his presence.

Lucius circled Alexie, like a vulture, brushing against her arm before he stopped in front of her. "What are you doing here?"

It was a question Alexie had asked herself a thousand times since she'd arrived at the asylum five minutes ago. Each time, she gave herself the same answer. She was trying to save the city, redeem two good men who had fallen off the righteous path, and stay a hero.

"I've decided to accept your offer."

"Good one." Lucius didn't smile, didn't scowl. He merely dismissed Alexie with a wave of his hand.

"Get lost," he said, walking away.

"Hey." Alexie grabbed Lucius by the arm and he spun to glare down at her. His fierce gaze rocked her courage. It made her miss the man's fearsome iron mask.

"I'm serious," she managed to choke out, almost convincing herself.

"You sound real serious." Lucius pulled his arm from Alexie's grasp and gave her a little shove. "You must think I'm stupid. Why don't I save you some time, draw you a map to my *real* hideout, maybe outline my end game for you? Then, you can send a big S signal in the sky and your super-buddies can swoop in."

"You know what, screw it. I was having doubts about this whole thing and you just made up my mind. Thanks, asshole."

Alexie turned from Lucius and stormed away from the asylum. A smile snuck onto her lips, but she held it back. Any second, Lucius would come nipping at her heels like the desperate dog he was.

"Wait," Lucius called out.

His voice carried on icy winds and slowed Alexie's steps. She looked back at Lucius, but he was gone. Just a long field of dead grass sat in front of her, leading to a decrepit asylum.

Alexie turned from the asylum and crashed against a hard chest plate. Lucius gripped onto the collar of her suit, and lifted her off the ground before she could work up an electric charge.

Energy swelled beneath her flesh as they soared through the air. The heat pricked her fingertips, sizzled her blood. She opened her fist to send a billion volts of pure electricity into Lucius when he stopped midair above the harbor.

"Don't do it," he said, lowering Alexie's boots into the icy water. "Lightning and water don't mix."

Alexie held tight to the bare skin on Lucius's wrists. "I might fry, but I'll take you with me."

"I can't trust you," Lucius said in a tone that incited more fear than anger. "And that sucks, because I really want to."

"It's not my fault you're an idiot."

"Why the change of heart? Did your friends step on your sparkly cape?"

"They're not my friends," Alexie said, despising every word that passed her lips. "They're my keepers. I don't fit with them, not the way I did with Cyrus." She forced the fear from her mind, and gazed at Lucius with warmth. "And you."

Lucius tightened his grip on Alexie. He lifted her feet from the water, drawing her close to his chest. Daylight blurred to swirls of rainbow waves, the air fizzled and popped, then her feet hit solid ground.

Alexie wobbled, clinging to Lucius as she fought to find her balance.

"What was that?"

The blur covering her eyes cleared to tall grass. They were back in the same place, standing in front of the asylum.

Once Alexie's legs steadied, she slowly let go of Lucius. "We weren't flying."

"No." Lucius stepped back from Alexie and hoisted his hands to his hips. "I can teleport now."

"How?"

"Uh-uh." Lucius crossed his arms. "You tell me something first."

"You're a giant di—"

"Something I don't already know. Come on, Lexie, don't you want to prove how useful you can be?"

Everything always had to be on Lucius's terms, which was the reason Alexie left the Grant mansion and never returned. This time would be different. She was stronger now, in both mind and spirit. Lucius would find that out the painful way, after she danced his little dance.

"Max found people, with powers. Like us."

"Really!" Lucius smiled, warm and genuine, which was much more frightening than his wicked grins. It was the look of the remarkable man she'd met all those years ago, the stare of a friend not a maniacal villain.

"Do you have names, locations?"

"No." Alexie held Lucius's stare, even though her knees begged to crumble. "I can get you a full list."

Lucius lifted his hand, and Alexie fought the urge to flinch. His fingertips glided along her cheek, leaving frosty trails on her skin.

"A gesture like that could help prove your allegiance," Lucius said in a whisper. The air around him shimmered then he vanished, leaving Alexie to sway in the harbor's icy wind.

Sweat beaded on Shay's palm but she didn't loosen her hold on the needle-nose pliers that chafed her skin. She couldn't move from her hunched-over position, didn't dare disturb the circuit board just below her. It had taken her twenty minutes to properly align the thin wire at the end of her pliers with the transistor on the tiny circuit board, and she wasn't going to so much as breathe until they were soldered together.

Her free hand slapped the workbench beside her. Something soft, something pointy, and something squishy grazed her fingertips before she found the soldering gun. Just as she brought the gun's tip to the wire's end, her cell phone beeped.

She flinched, which sent the soldering gun's red-hot tip deep into the circuitry. Smoke rose, tickling Shay's nose as she lifted the soldering gun from a melted hole in a one-of-a-kind golden circuit board.

"Great." A little piece of Shay's heart broke as she stared down at what equated to wire guts.

"Problems?" Max called out from across the lab.

Shay glanced at Max, who still lounged on her lab's couch. He lowered a magazine and sat up straight at the slightest hint of attention.

"You're still here?" Shay groaned. She had intended to say that without sounding like a jerk, and achieved the exact opposite.

"This is all so ..." Max lifted his hands then dropped them into his lap. "Fun?"

"Just go. Save some car from veering off a bridge, or pull a cat out of a tree."

"None of that stuff is going on right now."

"Do you have some kind of superhero sixth sense?"

"No." Max fidgeted on the couch. "I don't actually do those kinds of things. The police and emergency services workers are great in this city. Sometimes the fire chief calls and asks for help getting people out of burning buildings, but mostly I just wait around for the Grant brothers to attack."

Max returned to flipping pages in his magazine, and Shay rubbed her forehead. There was such great potential, wasted. Five people with incredible powers walked this Earth. Five people who could bring herds of cattle to the starving, deliver medicine to war-torn countries, and all they did was fight each other.

"You're distracting me, and I have so much to do."

"Look at all that." Max pointed at the table beside Shay, which overflowed with an assortment of mini containment grenades and laser, plasma, and sonic guns.

"You've got a huge pile of weapons. How many do you need?"

"All of them." Shay gave Max one of those *duh* glares, and he mirrored it right back at her.

"Who texted you?" Max tried to sound casual, but totally didn't.

"It's my boyfriend," Shay said without bothering to look at her cell phone.

"You have a boyfriend?"

The levels of shock in Max's voice should be enough to spark

Shay's temper but the look on his face, like *he'd* burned a hole through a gold condenser, balanced the rage scales.

"No." Shay picked up her cell phone, unlocking its screen. "I don't have a boyfriend. It's just Evie. She wants to meet for dinner, but I'm gonna have her bring Chinese here."

It wouldn't be anyone but Evie. Ollie had been the only other person to text her constantly, and he still refused to speak with her. She really missed him, but she understood why he stayed away. She'd only lived the life of a superhero for a few days and she'd almost died once, got abducted by supervillains, and let a murdered girl's soul control her body.

"Did you dump the guy, when you got famous?"

Shay stopped texting and looked at Max. "What guy? There was no guy."

"Like, recently, or at all?"

In Shay's experience, the best approach at purging the air of unwanted questions was to ignore them until they faded away. With that in mind, she lowered her gaze to her cell phone's screen and typed very slowly.

"You've … never been on a date?" Max asked, like the concept was absurd to him. "Or to a school dance?"

Shay tucked her cell phone into her pocket and looked down at the inventions on her workbench. "I've been busy."

"Doing what, living under a rock?"

"Following Evie to your battle scenes and watching her clean up your messes."

Max's grin dropped. He looked stunned, hurt, as if he'd been slapped, which was how it felt for Shay to speak such harsh words.

"I'm sorry. That was uncalled for."

"No. I …" Max rose from the couch. The magazine in his lap hit the ground, and the hotshot superhero actually flinched. "You're right to be angry. Your childhood was stolen. I guess, I never realized how much destruction my powers can cause."

"I'm not angry." Shay reached for Max then quickly drew back. "I was just teasing. I have a warped sense of humor."

She despised her big stupid mouth, more than ever. If Max's frown drooped any lower, she'd have to hug him if only to quell her own guilty conscience.

"I brought FroYos," Hetal said, walking into the lab with a large bag. "And I bumped into Alexie in the lobby."

Shay moved circuit boards around on her workbench, pretending to look busy. "Alexie's here now. You can take off," she said, glancing at Max. "I'm sure you have things and stuff to do."

"Right." Max's shoulders slumped. "Alexie—"

"Go," Alexie said. "Do whatever you need to. I'll hang here."

Shay kept her stare low as Max walked by her workbench. Once the thump of his boots drifted down the hallway outside her lab, both her heart and tight muscles sunk. She had wanted him to leave, until he actually left. Now, she wished he'd come running back in a whirl of flames.

"So, no FroYo?" Hetal asked, waving a small cup under Shay's nose.

"Yeah FroYo." A little binge of sugar and carbs was exactly what Shay needed to get her mind off Max and back on high-tech weaponry. "I hope it has sprinkles."

Shay got through half her frozen yogurt, and inventoried most of her weapons, when Alexie jumped up from a chair at the computer desk.

"Oh. Sorry, Alexie," Shay said, holding out her cup. "Did you want some frozen yogurt?"

"No. I actually forgot I'm supposed to be somewhere." Alexie hurried toward the door, without a glance to Shay. "You're good on your own, right?"

"Yeah." Shay grabbed a little steel ball off her workbench. "I've got enough firepower to take down the Deathstar, and the precision to hit the target from afar."

Hetal snickered but Alexie just stared at Shay from the doorway.

"We're good," Shay said, placing the highly lethal weapon back on the table. "Evie should be here soon with some grub so—"

Alexie waved Shay off, hurrying out the lab's door, and Shay shrank down.

"That was rude," she said, glancing at Hetal.

"Superheroes," Hetal muttered as she dug through the cluster of wire harnesses on the back workbench. "They're so mysterious."

Lucius stood up straight. A hint of vanilla filled the air, which was impossible while two levels underground and locked in the room Cyrus turned into a laboratory. It was Lexie. Her essence wrapped around him like a hug, and the scent of her hair filled his lungs every time she drew near. He closed his eyes, inhaled the sweet scent, and let his body travel to her.

A cool breeze struck his skin and he opened his eyes. He'd teleported much easier than before. An hour ago, when Alexie's sharp vibes disrupted his thoughts, it took him three attempts to transport from the bowels of the asylum to the hillside of weeds just outside the abandoned building. It had only taken him seconds this time.

He stood in front of Alexie, the siren who'd just lured him in from the sea. The shine in her electric-blue eyes, and snug fit of her sparkly suit put the sunset over the harbor behind her to shame. Every time he gazed at her he wanted to smile, but villains didn't have the luxury of letting out cheesy grins.

"Now, you can tell me how you do that," Alexie said, thrusting a stack of papers into Lucius's hands.

"What's all this, your memoirs?"

Alexie glowered. "The names, addresses you wanted."

Lucius thumbed through the pages, smirked, then ripped them in half.

"Hey. What the hell?"

"I already have this information." He tossed the torn pages to the wind. "I just wanted to see if you'd give it to me."

A snicker flew from Alexie's lips, and her body loosened. "Does that mean I passed your stupid test?"

"The first one," Lucius said, chuckling when Alexie groaned.

"Did I at least earn the right to know how you got the ability to teleport?"

He'd been hoping Alexie would press that matter. The woman didn't know it, but she just set herself up for the second test.

Lucius wiped his face clear, leaving only a touch of malice in his stare. "Every soul I devoured unlocks a new ability inside me. There are many, many things I can do now."

He searched Alexie's face for fear or disgust, but found pure intrigue. A person couldn't fake that level of interest, which meant she'd aced the second test with flying colors.

"Well." Alexie slinked closer to Lucius and glided her hand up his chest. "Aren't you lucky? All you have to do is slaughter everyone on the planet, and you can have a whole bunch of abilities you don't really need. Maybe, if you get enough, your skin can stretch out and burst like a giant gooey piñata."

"Hilarious." Lucius pushed Alexie's hand off his chest. "Don't get your righteous little spank pants in a bunch. I don't plan on absorbing any more souls, except Jenna and Max obviously."

"Obviously." Alexie strolled past Lucius and peeked through one of the asylum's broken windows. "What is your plan, assuming you have one?"

"I guess I can show you," Lucius said, blocking Alexie's view. "Since I don't mind killing you."

Alexie stood up straight, her fists clenched.

"If you betray me, that is." Lucius grabbed Alexie by the arm and pulled her toward him. Her body crashed against his chest, which knocked a tiny gasp from her lungs. "Cyrus is gonna be pissed when he sees you."

"You didn't tell him?"

Lucius concentrated on Cyrus. Time slowed, but the world raced before his eyes. Colors and shapes blended, streaking by in blurry swirls. His boots thumped onto the steel grate of their secret lab, deep in the belly of the old asylum. Alexie swayed in his grasp, and Cyrus jumped up from a workbench.

"What the ..." Cyrus grabbed a large pipe wrench and lifted his arm to swing it at Alexie.

"Stop." Lucius flicked his wrist and the wrench flew from Cyrus's clutch, sailed across the room, and crashed against the wall. "Lexie has decided to join our side."

"Good for her," Cyrus said in a sneer. "Too bad we don't want her. I'll wipe her memory then you can drop her ass in a volcano."

"I'm sorry," Alexie said, gazing at Cyrus.

"Sorry?" Cyrus rushed forward, stopping inches from Alexie. His fingers curled, his arms twitching at his sides. "Sorry for what—ignoring me when I asked for help, walking out on me when things got rough? Or is your pathetic apology for zapping me with two lightning bolts the day you broke my heart?"

Alexie didn't waver. Her gaze stuck to Cyrus, remaining blank yet soft. "I'm sorry you can't act like a grown-up for five seconds."

Lucius burst out laughing, and Cyrus growled.

"Enjoy it while you can, brother." Cyrus backed away, yet his hard stare stayed fixed on Alexie. "Because she's a treacherous bitch."

The insult didn't faze Alexie. In fact, she nodded. "Read my mind if you don't believe me."

"I already tried and can't, which proves there's something off about you."

Lucius grabbed Alexie by the sides of her arms. "Why can't he read your mind?"

"I don't know." Alexie wiggled her shoulders, unable to break free from Lucius's tight grip. "Ask his emotions, they're always clouding his powers."

Cyrus waved his hand, as if to swat the notion from the air. "There's nothing wrong with my powers."

"Try again," Lucius said. He released Alexie in a shove, pushing her toward Cyrus. "Concentrate."

Cyrus stared into Alexie's eyes and she didn't back down.

"Nothing," Cyrus said in utter shock.

"Yeah right." Alexie crossed her arms. "You can see the truth, see I'm in this with you two for real. You just don't want to admit it."

"The only thing I see is your smug face, and I'd like to punch it." Cyrus lifted his finger, pointing it at Alexie. "You did something, to keep me from your mind."

"Enough." Lucius stepped between the two. His wide body, and the thud of his boots, stopped the whiny complains.

This was ridiculous. He was a visionary, a mastermind who'd change the world, not the babysitter to two privileged super-brats.

"It doesn't matter if she's lying. I have more power than anybody who ever walked this Earth. Let Max and Simon come. Let them all come. No one can stop me now."

Alexie staggered back from Lucius. "You need to tone down the diabolical a notch."

"What, too much?" Lucius asked through a smile.

Shay dropped her screwdriver as the scent of greasy goodness surrounded her. Evie walked across the lab and set her tote bag on an empty table beside Shay.

"Ooh. Ling Fi's, my favorite," Shay said, dragging over a stool.

Evie unloaded little white boxes, stopping when Hetal crept out from behind a machine. "Oh, I forgot Hetal was here."

"It's okay. She can share mine."

"Actually." Hetal took off her lab coat, tossed it on a desk, and picked up her backpack. "I'm gonna head home for a bit, grab a shower, change of clothes."

"Take your time." Shay was happy Hetal finally decided to take a breather. The woman looked exhausted, more so than last night, and the day before. "You deserve a break."

Hetal waved as she walked from the lab.

"Good," Evie said, sitting across from Shay. "Now I can have you all to myself. Did you make a lot of weapons today?"

"Where's the sweet and sour chicken?" Shay checked the empty bag, as though that would make the food materialize. "You always get it for me."

Evie opened a few cartons, shaking her head. "They must've forgotten it."

"I'll just have some of your lo mein." Shay slid the chopsticks between her fingers, picking at the thin noodles. "Where you been all day? Simon texted me five times looking for you. Are you guys … is something going on between you two?"

"No. I have a boyfriend."

"You do!" Shay slammed her chopsticks down onto the table. She could no longer eat, not while gawking at Evie. "Since when?"

Evie set a box of rice on the table, pushing it aside. "For a while. I guess I never mentioned that, to you."

"Umm, no. Who is he? What's his name?" Shay leaned back to stare Evie down, only to see Evie actually was wearing plain gray sweats. "And, what's up with the sweat suit? Are you having some sort of identity crisis?"

"So, sweatpants aren't my thing?" Evie let out a long breath, almost a growl.

"Good one. Where did you even get them? I've never seen you wear anything that frumpy before. Hey, how do I even know you're you right now?"

Shay waited for Evie to play along, spill some secret only the two of them shared, but her sister just glared. A coldness overtook Evie's eyes, one Shay had never glimpsed before.

"You got me." Evie jumped to her feet, slowly circling the table. "Your sister's smart, feeding me crap information. I might thank her with a red-hot poker to the thigh when I get back to her cell."

"Who are you?" Shay hopped off her stool and backed toward the lab's door. "Where's my sister?"

"I am your sister."

Shay stared at the woman who wore her sister's face, but it wasn't Evie. This person disrupted the air with their jagged vibes. She should have seen through this impostor the second they attempted to masquerade in her sister's life. Max could tell something was off with Evie, even Hetal noticed, but not her. She'd been too busy playing scientist with all her shiny new tech and hadn't realized she'd been chatting it up with a stranger.

It might be too late, but she could see now. She could see a fake Evie walking right toward her.

The needle on Shay's fear meter spiked and she ran for the lab's door. Fingers curled into her hair, yanking. She cried out as the fake Evie pulled her away from the door by her hair.

A fist slammed against Shay's gut and she fell forward. Her knees crashed to the hard floor, which sent ripples of pain throughout her body.

The fake Evie smiled as Shay coughed on her knees, gasping for breath. She didn't think her sister's face could twist to form such cruelty.

"Please, don't," Shay cried out as she shrunk down, away from Evie.

"Don't what?" Evie picked up a metal pipe, lifting it high. "Don't do this?"

Instinct brought Shay's hands up, to block her face, and the pipe Evie swung bashed against her elbow. A wave of sharp prickles spawned from the hit and spread through her bones. Before a scream could pass her lips, the edge of the pipe cracked her cheek.

The bright lights of the room flashed to black. Shay fought to keep her eyes open but a heavy blanket of darkness fell over her, blocking the sound of her sister's laughter from her ears.

"Shay, Shay!"

The voice traveled through thick fog, dragging in slow motion inside Shay's head. It sounded like Max—like a stretched out, jumbled, panicky version of Max. Words and noises mixed with the throb in her temples. She forced her eyes to open, and white light rushed in to slap her already pounding brain.

People surrounded Shay. Their faces were blurry, but they were her friends. At least, on the surface.

"Can you hear me? Shay. Look at me." Max's voice, and his frightened eyes cut through the haze that fogged Shay's vision.

"There's blood everywhere," Hetal cried out.

"I know a doctor we can call," Simon said, kneeling beside Shay.

"She doesn't need a doctor." Max took off his hoodie and pressed it against the side of Shay's face. "Head wounds bleed a lot."

"I'm okay." Shay reached out and Max's hand slid into her own, holding tight.

"What if it's not you?" she said in a slur. "None of you could be you."

"Oh, God. She's brain damaged," Hetal shrieked, even louder and in a higher pitch than before.

"I'm calling 911," Simon said.

"Stop," Max yelled. "Just give her a second."

Max hovered over Shay, cradling her arm to his chest. "Do you know where you are?"

"My lab." Shay sat up and a wave of dizziness drove her back down to the floor.

"Don't try to move yet." Max lifted his sweater and cringed. "There's a long gash slicing all the way down your cheek."

"Don't tell her that," Hetal shouted.

"She can handle it."

Max wiped streaks of blood from Shay's face. Each swipe he took at her skin scraped like broken glass. She didn't know if she could *handle it.* The pain radiating in her head, and the series of events that led to said pain, were too much for any one person to bear.

"Who did this to you?" Max asked.

"I'm pulling up the security footage now," Simon said while typing on his cell phone.

Shay held onto Max and pulled herself to a sitting position on the floor. Once the room stopped pulsing and the vomit decided to stay in her stomach, she let go of Max's shirt.

"It was Evie. Except, it wasn't Evie." She laid her hand atop her cheek. It really had been split open. She lowered her hand from her face—not because her fingertips slipped on sticky blood and torn skin, but because the throbbing sting in her cheek amplified when touched.

"That doesn't make any sense," Max said, staring into Shay's eyes. "Maybe you do need a doctor."

"It *was* Evie." Simon turned his cell phone's display toward Max. A video streamed of the fake Evie person cracking Shay's head like a cantaloupe.

"That's not really Evie. That woman looked like Evie, sounded like her, even smelled like her, but the eyes and her smile were different."

Shay held her head, willing the throb of her brain into submission so thoughts could creep through. "She said the real Evie was in a cell. That my sister was smart for feeding her bad information."

"It could be possible," Hetal said. "There were a hundred and twenty-two other people we picked up on the energy frequency scanner. One of them could be a shapeshifter."

"Why would they target Shay, and how did they get their hands on Evie?" Max asked.

Strength returned to Shay's legs. She climbed off the floor, a bit too fast, and her knees shook.

"I was with the real Evie last night," she said, leaning against her workbench in attempts to ease the quake in her muscles. "I know it was her."

"Maybe Antiserum or Dr. Mayhem snuck into the building," Hetal said. "Left behind an imposter Evie then snuck out with the real one."

"Impossible." Simon clicked off his cell phone. "I just tracked Evie's movements for the last forty-eight hours, there was nothing out of the ordinary. Unless they learned how to teleport and popped into her bedroom, there's no way."

"Where's Lexie?" Max asked.

Simon shifted in place, staring into the far corner of the room.

"She was here earlier." Shay sat on a stool, since her knees wouldn't quit their quivering. "I'm not sure where she went, something she forgot to do. We need to find Evie." Her voice cracked and she took a deep breath.

The biggest temper tantrum neared the verge of eruption. She predicted foot stomping, waterfall tears, and a grainy shrill that could pierce a person's skull. "If Evie's in a cell, she's probably at the asylum. I was in a cell there."

Hetal hurried to the computer with the energy signature map

still on its display. "The scanner is picking up five blips at the asylum right now. I think the bad guys did some recruiting."

"We need to find Lexie, get over there now," Max said as he headed for the door.

"I'm going too." Shay hopped off the stool and her wobbly legs gave out beneath her.

Max grabbed Shay by the waist before the squeak of his sneakers could bounce off the walls. His secure yet gentle hold came with an electric charge, one that pumped her weakened muscles full of adrenaline.

Shay stood up straight and looked at Hetal. "Get the stem cell ointment we made this morning, I'm going to guinea pig it on myself."

"Awesome." Hetal ran across the lab, toward the small fridge. "I'm recording this for posterity."

The rush of barking orders gave Shay a very Evie feel, and she rode with it.

"You two." She pointed her finger between Max and Simon. "Find Alexie and suit up. We'll head out in fifteen."

Their stunned faces could've made the cover of *Superhero Weekly* with the title, *Caught in Headlights!* To grin now would shatter the authoritative façade, but if Shay held it in any longer she'd strain her lips. Thankfully, they walked away and she let a small snicker escape, despite the burn in her cheek.

Hetal hurried to Shay's side, juggling a camera stand, medical kit, and jars of neon green goo.

"I need some kind of suit," Shay said, looking at her blood-speckled lab coat. "Something badass, with pockets to hold all the weapons I plan on using."

After setting up the camera, Hetal grabbed her backpack from the desk.

"I was thinking the same thing." Hetal set her bag on the table beside Shay and pulled out a handful of leather clothes.

"You got me an outfit?"

"Actually, I made it." Hetal handed Shay a stretchy halter top then unpacked gauze and cotton swabs from the medical kit.

"When did you have time to make a superhero suit?" Shay peeked into Hetal's bag, running her fingers along the smooth leather of jet-black pants. "Are you a superhero too?"

Hetal's eyes grew wide and her body grew stiff.

"Wait." Shay pushed the backpack aside, weaving to catch Hetal's evasive stare. "Do you have an ability?"

"It's ... more like a disorder." Hetal cleaned the blood from Shay wound, leaving a pile of crimson-stained alcohol wipes on the table. "I have insomnia and when I don't sleep for a few days, I get hyper."

Shay didn't know what to say. As a science-minded person, she understood why Hetal didn't use pills to help her sleep. Brain cells were a terrible thing to waste. However, the friend in her wanted to see Hetal healthy. Working with dangerous equipment in a manic state definitely wasn't healthy.

"I'm not a freak!"

"I don't think you're a freak," Shay said with all honesty. "But I am going to make a sleep ray when this is over. Hit you with it when you overachieve."

A smile lifted Hetal's cheeks, but only for a moment. She slapped on a serious expression and opened a jar of stem cell ointment. "All right. I'm turning on the camera, so let's be real doctorly."

Shay nodded. She sat tall on her stool, pulled her hair into a bun, and then pointed at Hetal. "Hit it."

Lucius stood back and watched Cyrus stalk Alexie as she wandered around their makeshift laboratory. The parts used to build the machines in this room were no secret. They had all been stolen right under Max's pretentious nose. Any self-proclaimed superhero should be able to piece together what they'd been up to.

"What's this?" Alexie asked.

She stuck her head inside the only machine that could kill her within the room, further confirming Lucius's notion that Alexie was no hero.

"A nebula burst generator," Lucius said, admiring the way shock lit Alexie's already bright eyes.

"Dude," Cyrus yelled. He picked a metal rod off the table beside him and threw it at Lucius.

A twitch of one finger and Lucius stopped the rod midair and sent it crashing to the floor.

Alexie backed away from the machine. "You're gonna mutate people? So you can, what, eat their super-charged souls?"

"No, Alexie." Lucius kicked off the wall, glaring at Alexie as he strolled by her. "I'm going to ensure equality for all."

He glided his hand along the machine. The energy of the souls inside him triggered the magnetic plates within the chamber to hum, which vibrated the metal beneath his fingertips.

"You see." He lifted his hand off the machine, and it powered down. "Just like most pompous asshats, superheroes think they know what's best for everybody else. They'll let society spiral into chaos just to preserve their irrationally high morals. Cyrus and I are willing to do what it takes. To make the hard decisions."

Lucius had taken many lives, and each one haunted him. He didn't enjoy inflicting pain, but that's what made his cause so worthy. He—the soul taker—had sacrificed his own soul to do what he thought was right for the world.

"Eventually, every person *is* going to get in that machine. Most of them will die, but the ones who survive will live longer, happier, more meaningful lives. Think how wonderful the world could be with only super-powered individuals living in it. Cyrus and I are the real heroes."

Alexie snickered. "It's hysterical how everybody thinks they're the ones who are right."

She stared Lucius in the eyes, her gaze full of sorrow. "Equality is a pipedream. We all have powers, and we still fight each other. Each one of us thinks we're better than the other. Go ahead, try to deny it."

"Equality doesn't mean fairness," Cyrus said, as if he were talking to a child. "To think true justice exists is the pipedream."

"You're right, Alexie." Lucius held Alexie's stare, even though Cyrus huffed and grumbled beside him. "We have powers, and we still fight. But, while we're exchanging scrapes, people are dying."

There it was. Lucius had finally found the words strong enough to break Alexie's confident stance.

"If we all had powers, everyone could have an equal chance. A chance at survival."

"I'm ... surprised. I thought world domination or some kind of global hypnotizing scheme, but this is just—"

"Noble," Lucius said through a smirk.

"Extreme," Alexie said in a quaver. "But I like it. I'm actually excited about this. When do we get started?"

"There's a little kink."

"Lucius don't," Cyrus shouted. "I still can't read her thoughts."

"You guys need to trust me, or our little clique isn't going to work." Alexie walked toward Cyrus, standing in front of him. "Take my hand, try again."

Cyrus stood up straight. He looked at Lucius, as if seeking permission, but Lucius didn't budge. Emotions *had* always clouded his little brother's powers. Cyrus had to heal the tiny piece of his heart Alexie broke on his own, without pressure from Lucius.

"I guess." Cyrus took Alexie's hand and squeezed. "I've never had this much trouble before. I can read people from miles away."

Alexie stepped closer to Cyrus. "Your feelings for me are blocking you."

"There's someone in my life I care about far more than you, and

I have no problem getting inside her mind."

"I'm sure you find plenty of disgusting ways to use your power on her."

A grin lifted Cyrus's cheeks. "I did with you. You just don't remember, honey."

"Just read her already," Lucius yelled. He'd grown tired of the bickering, which sounded a lot like flirting.

Cyrus stared into Alexie's eyes. "It's all fuzzy. I can only see bits." He squeezed Alexie's hand tighter, drew it to his chest.

"She does want to be with us."

His head jolted to the side, like an invisible hand slapped him. He let go of Alexie and shoved her away. "Now I know why you dumped me."

Alexie reached for Cyrus and he stormed past her, glowered at Lucius, then stomped from the room.

"I'm sure you two will work that out." Lucius turned from the open doorway his brother just tore through. "We have more important things to deal with. I need your little scientist girl back."

"Why?"

"The machine's having a power issue. Cyrus is too close to the problem. We need fresh eyes."

"Shay's not even a real scientist, but she does have one in her pocket."

A ring chirped from behind Alexie's cape and she fished out her cell phone. "It's Simon."

"Answer it. Put it on speaker."

Alexie tapped the send button, keeping her eye on Lucius. "Yeah."

"I need you back here right away," Simon said, his voice blasting through the phone's speaker. "There's been an incident. We're moving on the asylum, hitting Lucius and Cyrus hard."

"I thought you wanted to try and make peace with the Grant brothers," Alexie said into the speaker, staring at Lucius.

"I do, more than anything. I miss Cyrus, our talks, the chess games, and Max is miserable without Lucius to boss him around. But, I don't think they'll ever come back to us."

Lucius turned his back to Alexie and clutched his chest. It had grown tight. He could barely breathe. His old friends missed him, not the villain Antiserum part of him ... Lucius.

"I'm close by," Alexie said into her phone. "I'll meet you at the asylum."

"We'll be there in fifteen minutes. Don't go inside without us."

"Yeah, yeah."

A beep rang out as Alexie ended the call, but Lucius didn't move. He couldn't look at Alexie. Hope had crept up on him, and it probably showed on his stunned face.

"Now what?" Alexie asked from behind Lucius. "Max and Simon are gonna come in here guns blazing."

Lucius forced the sentiment that clouded his mind to clear, and looked at Alexie. He'd been walking along the villain's road for far too long, had done things that shouldn't be forgiven. He couldn't turn back now.

"They'll come, and they won't find anything. Just meet them out front, play along. But first, tell me more about this scientist in the girl's pocket."

23

Shay tugged at her leather pants, which clung to everything. The holster fastened to her leg added to the smothering feel. Fortunately, the sonic blaster tucked within the leg holster was heavy enough to keep her pants from riding up her butt.

"This is kind of ... provocative." Shay looked at Hetal, who loaded a tactical vest with canisters of every shape.

"Don't worry," Hetal said with a wave of her hand. "The tact vest will cover your giant boobs."

Shay folded her arms over her chest, hiding the cleavage her halter-top magically created. "You shouldn't need to show this much skin to fight evil."

"All the heroines in movies do it." Hetal shoved the last weapon into the vest and scanned Shay over. "Looking like a sexy villainess will confuse the bad guy. When he's all stunned and drooling, hit him with a containment field."

"Yeah, right." Shay held out her arms and Hetal slid the vest over her shoulders, zipping it up.

"How do you feel?" Hetal asked. She ran her finger along Shay's cheek, which now had a thin scar instead of a gaping wound. "The stem cells worked pretty well, but I would've liked to see some more dramatic results."

Shay shook out the stiffness in her shoulders then smoothed back her ponytail. "I feel good, ready to kick some fake Evie ass."

"That's the spirit." Hetal patted Shay on the arm, then ushered her toward the lab's door.

"The last shot I gave you should kick in any minute."

They walked from the lab, rounded the corner in the hallway, and stopped in front of the elevator.

"The outfit and the weapons are going to make you feel indestructible." Hetal wagged her finger in Shay's face. "But you're not."

"Okay," Shay muttered as the stiffness slinked back into her every joint.

Hetal pushed the elevator's button and its door slid open. "Good luck, and be careful."

"Okay." Shay rocked in place. Her mind screamed to go save Evie, but her legs were not cooperating. "Just give me a little shove."

Shay flinched when Hetal's hand landed on her back, but it kicked her feet into gear. She stepped into the elevator and her throat sealed shut.

Her reflection shined on the metal walls around her. It was a total out-of-body experience, where she stared at a ferocious warrior. Except *she* was that warrior, carrying deadly weapons, and wearing the face of a frightened child.

The elevator's soft ping broke Shay's gaze on her own terrified face. She looked at the door as it closed on Hetal's worried eyes. The lift shot up, and Shay's stomach dropped down.

"I can do this," she whispered, staring at herself in the shiny wall. "You're hardcore. A hero."

Her little pep talk wasn't working. No matter how hard she tried, she couldn't transform her mind to fit the image that reflected off every surface around her. This look, these weapons, they'd be perfect for someone else. Someone who lingered unseen.

"Jenna, are you here?" Shay glanced over her shoulder. She actually expected to find Jenna waving at her with a sassy smile, but she only glimpsed herself.

The elevator swayed to a halt and Shay took a deep breath. She ignored the panic that disrupted her thoughts and lifted her chin high as the door slid open.

There were four levels in the rundown asylum, and endless hallways of cobwebs, yet Lucius knew exactly where to find his brother. Cyrus had developed a routine as of late. He'd wake up, scream at his inventions for a few hours, then go out back and smoke cigarettes. It used to be entertaining, but now the man's hissy fits neared the threshold of inconvenient.

A puff of white smoke wafted up from behind an ivy-laced wall and Lucius veered toward it. Cyrus flicked a cigarette at Lucius's feet the second Lucius walked into view.

"Max and Simon are on their way here. Mimic screwed up."

"Big surprise," Cyrus said as he knocked another cigarette loose from his pack.

"Can you do that thing?"

Cyrus lit his cigarette. "Of course. But no one alive should be inside the building when I do it."

"I have an errand to run. You'll have to deal with your girlfriend. They'll be here in ten minutes."

"I only need five." Cyrus tossed his cigarette into a puddle, bumping against Lucius as he strolled by.

"Hey," Lucius shouted, and a rumble quaked the concrete under his boots.

Cyrus glanced back at Lucius, his face twisted in pain. The agony trapped behind his brother's stare sucked the anger right out of Lucius, clearing space for the big brother vibe to sear into his chest. He stepped in front of Cyrus, and placed his hand on his little brother's wide shoulder.

"What did you see, in Alexie's mind?"

A snicker flowed from Cyrus's mouth, despite the anger clouding his stare. He pushed Lucius's hand off his shoulder, shaking his head.

"Brother—"

"Don't *brother* me." Cyrus jabbed his finger at Lucius's chest. "You win, again. She's in love with you."

"Who? Lexie?"

"That's why she dumped me, left with Max and Simon. She was running from her feelings, for you."

Lucius caught his grin before it could escape his lips, but the warmth spread throughout his body like a virus. "I thought you were over her?"

"I am, but it still stings."

In one of those over dramatic foot stompings, Cyrus walked into the asylum. Lucius couldn't think about repairing the rift between himself and his brother, or Alexie's feelings toward him ... or what his life could be like if he and Cyrus returned to Ling Enterprises. Those things were flights of fancy. He lived in reality, a lonely one he'd created through a series of tragic mistakes.

Lucius turned from the asylum—from his daydreams of a reunited Liberty Squad—and shot off the ground, soaring across the sky.

Max stepped off the elevator. The sight in front of him was enough to cement his feet in place, until Simon plowed into his back.

"Walk much?" Simon grumbled, brushing off his cape.

"Whoa," Max muttered.

Across the wide lobby, Shay stood beside the now broken fountain dressed in a killer outfit. It was sexy, too sexy. She shouldn't be allowed to wear anything so … tight.

Max tried to part his gaze from the curves of her hips, which he hadn't known existed before she'd squeezed into leather pants. There were a million things in this lobby besides the snug vest that cinched her waist, yet he couldn't see any of them.

"Seriously?" Simon stepped in front of Max, blocking his view of a girl he shouldn't want to gawk at. "That's not okay."

"If I were thirty-six and she were twenty-six, it wouldn't matter."

"Shay's not twenty-six. She's sixteen."

Max cringed. The words twisted his gut, which matched perfectly with his already jumbled mind. He completely understood everyone's aversion, felt it himself. A relationship between him and Shay would be wrong, on many levels, but he couldn't get fifty feet from her without melting. And the smile she flashed when Simon walked beside her … it ignited a blaze inside his chest.

It wasn't easy, but Max forced his stare to the floor and walked toward Shay. There had to be a way he could get her to stay behind. The visual alone. It was very distracting.

"Are you feeling okay?" Max asked Shay, even though his stare remained on his own boots. "You lost a lot of blood."

"Yeah." Simon peered into Shay's eyes. "Maybe you should stay here, rest."

"Hetal gave me a bunch of shots, B12, iron, a few other concoctions." Shay slammed her fist into her palm. "I'm wired, let's do this."

After that display, Max no longer wanted to leave Shay behind. He wanted to keep her close forever.

"I'll give you a lift." He held his hand in front of her, straining not to grin at her wide eyes.

Simon stepped between them and wrapped his arm around Shay's shoulder. "Let me. You wouldn't want to singe her hair."

The moment Simon walked away, Max glowered. He copied Simon's bulky strut while following them to the sidewalk. Shay glanced back at Max, just in time to catch his over exaggerated ape-like steps.

He froze. That didn't stop waves of embarrassment from washing over him, or did it erase the stupid look off his face.

Shay giggled and he shrugged. There was nothing he could do besides try to play it off as smoothly as possible. He was a moron, one who probably looked like a drunken monkey.

As Max stepped out the front door of Ling Enterprises, Simon pulled Shay close. The people on the sidewalk around them stopped to gasp, snap pics, and a spike of jealousy nicked Max's heart.

Wind gusted in swirls as Simon and Shay shot toward the clouds. It shouldn't bother him that Simon, of all people, had his hands wrapped around Shay. Shouldn't's didn't seem to matter to him anymore, not since Shay breezed into his life.

A prickling heat rose inside Max's body. The energy surged so fast it rocketed his feet off the ground. Flames ignited around him with a burst, propelling him faster through the air. All his thoughts drifted away, and instinct kicked in. The envy, self-loathing ... his broken heart veiled behind moments of weightlessness and freedom.

Max barreled toward a building and cut straight up, leaving a trail of fire along the window fronts. His smile spread with ease, turning into a laugh.

He sped toward the harbor, buzzing past Simon, and a big empty field rolled into view. There was no abandoned asylum, no rubble, not one trace a building had ever occupied the lot. Other than Alexie standing by the waterfront, only an acre of brown grass sat between the rows of deserted warehouses below.

The orb of flames around Max crackled, sizzling out as he landed beside Alexie. "What's this?" he asked, pointing at the nothing in front of him.

Alexie stared at the empty field where the asylum should be. "It was like this when I got here. I don't know. It's just … gone."

"Hundred-year-old asylums can't get up and walk away."

Simon landed in front of them and Shay staggered from his grasp.

"That fire thing on the building was awesome." Shay adjusted her slightly crooked tactical vest as she glanced around at the patch of tall grass. "Where's the asylum?"

"What's she doing here?" Alexie asked, doing a double take at Shay's outfit. "And why is she dressed like a commando?"

Simon grabbed Alexie by the wrist and pulled her aside. As they exchanged hushed shouts, Shay walked toward the open field that once housed a two-story, three-wing building.

"Where's the asylum?" she repeated in a louder more frantic tone.

"It was here yesterday," Alexie said.

"Evie," Shay yelled.

They all waited, silent, as though Shay's call would trigger Evie to appear. Seconds passed and only the sound of water slapping the harbor's concrete wharf rang out. Shay turned toward Max. Fear shrouded her stare. She looked so young with glazed over eyes, so vulnerable. Guilt flooded his mind. More than ever, he hated himself for being attracted to Shay.

"We'll find her," Simon said, patting Shay on the shoulder.

"Find who? What went down?" Alexie asked.

"Evie's been abducted," Simon said, glaring at Alexie. "Someone with abilities took her form, was impersonating her."

"That doesn't make any sense." Alexie looked at the grassy lot that used to hold the asylum. "Who would want to be Evie?"

"We think Lucius and Cyrus have been doing some recruiting," Max said. "They must know about the others with powers. Found some idiot who'll listen to their insane rantings."

"Yeah." Alexie ran her hand along the back of her neck, looking down at the ground. "I see how that could happen."

"I'm never gonna find her," Shay said, her voice barely resonating over the whistle of the harbor's breeze.

Max reached for Shay, caught Simon's disapproving head shake, then lowered his hand to his side. "We have to find Lucius to find your sister."

Shay stared at the long blades of dead grass that danced in the wind. "Evie must be so scared."

Evie's back rubbed against a van's hard metal floor as she kicked its side door. She was furious. She'd been locked in a damp cell, fed scraps, then handcuffed and tossed into a cargo van. There would be a reckoning. Nobody treated Evie Sinclair like this and got away with it.

Her hands were cuffed behind her back, and her balled fists banged against her spine every time she kicked the van's door, but that didn't stop her. Rage was a beautiful thing, especially when it fueled her body to keep fighting.

Evie kicked the door harder, and the handcuff's edge dug into her wrist. The sharp metal sliced her skin. Warm blood streaked down her palm and dripped off her fingertips. Her entire body ached, which only made her angrier. That anger gave her the power to kick the van's door again and again.

The door flew open and Evie rolled to her knees. Dr. Mayhem crowded her escape. His wide body blocked nearly all light from the world beyond the van's doorway.

"You've injured yourself."

Evie gasped, choking on the heart that now resided in her throat. "That voice," she said, mostly to herself. Even muffled through a shapeless black mask, she knew that voice. It belonged to a man who whispered words of love into her ear as he held her in his strong arms.

"Fitz," Evie said, breathlessly. "That's you, right? Fitzgerald. As in, Cyrus Fitzgerald Grant. That's you hiding like a coward behind that mask, right?"

He lifted his hand and Evie cowered down. Fabric rustled then his thin black mask fell to the floor beside her, but she didn't look. She couldn't see him dressed in a hard plastic suit, with a dark cape fluttering in the wind.

"Evie. You don't understand."

"Don't," Evie yelled. "Don't talk to me like you care about me."

"I do care about you. Look at me."

He bent down in front of Evie and she leaned away from him. Her back wedged into a corner of the van, and cool steel pressed against her cheek. A strong pull tugged on Evie's chest. Her body wanted to collapse against the man in front of her, but she forced herself to remain against the van's sharp metal side.

"Look at me."

Warm breath rushed over Evie's skin, leaving a hint of peppermint. It reminded her of sweet kisses from a caring man. Tingles ran through her body, and it made her sick.

Evie looked at Fitz, Cyrus … Dr. Mayhem, praying to God her look would kill. He didn't die. His body didn't shatter into a million pieces the way her heart did at this moment. He just stared at her with loving eyes, which hurt more than the handcuffs pinching her wrists.

"This was the only way I could save your life. I hope, one day, you'll be able to forgive me, because I do love you."

He sounded serious. Evie almost believed him.

"If you really love me, let me go."

"There's nothing to let you go to. In a year from now, regular people won't exist anymore. You'll thank me for this."

Cyrus moved away from the van's side door, leaving it open, and Evie hurried toward it. A hand clutched onto her throat, squeezing. She peered up, into Antiserum's iron mask.

Antiserum shoved Evie back into the van, then tossed a body onto the floor beside her.

"Don't say I never gave you anything," he growled, slamming the door shut.

24

Shay walked into the lab and unzipped her vest, fanning her sweaty skin.

"Hetal," she yelled.

Hetal didn't crawl from beneath a machine or poke her head over the wall of computers, which stopped Shay's steps in the middle of the lab.

"That's strange."

"Maybe she went home," Simon said.

Alexie hung in the lab's doorway, slowly backing into the hall. "Text me if you need me."

"Hey. Wait up," Simon called out, following Alexie from the lab.

Shay turned her back to Max. She peeled the heavy vest off her shoulders, dropped it onto her workbench, and hurried to pull on her lab coat.

"Hetal's bag is still here. She wouldn't go home without it."

"Maybe she ran to the diner."

Max's voice flowed right beside Shay's ear. She could practically feel him prowling close behind her, too close. An entire speech about the appropriate amount of personal space between two colleagues formed in her mind as she turned to face Max.

He stared at her from far across the room, looking awfully confused by her raised finger and wide-open mouth ready to reprimand, as he should be.

Shay shrank down, closing her mouth. Something, she had to say something to cover up her foolishness.

"I've been working up a theory on how to extract Jenna's soul from my body."

Instant regret followed the words that babbled from Shay's mouth. There were a million things going on right now and she chose to discuss that topic with Max, while they were alone.

"Is it dangerous?"

That was a good question, one that hadn't bothered to cross Shay's mind.

"I haven't really gotten that far into the equation yet. But I suppose everything's dangerous, in a way."

Max sat on the lab's small couch, hoisting his hands behind his head. "Ain't that the truth?"

"Back to babysitting duty?"

"No. I like hanging with you, watching you work. You take a pile of junk and turn it into something unimaginable. It's pretty cool."

Max's statement might have been the nicest thing anyone's ever said to Shay, in the most nonchalant way. The guy definitely mastered the mixed signals routine. Not even all the brains in her head could decipher his motives. She'd have to resort to drastic measures and have an actual, straight-up conversation with Max.

"What are you doing, here, with me?"

Max lowered his hands to his lap. He squirmed on the couch, its leather crinkling under his weight. "I don't … What do you mean?"

"Are you waiting for Jenna to come back? Have you been flirting with me, or are you like this with everyone? You do know I'm a junior, in high school, right?"

"That's, a lot of questions." Max leaned forward on the couch. He rested his elbows on his knees and stared at the floor. "I kind of hope Jenna never comes back. It hurts too much."

He looked at Shay, for a second, then his stare returned to the metal floor. "I have been flirting with you, and I feel really disgusting about it."

"Because I'm disgusting?"

"No," Max said, rising to his feet. "Because I do know you're a junior in high school."

Max finally locked eyes with Shay, and this time she looked away. His ridiculous hotness had been easy to overcome, but that gleam in his eyes when he stared at her quaked her knees every time.

"I wish I didn't feel this way about you," Max said, more to himself than her. "I look at you and try to see a bratty kid, but all I can see is a stunning person."

Max lifted his hand and Shay thought, hoped, he'd reach for her but he ran his fingers though his own hair.

"I won't flirt with you anymore, unless you flirt with me first. Then it's on."

"Umm. Okay." Shay wasn't exactly sure how she felt about that— terrified, hopeful, and a bunch more terrified. Either way, she'd be careful *not* to remotely flirt with Max in any way anytime soon. If only more people were around, then it'd be easier to accomplish this seemingly impossible feat.

"Where'd Simon go?" she asked, in an almost seamless transition of subject.

"I don't know." Max pulled out his cell phone, glanced at its screen, then shoved it back into his pocket. "Hetal should be back too. I think she lives in here now."

Shay headed straight to the nearest computer. "The beautiful elf who guards the lab." She typed on the computer's keyboard before her butt could sink into a chair.

"What are you doing?"

"I'm gonna hack the security cameras, see when Hetal left."

"Oh." Max rolled Shay's chair aside and pulled another over, taking a seat in front of the computer she'd been typing on. "Let a professional handle this."

"Excuse me." Shay scooted her chair back toward the computer, just enough to see its display and no closer.

"I'm in, but I do know Simon's password so ..."

"That's cheating, Mr. Professional." Shay would've smacked Max on the arm, but wasn't certain if that would be considered flirting. To be safe, she clasped her fingers together and placed her hands in her lap.

Max rewound the camera feed, stopping at the first sight of Hetal. "Here she is, at seven p.m."

"That's right after we left."

The screen flashed to gray fuzz then cleared to an empty lab.

"What happened?" Shay wheeled her chair beside Max, slanting closer to the computer's display. "The feed skipped ahead two minutes."

"It's some kind of interference. I'll back it up and slow it down."

Shay stared at the computer's screen as the clicks of a keyboard echoed throughout the room, the lonely, empty room. First Evie got taken from their suite while she slept, and now Hetal goes missing in the lab. Shay was running out of places that felt safe. Maybe that was the point.

"There." Shay pointed at a blurry image of Hetal, literally floating through the air. A white light flashed and Hetal disappeared. "That's just ..."

"I'm calling Simon."

The rough edges of metal handcuffs scraped Evie's raw skin as she rolled to her knees. Tires squealed. The van swayed as it started to drive at a fast speed, and her shoulder slammed against the locked side door.

A white lab coat gleamed in the seconds a passing streetlight lit the cargo van's back cab. The little body, which hadn't moved since tossed beside Evie, had to be Shay. Only a monster would want their little sister in this situation. In that case, she was a monster because she really wanted to see Shay's face.

Evie crawled closer to the motionless body. Streetlights flashed and she glimpsed brown skin.

"Hetal!" Evie used her shoulder to roll Hetal onto her back.

Not a groan, a mumble … not even a peep flowed from Hetal's lips. Evie dropped her head on Hetal's chest, grinning as the wonderful sound of a heart's strong beat filled her ear.

"Wake up." Evie nudged Hetal with her knee and still nothing. "Please."

A thin flap slid open in the metal divider that separated the back of the van and the front cab. Evie peeked through the slit, but could only see glimpses of city buildings as they sped by the windshield.

"She's been tranquilized," said a deep voice through the narrow slit in the divider. It wasn't Cyrus's gentle tenor. The man who'd spoken to her had a rigid tone, one that seemed to chill the air.

Evie leaned against the divider. Her handcuffs pressed against her back as she ducked to see into the driver's seat.

"You must be Lucius."

The man behind the wheel didn't answer, but Evie could see a hint of a smile lift his stubbly cheek.

"I know you as Corbin, since that's what Fitz called you every time he ranted about his overbearing brother."

Lucius glanced at Cyrus in the passenger seat. "You used our middle names?"

"Yeah. Nobody knows who we are."

"You could've used any names, but you didn't want to lie to her."

The flap in the divider slammed closed, which muffled out the rumble of their voices. Evie pressed her ear against the divider's cool metal. Over the hum of tires, she couldn't hear a thing.

Cyrus had to care for her. All those nights he snuck into her condo after Shay went to sleep, the hours they spent together talking, laughing, cuddling in each other's arms couldn't have been faked. He cooked for her, rubbed her feet while watching TV shows he hated, helped her find investors for the ... Superhero Policing Unit.

Of course. It was always about superheroes. She split the real heroes focus, distracted Simon, Alexie, and Max for the villains. She was a villain. No, she was the enabler of a villain. Oh God, no, she was the girlfriend of a supervillain.

"Look, right there." Shay's voice echoed throughout the lab as she pointed at the computer's screen. "It's a person, holding Hetal."

Simon leaned over Max's shoulder to stare at the fuzzy camera feed, which played in slow motion on a computer's display. "There has to be a way to clear up this video."

"I'm running it through a series of filters," Max said, typing at a mile-a-minute. "And ... there."

He hit the enter key and the video reset, playing in mega-slow motion. "It's going frame-by-frame, at half-speed. This is the frame."

They all leaned closer to the computer, bumping heads.

"You can see Hetal," Max said, his finger hovering in front of the screen. "She turns, like she heard something, falls to the ground, levitates, and ..."

Shay strained to keep her eyelids open, afraid to blink and miss the whole thing. The video flashed. A faint silhouette of a dark figure showed on the screen. The staticy shadow of a person picked Hetal off the ground. Then, they were both gone.

"Antiserum," Shay said, not really sure why. She'd only seen a millisecond of a maybe-person holding Hetal, but she knew it was him. His creepy vibe still clung to her lab.

"Do you have a picture of Dr. Mayhem without the mask?"

"Yeah." Max typed while glancing at Shay. "What are you thinking?"

"It's kind of crazy." A picture popped onto the screen and Shay's jaw dropped. She recognized the man's honey-tinged eyes, his dimples that spawned dimples. "I've seen this man before."

"When you were taken?" Simon asked.

"Yes, but no. In my condo, two months ago. I got up in the middle of the night to use the bathroom, and he walked out of it. Then crept into Evie's bedroom."

Both Max and Simon turned to stare at Shay. The mixture of confusion in Simon's eyes and the shock on Max's face was hilarious, but this wasn't a laughing occasion.

"What?" Shay said in a bark. "Evie's been sneaking football player-looking dudes in at night since she was sixteen. It was kind of pointless after the accident, since nobody was there to care what she did."

Max leaned back in his chair. "Did Cyrus see you, say anything?"

"Yeah. He shushed me, so I hated him instantly."

"Naturally," Max said.

Shay nodded, even though Max was taunting her. "He said he was invisible. That I didn't see him. I completely forgot about it until just now."

She looked at the computer, at that man's smile. Cyrus Fitzgerald Grant, the esteemed Dr. Grant, the terrifying Dr. Mayhem, would need a new title added to his bio: the soon-to-be dead man who messed with her sister. "Invisible. This profile says Cyrus has a PhD in astrophysics."

"And mechanical engineering," Simon said with a hint of awe. "Cyrus is a genius."

"Why?" Max asked.

Shay shooed Max away from the computer. She minimized the photo of Cyrus and opened the map with the energy signatures.

"There's still a bunch of blips at the asylum's location. They made it invisible. That's how Antiserum got in here to take Hetal, and Evie, why we couldn't see the asylum."

Simon shook his head. "Invisibility is not possible."

"Anything's possible. With certain metamaterials, one could alter wavelengths, distort visible light."

The wheels in Shay's brain kept turning. She could almost see the lens, wires, and transistors come together to form this theoretical creation.

"Gradient-index materials could reduce the diffraction limit, drop the perception of an image well below minimum resolution."

Max looked lost, more so than Simon. "In English?"

"They made a cloaking device," Shay said in a groan, which seemed to be simple enough for the dummy crowd to understand. She missed Hetal. She really missed Evie. She'd even take Alexie over these two lunkheads.

"Where's Alexie?"

A string of Mandarin grumbles burst from Simon's mouth as he looked away.

"Are you guys breaking up?" Shay asked, weaving to catch a glimpse of Simon's face. "Is that why she's been scarce?"

"Ha!" Max snickered. "That's a good one."

Simon glared at Max. "Her aunt's sick, Parkinson's."

"Oh. I thought Alexie grew up in foster care. Isn't that how she met Max?"

Max crossed his arms. He looked beyond Shay, at Simon's flustered expression.

"Right," Simon said, softly. "Her friend then."

"I'm not trying to get in your business." Shay typed a quick code on the computer's keyboard, which switched the map to a live satellite feed. "Look, the asylum's visible again. I think we should go back. We can sneak in and rescue Evie and Hetal. Lucius and Cyrus won't be expecting us."

Simon glanced at his cell phone. "It's almost midnight. And Alexie—"

"We won't need Alexie," Shay said. The whininess in her own voice annoyed even her, but she was helpless to tone down her desperation. "It'll be easier in a small group. No fighting, just a quick smash and grab."

"No," Simon said, and Max snorted. "We should get some rest, wait for Alexie, and go in as a team."

"But—"

Max placed his hand on Shay's shoulder. "Simon's right. We should wait."

"Fine." Shay threw herself back into her chair, its squeak lost under her huff. "It's stupid, but whatever."

"Will you be all right tonight, on your own?" Simon asked.

"I'll stay with her," Max said.

More grumbles erupted from Simon's mouth, this time a colorful mix of slurs in English and Mandarin.

"What?" Max held his arms out at his sides as he rolled his chair away from Shay. "I meant on the couch."

"Sure you did," Simon grumbled on his way out of the lab.

"Hey," Max called out before Simon could round the corner. "Don't lecture me from your closet."

"Closet?" Shay said.

"You know what?" Max knelt in front of Shay and a sly gaze flared within his eyes. "I think you're right. It would be a good idea to sneak over to the asylum and grab our girls back."

Shay scooted to the edge of her seat, a grin puffing her cheeks. "Yeah?"

"Yeah. Thirty minutes, and Simon should be passed out. Then we'll head over, get your sister back."

"And my assistant." Shay jumped up from her chair. She hurried to her workbench, switching out her lab coat for a tactical vest.

The van rocked to a stop and Evie fell to her side. It was impossible for her to gain a sense of balance with her hands cuffed behind her back, especially when a madman was at the van's wheel.

A soft groan erupted from Hetal's mouth and Evie shuffled back to her knees. The chain of her handcuffs clinked as she leaned over Hetal.

"Hetal," she whispered and Hetal's garbled moans grew louder. "Can you hear me?"

"What happened?" Hetal asked in a slur. She stayed flat on her back, rubbing her eyes in slow jerky motions.

"I need you to get up. We have to fight."

"Fight?" Hetal mumbled. "Evie? You've been rescued."

"No. You've been abducted."

"What?" That seemed to spark a fire under Hetal, as she sat upright with a jolt. She rubbed her head, looking around the dark empty van.

"Is this where you've been, in the back of a van?" She grabbed the handle on the side door, only to find it locked.

"No. I was at the asylum. I have no idea where we are now."

Hetal drew her knees to her chest and held herself tight. "What do they want with us?"

"Nothing good I'm sure. I'm handcuffed." Evie turned to show Hetal the new, uncomfortable jewelry she'd acquired. "I need *you* to fight."

"Me?"

"Yes, you." Evie strained to display courage as she stared at Hetal, instead of the fear that actually gripped her. "When the door opens—"

The van's side door slid open. Lucius crowded its doorway in his clunky plastic suit, but he wasn't wearing his mask. He looked more sinister without it. Evie could easily excuse the malicious things Antiserum did when he looked like a monster, but without the mask he was just another person—a man—the man responsible for her parents' death.

"What?" he asked, a light smile on his lips. "I'm curious to know, what should she do when the door opens?"

"Grab that metal shard at her feet and jab it in your neck," Evie said in a snarl. She glanced at Hetal, then at the pointed piece of steel right next to Hetal's unbound hands.

Hetal's shoulders grew stiff. Her eyes widened and Lucius laughed.

"It wouldn't do anything." He picked the razor-sharp slice of metal off the van's floor. "Except get the girl killed."

Streetlights shined on the jagged shard as he lifted it high. He slammed the metal's sharped end against his own palm and it bent, folding in half, without leaving a scratch on his skin.

"That's fine," Evie said, holding a harsh glare. "My sister's gonna track you down and blast your ass to bits."

"Hey, Cyrus," Lucius yelled over his shoulder. "Your woman's kinda cute, tough."

His grin dropped. He clutched onto Evie's shirt and yanked her toward him. "I hope little sis *does* show up. She has something that belongs to me."

Cyrus appeared over Lucius's shoulder, and Evie's eyes lit up. For a second, she'd forgotten he was the villain responsible for her captivity.

"Keep your hands off this one." Cyrus pushed Lucius away from the van's door and took Evie by the arm. She gazed into his eyes, silently begging him to stop—to let her go and act like he loved her.

"Come on," he said, tugging on her arm.

Evie looked at Hetal, who was cowered in the farthest corner of the van, then back into Cyrus's deceivingly gentle eyes. "Fitz, please, help us."

"His name is Cyrus," Lucius said in a growl. "Or Dr. Mayhem if you prefer."

That man's cruel voice rattled Evie's nerves but she didn't waver. Her affectionate stare on Cyrus didn't break, and the temporary backbone she grew remained firm.

"You don't have to do everything your brother tells you. It's okay to think for yourself, to do what you feel is right."

Cyrus glided his thumb along Evie's cheek. "I'm not gonna hurt you. I'm going to give you powers, like me, then I'll let you go. I promise."

"What?" Hetal shouted. "You can't. It could kill her."

Evie backed deeper into the van. "It's not what I want, Fitz. It's not."

Regret crossed Cyrus's face, right before he pulled Evie from the van. She fought against his crushing grip, swung her bound arms from side to side.

The dark shadow of a tall tower fell over Evie. She stopped struggling to stare at the building in front of her. "We're back at the asylum?"

A scream cut through the icy air. Evie looked over her shoulder as Lucius pulled Hetal from the van.

"What's going on here?" Alexie yelled as she stepped from the shadow of the asylum.

Evie grinned, almost cheered at the sight of Alexie's ornery face. "Thank God. Zap these two jerkbags and get us out of here."

Alexie groaned. She walked around Evie, without a glance, and stood beside Lucius. "I don't understand why we need Evie. You should let me get rid of her."

"Alexie?" Evie all but whimpered. The fire in her veins sputtered out. This couldn't be happening. She'd taken a van ride from reality and got spit out in a bizarro world where Electric-Luxie, the poster-girl for all things righteous, was a villain.

"Evie is Cyrus's new woman," Lucius said through a smile. "He actually loves this one, instead of lusting after her like he did with you."

"Clearly," Alexie said, somehow cramming a boat-load of sarcasm into her one word. "You're supposed to abduct and torment the people you love. I forgot."

Alexie finally looked Evie in the eyes, but only for a second. "Have they treated you half-decent at least?"

"Traitor." Evie kicked Alexie in the shin, then resumed her wild struggle against Cyrus's tight clutch. "I knew there was no such thing as a hero."

Lucius chuckled. His laughter stung Evie's ears and she stopped struggling. He enjoyed her misery too much. She'd blot the sun from the sky if it would end that man's pleasure.

"One day, you'll understand," Alexie said, softly, staring at the dead grass beneath her boots.

"You all say that," Evie shouted with spite. "Because none of you have a single valid reason for anything you do. Then, when something convenient happens, you pretend like you planned it all along. Heroes, villains … you all super-suck."

"Yeah. Well, you're about to join that club," Cyrus said as he dragged Evie toward the asylum, despite her kicking and screaming.

A gust of air blew across the rooftop, rocking Shay in place. She peered over the side of Ling Enterprises and a twinge of fear flared within her chest. The icy wind whipped her ponytail against her neck as she strained to see the sidewalk, 113 stories below the roof's edge she stood upon.

"I don't know," she said, looking at Max. "Are you sure about this? I don't want to get burned."

"The fire won't touch you." Max offered his hand to Shay. "Trust me?"

Of course Shay trusted the superhero, but the man behind the suit ... that was still up for debate.

A flurry of tingles erupted in her chest as she moved her hand toward Max. Those tingles spiked the moment she slid her palm into his.

Max pulled Shay close and their chests collided. Heat ignited from the slight contact, surging throughout her body in such a delightful way. Her breaths went into overtime when Max clutched onto her waist and a smile attacked her lips.

This wasn't flirting. Shay definitely was not flirting.

"Ready?" Max asked.

Before Shay could answer, Max threw them over the side of the building. A yelp rose in her throat as windows zoomed by, but she managed to hold it there. Frosty air hit her skin like a slap, nipping at her cheeks. She buried her face in Max's chest and an explosion propelled them upward.

Wind no longer chilled her skin. Instead, a warmth radiated from all sides. The force of high speeds still tugged her body, but Max's arms held her snug to his side. She never felt so safe. Her brain knew she soared between skyscrapers, hundreds of feet off the ground, yet her nerves remained completely calm while caught within a superhero's grip.

Shay peeked over Max's shoulder. An orb of crimson fire encased them. The flames didn't cover Max's body. They twisted in slow motion around him, cocooning them both in a bubble of fire. It was hypnotic the way each tiny flame danced, whirled, bled into one another, as though the winds of flying fed them.

"Don't touch it," Max said, his breath rushing over Shay's neck.

Her hand jerked back. She hadn't even realized her fingers reached for the fire until his voice pulled her from the flame's lure. The weight on her stomach lifted and solid ground rushed in to tap the soles of her boots.

"Whoa." She staggered away from Max, patting herself down for a quick stray-flame check.

"Cooler than flying with Simon?" he asked.

"Way."

The veil of night lifted the longer Shay stared into the darkness around her, and the splash of water filtered into her ears. Once she glimpsed the asylum, it was impossible to miss. The broken glass on the building's many windows gleamed in the moon's light.

"What's the plan?" she whispered to Max.

"I thought you had one."

"No," Shay said, louder than she should have.

"This was your idea."

"Ideas are supposed to come with plans?"

Max snickered. "Come on." He hunched low and crept through the tall grass. "We'll wing it."

Shay clearly wasn't as smart as the tabloids claimed. A smart person would've run, hid, and waited for help, but she followed Max right toward the enemy's lair.

The girl Lucius dragged through the asylum pounded her fists against his chest, dug in her heels as they walked, but it did nothing to slow him. He pulled Hetal down crooked stairs, through dark hallways, and into the musty basement with ease.

"You were my role model." Hetal looked around Lucius, at Alexie straggling far behind in the dark corridor. "I even have a *What Would Electric-Luxie Do* bumper sticker on my car. I'm scraping that sucker off, because I no longer care what you would do."

Hinges squealed as Lucius opened the thick steel door to their secret lab. He shoved Hetal inside. She tried to run back out the door but he kept pushing her farther into the room.

Once Hetal spotted the nebula burst machine, she froze in place. The machine's golden panels, coiled transistors, and ionized plated arms stopped her from spouting out her constitutional rights so she could gawk.

"What am I doing here?" she asked, running her fingers along the machine's curved side.

Lucius nodded at Alexie, giving her the go-ahead to deploy her good cop routine. He knew it wouldn't work, but Alexie had to fail to learn.

Alexie clasped her hands behind her back, beneath her sparkly cape, and offered Hetal a soft smile. "We need your—"

"Not you," Hetal sneered. "You're a betrayer, a snake in the grass. I'd rather receive demands from someone less evil."

Lucius watched as Alexie's confident stare gave way to defeat. He didn't enjoy shattering her beliefs, but she needed to see the truth—that nothing significant could come from being polite and proper.

He walked toward Hetal and the girl shrank down.

"You tell me why you're here," he said, gesturing at the machine.

Hetal crept past his outstretched arm. She studied the control panel beside the machine, inspecting every wire that ran from the oversized chamber.

"The construction is magnificent." Hetal had that look in her eyes, the same look of wonder Cyrus got every time he stared at the machine. "This equipment has everything needed to radiate a person to their core, just like the blast that hit Max in space. Except, it's missing its most vital component."

Hetal turned her back to the machine, crossed her arms, and lifted her chin. "I won't help you."

"I don't *need* your help." Lucius curled his fingers into fists, straining to contain his anger. "But you will help me."

"Or what?" Hetal's eyes grew wide the moment the words slipped past her lips, and she slapped her palm over her mouth.

Lucius lifted his cell phone for Hetal to see. A series of pictures flashed on its screen. Hetal's mother tending to a garden. Hetal's little sister waiting for the school bus. He'd taken these pictures from afar, and he had no intention of harming these people. The girl who shivered in front of him didn't know that.

"They can have very unfortunate accidents."

Tears welled in Hetal's eyes. "Is this what you do now, Electric-Luxie? Kill innocent people to get what you want?"

Alexie lowered her gaze to the steel-grated floor. "There's no such thing as innocent."

"I can't believe this."

Lucius grabbed Hetal by the shirt, pulling her face right in front of his. "If this machine doesn't have a constant power source, your friend Evie will emerge a mutated fluke. That, you can believe."

Shay crouched under a broken window. The asylum's frigid wall shocked her bare arm as she pressed against it, sending flakes of stone to the ground.

Max peeked inside the asylum then dropped back down beside Shay. "Do you remember the layout? How to get to the cells?"

"Maybe."

Max stared at Shay with disapproval as he rose to his feet.

"I'm sure it'll come to me," she said in a hushed shout.

"Great." Max climbed inside the window, then reached his hand out to help Shay.

She slapped his hand away and jumped up onto the sill. She didn't need help climbing into a first-story window. She needed Max to use his superhero magic to locate her sister in a giant, ghostly asylum.

In near silence, Shay swung her legs inside the window and hopped to the cracked floor. Max dipped his head to the only doorway in the small room they'd snuck into, motioning for Shay to lead the way. She didn't have any powers, had never actually fist-fought anybody before. It wasn't even her who had run through the halls of this decrepit asylum. That had been Jenna. Despite all that, she crept across the room.

Shay pulled the sonic blaster from her leg holster with barely a sound. She held the weapon to her chest as she neared the doorway. After a deep breath and a quick mental lecture to be brave, she peeked into the hallway.

It was empty. Well, except for the thick layer of dust that covered every splintered surface, the abandoned stretchers pushed against the cracked walls, and the chill of wickedness in the air, the hallway was empty.

Left, a soft voice rang out. Shay turned toward Max, pulling him close. "Did you hear that?"

Max shook his head, and Shay walked into the hallway.

"Left it is," she mumbled to herself, heading down the left corridor. Broken tile crunched under her light steps. She was sure the sound blared throughout the building, but the baddies didn't swoop in to beat her down so she continued walking toward the end of the dark hall.

"Familiar?" Max whispered.

Right, said the soft voice, clearer, squeakier, in a very Jenna-ish tone.

"Sort of," Shay said to Max, as she followed the directions Jenna gave her from within her mind. "This way."

A distant crash vibrated the floor and Shay stopped short. Her finger twitched, sliding to the trigger of her sonic blaster.

Second door on the right.

"Come on," Shay whispered to Max, opening the only steel door in the creepy hallway.

225

Cyrus walked into the holding room. His legs fought each step. He hated the sight of Evie locked in a filthy cell, but he couldn't bear the thought of her trapped in this dark room alone. If only she'd listen to reason. The world was about to change, become more dangerous … unpredictable. Those without powers could never survive the frenzy, not once every idiot in the city started tossing fireballs or punching down skyscrapers. He couldn't let Evie die under a pile of rubble the way her parents had at his brother's hand.

The thought doubled his pace into the dimly lit room of barred cells and narrow solitary chambers. Whatever it took to get her in that machine, he'd do it. He wouldn't use his powers, but he'd shove her inside the nebula burst generator and lock its door to keep her safe.

"Cyrus," Evie called out, her shaky arm reaching through the bars.

Without thinking, Cyrus rushed to Evie.

"Are you hurt?"

He held her hand to his chest, looking at the welts on her wrist left by handcuffs.

"Yeah I'm hurt. You put me in a cell."

"It's for your own good."

Evie pulled her hand from Cyrus's grasp and held onto the iron bar in front of her. "I don't get how taking me from my room in the middle of the night and dumping me in this rat hole is for my own good."

"Lucius *will* transform every person who carries a mutative strand in their DNA, whether I help him or not. Once the city is packed with fools wielding powers, regular people won't be safe. I'm making sure you're not one of those regular people anymore."

The anger melted from Evie's face every time her gaze flashed to Cyrus. "And I have this mutative strand?"

"Yes. I ran the test twice, you're SP positive."

"SP?" Evie asked.

"Superpowers—it's what I'm going with until I think up something witty."

Evie didn't crack a smile, didn't say a word or even move a muscle.

Although only seconds had passed, it seemed like an eternity before she looked at him.

"You know," she said, leaning against the bars. "I've always dreamt of having superpowers."

Cyrus waited for the inevitable *but*. It never came. Instead, Evie reached through the bars and glided her hands up his chest.

"I'll do it," she said, gazing into his eyes. "I want to do it."

"Seriously?"

Evie nodded, lightly, keeping her gaze locked on Cyrus's face. "Read my mind."

"No. I won't use my powers on you, ever."

Evie's grin drew Cyrus closer. His forehead pressed against cool metal as he held her through the bars that separated them.

"I love you, Cyrus."

She rose to her toes and kissed him. The moment her lips touched his own, he jolted back. He knew Evie's kiss. It was soft and feathery as it floated in to caress his mouth. The slobbery mess that sloshed along his face was nothing like Evie's kiss.

"Mimic." Cyrus wrapped his fingers around Mimic's neck, and yanked her forward against the bars. "Where's Evie?"

"What's wrong, sweetie, don't wanna play with me? I'm pretty enough, just your type."

Cyrus squeezed Mimic's throat. His mind saw Evie even though he knew it was Mimic's windpipe he crushed. The visual shook his fingers, yet he squeezed the neck in his grasp and lifted Mimic's feet off the ground.

"Where … is … Evie?"

Mimic clawed at Cyrus's hand, gasping, and he loosened his clutch. She fell to her knees, cradling her new set of puffy finger marks.

"Solitary," Mimic said between pants and hacks.

Cyrus nearly choked on his rage as he stomped across the room. He should've broken the fluke's neck, done the world a favor.

"Hey," Mimic yelled. She pushed the barred door open and

227

walked from the cell. "Evie will never love you, never understand. You don't need her. I can be her for you, but better."

The already boiling rage that scorched Cyrus's mind twisted into a seething fury. Red. All he could see was red, and the long metal surgical table in front of him.

Cyrus grabbed onto the table's jagged edge, ripping its bolted legs from the ground. Before the snap of metal could bounce off the walls, he hurled the rusty slab at Mimic.

Mimic ducked as the table soared overhead. Her entire body shook when the table crashed against the stone wall, quaking as it banged to the floor.

"Don't *ever* compare yourself to Evie again." Cyrus stood over Mimic, who cowered in the filth. "You could never be her. Change your form."

The air shimmered around Mimic, gave off a heat that reeked of burnt electrical wires. Evie's body blurred, shrinking down to one of a little girl. Mimic rose off the floor, a small child who barely stood waist-high to Cyrus. Her now innocent eyes gazed up at him, and she folded her tiny arms across her small chest.

"Sorry," she said in a meek, squeaky voice as she hurried from the room.

Cyrus stared at the façade of a child. Her bright red dress gleamed in the gray hallway, and her two long braids tapped her back as she skipped along on little legs.

The idea of Mimic parading around as a child sickened him. He'd just reached the end of his limit with that monster. When this human race makeover thing was complete, he'd be sure to rectify his brother's mistake of a creation.

Shay inched down fractured metal steps. They creaked beneath her feet, thundering up the narrow stairwell as she crept down it. At least, in her mind they did. These stupid stairs were loud. This narrow stairwell, with its giant crack running all the way down the mold-splattered wall, ruined her love of stairwells, which only added fuel to her already enraged flame.

Once she stepped on the bottom landing, and her feet returned to un-squeaky ground, her entire body unwound. She reached for the door, desperate to flee this dark cramped space, and Max grabbed onto her arm.

"I hear a child," he whispered.

"That's—"

A little girl's giggle echoed from behind the door in front of Shay, followed by the clickety-clack of skipping shoes. The tap of hard soles grew louder, and Shay leaned away from the door. Another giggle rang out from what could've been right beside her. Then, a song. It was a happy tune from Shay's childhood, sung by a ghost girl's mousy voice in a rundown asylum of decay.

Shay had become paralyzed with fear, even after the eerie voice drifted away. "Really creepy," she said in a hush.

"Should we ..." Max rocked in place as he stared at the door. "Rescue her?"

"I don't think that was a regular child."

Max nodded, relief washing over him. "Shapeshifter?"

"Or a poltergeist, but probably the shifter."

Max grabbed the door's knob and glanced at Shay. "Which way do we go?"

"Right ... right?"

"You're asking me?"

"No." Shay turned her back to Max, shielding her face. "Right?" she said beneath her breath.

Yes. Right. Can't you do anything on your own?

Shay grumbled at Jenna's snippy tone, which echoed in her head. She turned back toward Max, nodding. "Yep. Go right."

The suspicion in Max's gaze grew deeper, and Shay shrank down.

"What?" she asked, as softly as one could bark a question.

"What's up with you?"

Shay crossed her arms, and the sonic blaster in her hand banged against her hip. "What's up with you?"

"Nothing. I'm not the one talking to myself. Maybe we should go. This was a bad idea."

"Evie."

"I know it's hard, but we'll get—"

"No." Shay waved her hand, which cut off Max's clueless train of thought. "Someone just said her name."

They both pressed an ear against the door, staring at each other while listening to the muffled peeps on the other side.

Evie flinched as the hood was yanked off her head. Her eyes hadn't yet adjusted to the onset of light, but she glimpsed a blurry figure standing in the narrow doorway in front of her. She scurried backward. Her handcuffs slammed against the wall, the metal gouging straight to her bone. She held in her cry, denying whoever came to torture her their satisfaction.

"Evie!"

Cyrus rushed to Evie's side and she almost dove into his arms, but it wasn't the same man she'd come to care for. That man didn't wear shiny plastic armor. The person whose hands held her at night weren't covered by thick leather gloves. This was some other man staring at her. A supervillain, Dr. Mayhem, and he gazed at her with the tender stare of a man she trusted.

"I'm sorry," Cyrus said, unlocking Evie's cuffs. "I didn't know that bitch was gonna do this to you."

As soon as Evie's hand slid free from the shackles, she slapped

Cyrus across the cheek. "How dare you play the worried boyfriend card? Look at this."

She shoved her bloody wrist in his face, resisting the urge to wring his neck. "Look at what you did to me. And I'm so thirsty, and dirty."

Cyrus reached for Evie and she leaned away from him, wedging herself into a corner. "Don't touch me."

"Can you walk?"

Evie just stared at Cyrus. Any answer she gave would be the wrong one. It always was with the good-looking, evil types.

Cyrus stood up in the skinny room and backed away from the open door. "Come on."

"You're letting me go?" Evie jumped to her feet and hurried out the tiny concrete cell.

"Yes, after you get in the machine."

"No." Evie pounded her fists against Cyrus's chest, hurting her hands more than his solid chest plate.

"Dammit, Evie." Cyrus grabbed Evie's arms, holding them down at her sides. "I just said a bunch of romantic shit to you. Except it wasn't really you, it was that stupid shapeshifter."

"I don't care." Evie's body shook but she held her chin high. "I don't care what your twisted excuses are, how much you think you love me. You have no idea what true love is. I would never force someone I loved to change who they are."

"I'm not changing you. I'm saving you."

Cyrus tossed Evie over his shoulder like she was a sack of potatoes. She kicked, punched, screamed, but he didn't slow his steps from the room.

Evie's screams pierced Shay's ears, sending a shockwave of panic throughout her body. She yanked the stairwell door open, nearly clobbering Max with its edge, and ran into the hallway. She didn't know, didn't care what was on the other side of the door. Evie cried for help and neither her mind, body, nor her soul could ignore it.

In a skid of dust, Shay stopped short in the tight hallway. She stared down the dark passage at Cyrus, who had her sister slung over his shoulder. His lips lifted into a grin and she raised her sonic blaster.

"You shouldn't have come here, girl," he said.

Evie stopped punching Cyrus and peeked over her shoulder, trying to catch a glimpse of Shay.

"Put my sister down," Shay said though clenched teeth.

Max stepped beside Shay. He lifted his hand and a ball of flames ignited in his palm. "It's over, Cyrus. Simon and Alexie will be here any minute. If you let Evie go now, you'll have time to slither away."

Cyrus chuckled. He pointed at Max. "Go to sleep."

A yawn burst from Max's mouth. He staggered to the side, then fell over like a freshly chopped tree. His limp body crashed against the stairwell door, knocking it open. He thumped to the ground inside the stairwell and the door banged to a close, shutting away his sleeping body.

Terror struck Shay, wrapping around her to block off the flow of air. The sonic gun shook in her hand, growing heavier by the second. She glanced at the closed door, and the superhero she knew slept right on the other side of it, then at her sister still dangling over the villain's shoulder.

"Come here, Shay."

Cyrus's smooth voice flowed down the hall, but thanks to Hetal's device in Shay's pocket, did nothing to compel her.

Shay stood up straight. "No."

A grin swept her lips as shock filled Cyrus's gaze. This was her chance. The man's defenses were down, doubt swarmed his expression. A very convincing bluff could end this confrontation, without her gruesome death.

Shay held onto the butt of her gun with both hands and took aim. "This gun has a very precise laser, and I'm a great shot. You don't need both of your eyes, do you?"

Cyrus lowered Evie from his shoulder. He set her feet down on the floor and held her in front of him by the back of her neck.

"Is this what you want?" he asked, peeking out from behind Evie. "Come and get her."

"Don't," Evie yelled. "Just go, run."

The bottom of Shay's stomach dropped. She couldn't go anywhere. The fear within her sister's gaze wouldn't let her move.

"I'm not leaving you."

She tucked the gun back in its holster. There was no way she could use the sonic blaster in this cramped hallway, not without hitting Evie. The electro-pulse darts in her vest pocket, however, were a different story.

In one of those silent conversations only sisters could have, Shay told Evie to duck. Evie's expression held the reply of *Hell no, you're freakin' crazy* and Shay flashed a *Yep* smirk.

"Okay," Shay said. She leaned against the wall to get a better view of Cyrus. "Just don't hurt her." She slipped her hand into her pocket and pulled out a thin metal rod. It looked harmless, like a fancy pen, but it shot multiple fifty-thousand-volt pulse darts.

Shay took a step toward Cyrus, then another. The closer she got to him, the more weak spots she found in his armor. He'd forgotten to fasten a strap on his side, which left a wide-open target for her pulse dart.

The second Cyrus blinked, Shay raised her arm. She pressed the button on her dart gun and two pointed chips sailed down the hallway.

Evie curved to the side, as far as she could with a hand wrapped around the back of her neck. The shiny darts flew passed her waist and stuck into Cyrus's side.

Cyrus locked stiff as a web of white lightning scattered from the darts in his flesh. The electric charge traveled along his body, flashing and crackling. When it rode up his arm, Evie broke free from his grip. She dropped to her hands and knees, and Shay ran to her side.

"Are you okay?" she asked, wrapping her arms around Evie's slightly shuddering body.

"Yeah." Evie's teeth chattered, her shoulders twitching. "It shocked me a little, but I'm good."

A roar erupted from Cyrus's mouth. He tore the darts from his side, tossing them to the ground beside Shay. His body shook, but his glare held firm. He reached for Shay and fell to one knee.

"We gotta move," Shay yelled, dragging Evie backward down the hallway.

Cyrus rose to his feet, growling, and Shay pulled a containment grenade off the front of her vest, its pin dangling from her zipper. His eyes grew wide as she tossed the round canister at his feet.

A bright light blasted from the grenade, and blew up to form a bubble around Cyrus. The burst of energy knocked Shay to the ground, right beside Evie.

She sat up and her nose nearly touched the transparent containment field. Cyrus stood over her, but he couldn't touch her. He was trapped within an orb of electromagnetic energy.

Cyrus slammed his fists against the barrier between them, and a yelp flew from Shay's mouth. She scurried backward on the floor, kicking up a cloud of dust as she hurried away from the raging man who beat the containment field imprisoning him.

Shay couldn't hear his shouts, or the thump of his fists as they crashed against the sturdy field of entwined light, but she could see his fury clearly.

This time, her containment field didn't falter. A supervillain pounded his extra strong fists against the field's hazy surface, and it did nothing except spread ripples of blue light around the smoky orb.

The smile wiped from Shay's lips when she looked at Evie. Her sister sat on the filthy ground, covered in cobwebs, staring at Cyrus.

Shay knelt beside Evie, caressing her sister's back. "What did he do to you?"

Evie reached for the forcefield in front of her and Cyrus stopped attacking it. Then, Shay saw the most unexpected thing. Love. It shined in Cyrus's eyes as he gazed at Evie.

"He really, really hurt me," Evie said. She dropped both her stare and her hand to the broken tile below her knees.

"Let's get out of here." Shay helped Evie to her feet. For some reason, Cyrus smiled at her. He was stuck inside *her* containment field, yet he held a cocky smirk.

Shay turned from Cyrus's smug grin, and a large hand grabbed onto the front of her vest. The shock in her eyes reflected off a plastic chest plate as her feet were lifted off the ground.

Lucius had a firm hold on her. She could feel the chill his body emitted before she even looked up at his sinister face.

"Release my brother, or I'll snap it." He gestured at his other hand, which clutched Evie by the throat.

"I can't," Shay said, reaching for the sonic blaster in her leg holster. "It's time released. Twenty minutes."

Lucius growled and his grip on Shay tightened. She wrapped her fingers around the sonic blaster's handle, just as Lucius slammed her head against the wall. A flash of white cloaked her vision, then a veil of darkness covered her.

27

Max stretched out, rolling onto his back. He'd just had the weirdest dream. It had to have been a dream. He wasn't stupid enough to bring Shay to the asylum, to battle supervillains, without back-up.

The scent of musty air filled Max's lungs and a cold stone floor chilled the back of his head. He *was* at the asylum.

"Shay," Max called out, sitting up on the dusty floor.

Her voice didn't sing in his ears. He looked around the dark stairwell, but her soft brown eyes were nowhere in sight.

Max jumped to his feet and sprinted into the hallway. Cyrus stood alone at the far end of the dark corridor. A smile spread across Cyrus's lips. The man taunted Max with that crooked grin, and it was all he needed for his fist to burst into flames. He ran, full force, and swung his fire-encased knuckles at Cyrus.

His punch landed on what felt like a ten-inch thick titanium wall. A vein of blue lightning spread from beneath his fist and crackled around a now misty sphere.

He backed away from what he imagined was one of Shay's many weapons. An itchy prickle bit at his hand, and he rubbed the split skin on his knuckles until it healed and the burn faded.

Cyrus opened his mouth, his head tilting back. It looked as though the man were laughing, but no sound flowed in the tight hallway.

Max lifted his middle finger, backing away from Cyrus, and Cyrus tapped the watch on his wrist.

Lucius released his grip on Shay's unconscious body and she thumped to the steel grate floor of his lab. The other one, Cyrus's girlfriend, squirmed and scratched at his hand. She was such a rude woman. He didn't know what his brother saw in her. True, he was throttling her neck; but still, her behavior was unbecoming of a guest in his secret lair. He released his grip on soft skin and the rude one dropped from his sight.

"Shay," Hetal yelled, hurrying across the room.

Lucius waved his arm, using his powers to fling Hetal into the machine. "Get back to work."

Hetal sunk elbow-deep into a nest of jumbled wires but her attention stayed on Shay and Evie. "Is she alive?"

"Yeah," Evie called out, pulling Shay into her lap. "Are you okay?"

"This is touching," Lucius said, looking between Hetal and Evie. "Now shut up."

Alexie walked beside Evie and pointed at Shay. "Where did *she* come from?"

"I found her in the hall. She trapped Cyrus in some kind of forcefield."

"If she's here, Max and Simon won't be far behind."

"Then I guess we better hurry. Hetal." Lucius's shout caused the girl to bump her head on the machine before she jumped to her feet.

"Five minutes?" she said, in more of a question than an answer.

"Lucius." Alexie glided her hand up Lucius's arm, leaning close enough to fill his head with vanilla musk. "Maybe we should consider a truce. I think, if we're willing to compromise on the whole forcing people into the machine aspect, Simon and Max would get behind this plan. The five of us could accomplish much more if we banded together."

Lucius grabbed Alexie by the waist, bringing his lips right in front of hers. "What a disappointment. I thought you were a fighter."

"Fine." Alexie pushed off Lucius's chest. She strolled across the room to stand over Evie and Shay. "Then I guess we'll fight."

Max followed the echo of voices. The hallways in this asylum twisted and turned, branching off to loop back around again. He'd already hit one dead end chasing shouts from nowhere.

Just as he considered flying through these corridors, and torching the chipped paint from the walls as he soared by, Hetal called out Shay's name.

Max ran down the hall on his left, slowing at the sound of Lucius's bark. This was it. Through the open door beside him, a villain waited for a hearty beatdown.

His fingers curled into a fist, trailing flames. He stepped into the doorway, got one glimpse of Alexie, and froze in place. The woman was no prisoner, she wasn't even angry. In fact, she rubbed on Lucius like a cat in heat.

Max ducked back into the hallway. He leaned against the wall, fighting to catch his runaway breath. Alexie, a villain? Sure, she had a mean streak, but the woman knew right from wrong. Alexie had always wanted to protect the innocent.

Max gripped onto the doorway and peeked back inside the room that looked like a crazed scientist's scrapyard. Alexie was nose to nose with Lucius, locked in what looked to be ... a kiss?

A stab of betrayal sliced into Max's gut, cutting so deep it pushed him back against the wall in the hallway. Poor Simon. Lexie was only his cover girlfriend, but it would still be a tug to the cape. Max slipped his hand into his pocket and clutched his cell phone. This call home was going to be a doozy. *Oh, hey, Simon. I did that thing you told me not to do and now Shay's in trouble. BTW, Lexie's evil.* It would probably flow better in a text.

Max pulled his cell phone from his pocket. When the words *No Signal* flashed on his screen, he almost smashed the piece of crap tech against the wall.

There was no easy choice for him to make, no right decision. He could fight two, three, possibly four villains solo and likely get Shay killed. Or, he could go get Simon and completely miss Shay getting killed. Both options sucked. Supervillains totally sucked.

The grind of Max's clenched teeth became eclipsed by the sizzle of fire. He looked at his hands. Flames surged from his fingertips, rolling up his arms in waves. He had to get Simon before he made another mistake.

Evie stroked Shay's cheek with one hand while reaching for the sonic blaster in Shay's leg holster with the other. Lucius stood over Hetal, shouting like a child. The hissy fit terrified Hetal but provided the perfect distraction for Evie. Her finger brushed the weapon's handle, and Alexie knelt beside her. She froze, even her lungs seized.

"Listen, Evie—"

"Get, away from me," Evie said in a whisper, keeping her eye on Lucius.

"I just … wanna explain. I might not get another chance. You know how I dated Cyrus a long time ago. Well, I didn't break up with him because he went darkside. I was always, really into Lucius and I thought it'd be the perfect—"

"Oh my God. Save it for the judge, because you're definitely getting a subpoena on this one. And, ew."

An angered shout echoed from the hallway and Evie cringed.

"Sounds like the beast broke free from his cage." Alexie took the sonic blaster from Shay's holster and rose to her feet. "I'm so glad Cyrus is *your* problem now."

Thick gray clouds floated around Shay. Each time she waved a puff of smoke away, another would drift in to take its place. There were people in the distance, behind the billows of fog. She glimpsed tiny hints of color—an arm, a metal floor, wires—but they existed far beyond the gray haze around her. If she could just beat back these stupid clouds of smoke, she could see what was on the other side of them.

"You're wasting your time, and energy."

"Jenna?"

It had been Jenna's voice, ringing out clear as day, but Shay's hands found nothing when she groped the haze in front of her.

A finger tapped Shay on the shoulder and she turned, staring at the legendary girl that actual statues were made of.

Shay threw her arms around Jenna, hugging tight. "Thank you."

"For what?" Jenna asked.

"For helping me so much. For being here."

Jenna patted Shay on the back, lightly, as if she were touching a foreign substance. "No worries. Not like I have much else to do, besides swat at clouds."

Shay drew back from Jenna, but not far. "Where are we?"

"My crib. Inside your consciousness, or subconsciousness. Whatever. Not a scientist."

"Well, I guess, technically—"

"Not wanting a science lesson either." Jenna held a serious expression, and Shay giggled. With that hard stare, Jenna looked exactly like the picture on the trading card Shay kept in her binder at the lab.

"This place is horrible." Shay looked around at the hollow void that seemed to exist for the sole purpose of collecting gray smog.

"Sorry my insides are so bland."

"It's not usually this foggy." Jenna waved her hand, clearing a small space around them. "Except when you're sleeping, but then the haze has colors so it's cool."

"I got knocked out."

"I know. Lucius is a dick."

Shay gasped, turning her dropped jaw to Jenna.

"What? It's true."

"Yeah it is," Shay said through a snicker. Jenna really was special, way cooler than she could ever be. No wonder Max spent the last ten years missing her.

"I figured out how to remove your soul from my body."

"Really?" Jenna's eyes grew wide, and a bright smile crept across her lips for a split-second.

"Yeah, but I don't know where you'll go once I set you free." Tears welled inside Shay's eyes. It took all she had to keep them at bay, to keep herself from weeping like a baby.

"Anywhere has gotta be better than here. You're scared for me?" Jenna wiped a tear from Shay's cheek. "I'm not scared. I'm ready to move on."

"So you want me to do it?"

Jenna held tight to both of Shay's hands. Her mouth opened but the words were lost under a howl of wind. White light pulsed. Every flash clouded Jenna, blurring her face in its glare.

Shay squeezed Jenna's hands, but they were ripped from her grasp. She flew away from Jenna, through whips of gray smog, faster and faster into a blinding light.

28

Max ran into Simon's penthouse. He barged into the bedroom, where Simon slept like a log, and flipped on the light switch. "Dude. Get up."

"What?" Simon sat up in bed. He didn't look startled, then again this wasn't the first time Max had woken his buddy in such a manner. "What's happened?"

Clothes fell from their hangers as Max tore through Simon's closet, searching out yellow spandex. "I messed up." He pulled Simon's suit from a hanger then tossed it on the bed. "I took Shay to the asylum and now Lucius has her."

"Aw, hell." Simon tossed his blanket aside and climbed out of his bed. "Can't you act like a responsible adult for two seconds?"

"Don't know, never tried."

Max stole small glances at Simon, who wiggled into his suit, while pondering which words to use in what combination. As usual, he came up blank.

Simon shoved his foot into his boot and bent to tie its laces. "What?"

"It's Lexie. She's there too ... with Lucius."

Max watched Simon adjust his cape. Not one hint of a reaction crossed the man's face.

"You don't seem surprised."

A huff and a brow crinkle was the most Simon gave away. "I own a global communication conglomerate. There's not much that gets past me."

"Does that mean she's our enemy now? Are we supposed to fight her?"

Simon rubbed the back of his neck, avoiding Max's stare. "I asked Lexie to spend some time with Lucius and Cyrus."

"You want them back in the group?" Max yelled.

Simon shook his head, but the guilt that gripped his expression told the truth. Betrayal hit Max like one of Simon's super-powered fists. He would've ended this feud with the Grant brothers years ago, forgiven Lucius and been able to set Jenna's soul free, but was afraid to lose Simon and Alexie.

Flames ignited in Max's hands. He couldn't help it, couldn't extinguish them. The ache left behind by his friend's treachery burned too hot, and the fire was the only thing to soothe it.

A look of true remorse crossed Simon's face. "This is why I didn't tell you. I didn't want to upset you for nothing. Lexie says it's not even working."

Simon reached for Max, got singed by one of his flames, then drew his hand back. "Please, Max, don't be angry."

The fire that blazed between Max's fingers fizzled out to puffs of smoke. It would be hard to hold a grudge against Simon, even though he'd like to. He hadn't met another person as sincere, as pure as Simon. That kindness often got Simon in trouble, but not with Max. Max could see the good intentions behind his friend's misguided actions, but that didn't mean he had to let the guy off the hook easily.

"Come on." Max ran for the balcony's sliding glass door. "We can discuss this later, the *three* of us."

Cyrus stomped down the narrow hallway. Tile shattered, shooting out to smack the walls as he stormed through the asylum. He could still smell Max. A sickening mixture of valor and high-priced cologne wafted in his hallways, tainting the air.

Cyrus rounded the corner and hurried into his lab. Max was nowhere in sight, but there were people scattered around the room and each one of them stopped what they were doing to give him a wary look. Even the prisoners, who were supposed to have fear in their eyes, stared at him with confusion.

"Where is he?" Cyrus balled his fists tighter, walking to the center of the lab. When spotting Shay knocked out on the floor, his nails undug from his palms. If Max had been there, his precious little Jenna vessel would be gone.

Lucius stepped away from the quivering girl he'd been shouting at, who'd been working furiously to splice the nebula burst machine into the city's power grid. It wouldn't work without a regulator, or else Cyrus would've done it by now.

"Who?" Lucius asked, glancing around the lab.

"Max. I put him to sleep in the stairwell. He went down the hall right after you left."

Alexie stood in front of Lucius. "Are you sure you want to keep fighting? We can leave right now, weigh out options. Cyrus, don't you think we should leave?"

"Yes." Cyrus did want to flee from this depressing asylum, but not until he completed the task that had ended the only relationship he ever truly cherished. He'd already lost Evie and it wouldn't be for nothing.

Cyrus hurried across the lab, toward Evie. "Right after I put her in the machine."

"No," Evie yelled as Cyrus latched onto her arm. He pulled Evie to her feet and Shay clunked to the steel-grated floor.

Evie's fists bounced off his face. It didn't seem like she was doing much damage, but each hit bruised his soul far more than it could ever sting his flesh. He hated himself—hated Evie for struggling so much. Hate was all he had left, so he dragged the woman he loved across the room against her will.

Max soared toward the asylum, leaving a trail of flames in the night sky. He'd already decided to forgive Alexie for sneaking around with villains behind his back, and he could never stay mad at Simon.

Alexie and Simon had taken him in when he returned from space with powers, after society turned its back on him. They helped him rebrand his image, and put him on the path of a hero. They were family, Simon and Alexie, the only family an orphan like Max ever had.

Far below the dark clouds Max flew through, in the shadows of the asylum, a figure climbed out a window and down the building's side. Golden hair gleamed in the hint of moonlight, and Max slowed his speed. He hovered at the treetops, watching as Shay crept away from the asylum.

She spotted Max's flames in the sky and ran toward him, waving her arms franticly. That sizzle didn't burn in Max's chest when he gazed down at her, as it had every time since the first time he set eyes on Shay in that stairwell.

The person who signaled Max wasn't Shay. He'd bet his life on it.

Flames surged around his fist, which he held out in front of him as he barreled toward the Shay impersonator. The body shifted into Lucius just before Max's knuckles crashed against its chest.

Max touched down in the tall grass, nice and gentle, as the shapeshifter launched backward through the air. Its body thumped to the ground, tumbled across a sloped field, and landed on its back as an unconscious *young woman.*

The girl couldn't have been more than twenty. She was kind of cute too, dark skin, wavy hair. Max felt like straight up crap. He'd never hit a girl that hard before, but at least she took the impact in Lucius's form.

"How did you know?" Simon asked, landing beside Max.

His heart would've thumped against his chest if that person had been Shay. Tingles would've nipped at his skin from the inside-out, but he couldn't tell Simon that.

"I just knew," he said, staring at the sorriest excuse of a villain he'd ever knocked out.

"You got lucky."

Max let out a long, shaky breath. "I know. This thing irks the hell out of me."

"Well, I think you broke it."

"Good." A burst of flames erupted around Max's clenched fists as he turned toward the asylum. "Let's go break a bunch more stuff."

A hand slapped Shay on the cheek. It wasn't a malicious hit, more of a loving tap, but it synchronized with the throb in her head perfectly.

"Wake up, Shay." Hetal's voice trickled into Shay's mind, blasting over the buzz in her ears. "They're putting Evie in the machine."

"You," Lucius said, which snapped Shay's eyes open. "Power it up."

"I can't," Hetal said in a whimper. "The wires to the power grid weren't thick enough. They melted."

Shay didn't move. She probably could. Her fingers curled into fists when her will commanded it, but she could feel Lucius staring at her and that kept her body from budging.

"Useless human. I'll do it myself."

The thump of boots moved away from Shay. Glass shattered, and then she heard the one thing that could override the pain that radiated from the hit she'd taken to the head.

Evie screamed for help from what sounded like the bottom of the ocean. It was her name. Evie screamed Shay's name, and the sound triggered a torrent of spikes to jab at Shay's every muscle.

Flashes of blue and green light reflected off the broken medical equipment scattered around the lab. It stung Shay's eyes as she rose to her knees. The light pulsed from tiny sparkling balls, and those balls swirled around Lucius.

"Shay!" Hetal helped Shay to her feet.

"What's happening?"

"Evie's in the machine." Hetal pointed, beyond the backs of Alexie and Cyrus, at Evie locked within the nebula burst generator. Evie pounded her fists against a small window on the large golden chamber's door, her shouts barely escaping the sealed machine.

"And Antiserum's devouring souls. He's gonna power it up any second."

The shimmering orbs of light around Lucius fused into his chest. He held his hands out at his sides, tilting his head back as power lit his body in a white glow.

"The hell he is." Shay reached for her sonic blaster, finding an empty holster. "Crap."

Lucius laid his hands on the machine and a cascade of colorful switches blinked to life on the nearby control panel. Arms of lightning spread from his touch, covering the entire machine in a web of electrical bolts. The floor below Shay's boots quaked as a low hum rumbled from deep within the machine.

Evie stopped banging the door's little window. Her fingers curled into her hair, and a look of agony twisted her face. Shay patted the pockets of her vest. One containment grenade and an electro-pulse dart was all she had left.

The machine groaned, louder and louder. Its thin arms started to rotate around the chamber, and Shay pulled the weapons from her pockets.

Alexie turned away from the machine. Her gaze connected with Shay, and Shay glimpsed fear. It wasn't a selfish kind of terror, more of an *Oh God, what have I done* woe.

At this point, Shay didn't care about Alexie's guilt or sorrow. Her sister doubled over in pain, trapped inside a chamber of twirling magnetic arms that Lucius powered with the tangle of electric bolts streaming from his hands. Evie was all that mattered.

Shay bit down on the containment grenade's pin and ripped it out of its safety lever with her teeth, spitting it to the ground. Before the little metal loop could clink against the steel floor, she tossed the bomb across the room.

A translucent field surrounded Alexie and Cyrus, locking them in place and out of Shay's way. She turned from the containment orb, which rippled as Cyrus pounded his fists against it, and aimed her EP shooter at Lucius.

She could barely see him beyond a whirling electrical storm, which surged from his palms and fed the machine. Strobes of light fluttered her eyelids. One by one, a row of red indicators on the machine's control panel blinked to green. It was a countdown to her sister's death by mutation, and it clouded her mind.

"Do something," Hetal yelled, nudging Shay's arm.

"If I shoot Lucius, the electric pulse could surge the machine and fry Evie to dust." Just the thought caused Shay's hand to tremble and her finger to move away from the weapon's button.

"Aim for the floor, at Antiserum's feet. The discharge should blow him back."

"Should?"

Shay searched through thick splinters of lightning, straining to glimpse Evie beyond the bursts of blue flares. She couldn't see Evie. The supervillain who killed her parents was going to irradiate her sister, and she froze like a faulty hard drive.

"The last toggle's gonna trip," Hetal screamed. "You have to shoot now."

Shay's entire body shook beyond her control. The glare of light brought tears to her eyes. It had to be the light. It couldn't be bone-shattering terror. She definitely wasn't crying because she was scared she'd miss her only shot, or worse, hit Lucius and disintegrate her sister to tiny specks of microscopic Evie.

"Shay. You have to go now, now."

Hetal's voice hadn't registered. Shay couldn't hear anything over the roar of the machine's arms as they spun, or above her own mind screaming out calculations.

"Now!"

As the last toggle flickered between red and green, Shay pressed the button on her EP shooter.

29

An electro-pulse dart flew from Shay's pen-shooter. The little chip crackled with electricity as it sped toward Lucius. It struck the metal floor at his feet, and then exploded in a burst of energy. The blast flung Lucius across the lab, and sent Shay teetering.

As she toppled to the floor, the containment field around Cyrus and Alexie sputtered out. She braced for hard ground as she fell backward to the floor, but landed in soft arms.

"Gotcha," Max said, holding Shay tight. He whisked her up and onto her feet as Simon walked into the room, standing at her other side.

Blood surged through her veins as she stood between two superheroes and stared at a pack of supervillains. She felt as strong as Mr. Amazing himself. Her spine remained stiff, even as Lucius climbed off the floor to snarl at her, until she remembered she had no weapons.

"Looking for this?" Alexie said, lifting Shay's sonic blaster. "Here, take it."

Alexie tossed the sonic blaster to Shay. She flinched as the clunky metal gun sailed toward her chest, but she actually caught it—despite a little fumble—then pulled it close.

"Lexie?" Lucius said, a heavy layer of hurt shading his eyes.

"Sorry, Lucius." Alexie slammed her electric-laced fist against Cyrus's face. She jogged across the room, to the hero side, as Cyrus fell to the ground. "Your brother was right. I *am* a treacherous bitch."

"No," Lucius shouted. "You're a dead treacherous bitch."

Cyrus jumped to his feet as Lucius rushed toward Alexie. Shay lifted her blaster, but Simon ran in front of her to kick Lucius in the gut.

In one blink, the scene erupted into an all-out brawl. Max charged Lucius, punching the man with fire-encased fists. Alexie strutted toward Cyrus, her arms stretched out, shooting streams of lightning from her fingertips.

Shay wasn't worried about the people fighting. These guys beat each other down on the daily. Her sole concern was for Evie. She weaved to see beyond Simon, who took a hit from one of Lucius's black energy balls, to peek inside the machine's small window. There was no hint of Evie within the chamber. The little window only showed a flicker of yellow lights.

Shay ran toward the nebula burst generator and Max crashed to the floor at her feet. Steel grate bent around his body, the floor crimping up and tripping her steps.

The crackle of Alexie's lightning cut off behind Shay. Without the sizzle, and other than Simon's grunts and the slap of fists hitting skin, an eerie hush clung to the air.

Shay peeked over her shoulder. Cyrus had seized Alexie by the throat, and lifted her feet off the ground. With the hand that wasn't throttling Alexie's neck, Cyrus reached into her pocket and pulled out a tiny silver device—Hetal's brainwashing-blocker. He dropped the thin metal disk to the floor, then crushed it under his heel.

"Why don't you just die," Cyrus said, staring into Alexie's eyes.

Alexie's arms flopped to her sides. Cyrus released his clutch, and her limp body thumped against the floor.

"No," Shay yelled. She pointed her sonic blaster at Cyrus and pulled the trigger without hesitation.

Twenty gigahertz of ultrasonic waves rushed toward Cyrus, disrupting the air around him. He ducked, but it struck his chest and threw his body into the solid wall behind him.

Shay dropped to her knees beside Alexie. She latched onto the dead woman's cape straps and shook. "Come back to life."

Shay didn't have brainwashing powers like Cyrus. She didn't have any powers, but she couldn't help herself from trying. Alexie's eyes remained empty and Shay looked away, right into Max's broken gaze.

"I need a defibrillator," Shay yelled. "Any kind of electric charge."

She'd given Max very specific instructions, yet all she got from him was a blank stare.

"The wires, on the wall behind you," Hetal called out from her hiding spot in the lab's farthest corner.

Max ripped two thick wires from the wall. Tiny blue arcs hissed from their frayed ends, cascading around his hands.

The ground shook as Lucius slammed Simon against it. Simon slid across the floor and crashed into a steel table, which flattened like a shiny pancake.

Lucius leapt across the room. He landed atop Simon, cracking the fractured walls of the asylum even farther apart, and started punching the downed superhero.

"I gotta help Simon," Max said, shoving the wires into Shay's hands. He kissed two of his fingers and placed them on Alexie's forehead before soaring off in a burst of flames.

Shay knelt over Alexie. The wires in her hand spit bright white sparks, which bit at her skin in every place they touched.

"I'm not afraid."

The floor trembled beneath Shay as an explosion rang out across the room, but the quake paled in comparison to that of her own muscles.

"I'm not afraid."

The wire's severed tips crackled as Shay brought them just above Alexie's heart. She was afraid, but she wouldn't let fear keep her from trying to save a life.

Shay pressed the wires against Alexie's chest. Alexie convulsed on the floor. Her limp arms flailed, slapping the steel grates below her. A hint of red returned to Alexie's blue lips and Shay lifted the wires from her chest.

Alexie gasped, in more of a watery gargle than an intake of air. She sat up with her fist high, wobbling.

A thousand volts of electricity sizzled from the wires in Shay's hands. It kept her from hugging Alexie, but it couldn't deter her from smiling. "You're okay. Right?"

Alexie's eyes grew wide. Her already balled fist drew back, and all the little hairs on Shay's arms stood up. A monster was behind her. She could feel his rage, which jacked up the heat in the entire room.

Without looking, or thinking twice, Shay spun around and thrust the wires in her hands outward. She wasn't expecting the sensation that clutched onto her when she electrocuted Cyrus. To see agony in his eyes, to bring his super-powered body to a shuttering halt, felt amazing and she hadn't been expecting it.

Shay's palms slid up the wire's smooth rubber casing as she pressed them against Cyrus harder. His body launched from the tips of the two arcing wires. He shot backward, crashing against the same fractured wall as before, and then fell face down on the floor.

This time Cyrus would stay down, that is, if the supervillain ever got up again. Shay may have just killed a man, a man who tortured her sister, and she didn't know if she could care about that.

"You brought me back," Alexie said through chattering teeth.

Shay tossed the wires aside and held out her hand to help Alexie off the floor. "I owed you one."

As soon as Alexie looked semi-steady on her feet, Shay ran toward the nebula burst generator. She had to see inside the machine. Even if her sister had been atomized, left as a pile of glittery flakes, she had to witness it with her own eyes.

Shay grabbed onto the machine door's top lever and unlatched it. Max crashed against the machine, right beside her, denting its side. Shay jumped back as Max landed in a heap.

The air grew thick, ice-cold. Lucius could be behind her, or beside her … his frosty vibes rippled the air all around her, making it impossible to trace their origins.

She lifted her sonic blaster and Lucius teleported directly in front of her. The shock of seeing a man materialize from thin air stunned Shay still.

Lucius snatched the weapon from her grasp, leaving her in a sway. With one large hand, he shattered the gun's barrel in a shower of sparks. With the other, he grabbed Shay by her throat.

"I'm weak," he said, lifting Shay off the ground. "And you have *two* souls."

Shay kicked her feet. She scratched and punched Lucius in the face, and all the while a force tugged at her chest. She couldn't scream, couldn't pry Lucius's fingers from her neck.

Oxygen wouldn't flow past the airways Lucius crushed, and unseen talons ripped, clawed … shredded Shay's insides. Lucius was taking her soul. The man was tearing her very essence from her body and she couldn't stop him.

I have an ace up my sleeve, Jenna whispered in Shay's mind. *It's a wild card. Let it out?*

"Hell, yeah," Shay managed to garble before falling under a gray haze.

255

Max peeled himself off the now mangled floor of the makeshift laboratory. An orange fog clouded his vision and he rubbed his eyes, except it wasn't a fog. He should've recognized that glow immediately. The intense heat that stung his skin and the orange tinted, flame-laced winds had been his world ... once.

"Jenna," he whispered, looking up at the flashes of orange light.

Shay hovered above his head, with Lucius dangling at the end of her grasp. The tips of her blond hair blazed in orange flames, and her eyes burned a bright shade of red. Solar winds whirled around her, flinging bits of broken metal across the room, yet Shay floated gently in place midair.

"What is that?" Simon asked as he limped to Max's side.

Alexie stood on Max's other side, leaning against his shoulder. "That's Jenna's solar winds, but the red eyes and orange hair is different."

Coils of glimmering orange light circled Shay, growing dimmer by the second. She released her grasp on Lucius, and he crashed to the steel grate floor in front of Max.

The thud of his limp body bounced off every wall. When his head rolled to one side, Max was sure the man had died and it brought a great sadness to his soul.

A gust of wind blew around Shay, spreading out to tear through the room. Every loose object on top of each rusted metal table took to flight. Glass beakers crashed against each other, shattering. Tools and broken metal lodged into walls and machines.

The blistery air swirled faster. Its heat scorched Max from the inside out, no matter how far back he stumbled from Shay. He was Firestorm, the unburnable man of flames, but this heat was different. It wasn't the fuzzy warmth of a fiery blaze that attacked him. The burn he felt was sheer radiation, like standing atop the sun, and it pulsed from an orange orb that surrounded Shay.

Max lifted his arm in a measly attempt to block the torrent of super-heated gusts as Shay landed in front of him. Then, it all stopped. The floor didn't quake under a thunderous growl, a sweltering breeze didn't cook his skin, but he wasn't ready to look at Shay. He didn't know which girl, which love he'd find when staring into her eyes.

"Dude." Alexie jabbed her elbow into Max's ribcage then pushed him forward. "Say something. She's your girl."

Slowly, Max lifted his gaze to Shay's face. The glow of her crimson eyes stunned him. It was Shay's face, Jenna's power, and the eyes of a demon. He didn't know what or who he was looking at.

"Jenna?"

She tilted her head to one side, and that was as much as her stiff body moved.

"Shay? Is that you?"

"I am no human," she said, in the strangest voice that echoed in both high and low tones. "I am the power that dwelled within, given speech. I am pure energy pushed forward and animated to life."

Her stare turned harsh. "And I want more."

"Do something," Alexie said in a panic, shoving Max closer to Shay.

Max had battled with the alien powers inside himself, once, when they'd first manifested. He would've lost his battle, been consumed by energy if not for Lucius. But, Max couldn't bring himself to deploy the tactic Lucius had used on him.

A surge of red flared through Shay's already glowing eyes. She reached for Max and he cringed. Shay shouldn't have powers clouding her mind, but she did and he had to stop them before they devoured her.

Max drew back his fist and clocked Shay square on the jaw. A sharp ache pierced his heart as his punch dropped Shay to the floor, knocking her out like a light.

"I could've done that," Alexie said.

Sorrow filled the new crack in Max's heart as he stared down at Shay lying unconscious on the ground. Power could no longer infect her mind, because her mind was out cold. He could only hope Jenna's power returned to whatever void it'd slithered out from before Shay awoke.

Shay groaned. There it was again. A tap, tap, tap struck her on the cheek, and it ripped her from puffy gray clouds then dropped her onto a cold floor.

"Stop hitting me," she said, swatting at the hand tapping her cheek.

"Shay," Max cried out.

The quiver in Max's voice told Shay something was wrong. Jenna's wild card must have lived up to its title, and someone must've slugged her in the face because her jaw throbbed.

Shay sat up, too fast, and bashed her forehead against Max's nose.

"Ow." Max rubbed his face as he scooted back from Shay. "Slow down, slugger."

"What'd she do?" Shay looked around the lab; the metal strewn, hole in the floor, everything scattered everywhere lab.

"Who?" Max asked.

"Jenna."

"That wasn't Jenna." Max climbed to his feet and stood between Simon and Alexie.

Three superheroes stared at Shay with suspicion, as if anticipating her to jump up off the floor and attack.

Simon lunged toward Shay and yelled, "Boo."

Shay yelped with a start, and then whacked Simon on the arm. "What the hell?"

"Fear triggers superpowers," Simon said, plainly, as though that would explain why he'd scared her.

"I don't have superpowers."

"Jenna does." Max offered Shay his hand, helping her off the floor. "She pushed her powers to the front, and they didn't want to let go. I had to …"

He frowned as he glided his fingers along her jaw. It had been the lightest touch, yet it stung like a million tiny pinpricks.

"… put the smack-down on you."

"I gave Jenna permission." Shay hadn't been left with a choice. Lucius was going to kill her, and she had to—

Panic struck Shay in waves. There were many people staring at her with concern, and none of them were Evie.

Shay ran toward the nebula burst generator, despite the quake in her knees. As she reached its wide-open door, Hetal walked out of the machine with one arm around Evie. Her sister walked, blinked, looked at her.

A giggle burst from Shay's mouth. Evie was alive. She looked pretty angry, but alive.

Shay wrapped Evie in a big hug. "Sorry." She held tight, but couldn't stop the shake of her sister's bones.

"Why are you sorry?" Evie pulled back from the snug embrace just long enough to wipe away Shay's tears.

"I let Cyrus take you, put you in that machine."

Evie's body grew stiff. She stepped back from Shay, glancing around the room. "Where is that bastard?"

Once spotting Cyrus face down under a pile of rubble, a groan trickled from Evie's mouth. "Are they … dead?" she asked, nudging Lucius with the tip of her foot.

"No," Simon said. "Just out cold."

Shay could've swore she saw a smile on Evie's lips but it flittered away as quickly as it appeared.

"You guys got them," Evie said, her gaze lingering on Cyrus.

"No. Shay got them," Hetal said with a bit too much excitement. "It was awesome! She shot badass weapons, her eyes glowed. There was orange fire. I got the whole thing on vid."

Hetal held up her cell phone, showing a shaky video of Shay floating midair on its screen.

"Can I borrow that?" Evie seized Hetal's cell phone, without bothering to wait for an answer. "I've got to call this in, get an SPU team over here."

Alexie slapped her hand on top of the phone in Evie's grasp. "Why?"

Evie smacked Alexie's hand away. "Aren't you supposed to be evil?"

"I was undercover."

"Yeah right." Evie glanced at Simon. She was obviously unsatisfied with his nod, because she looked at Shay. Since Shay had no idea what was going on, all she could do was shrug.

"I would've told you," Simon said, ushering Alexie back from Evie's face. "But you weren't you."

Shay eyed everyone in the room, looking for anything unusual. "Where is that shapeshifter?"

"I knocked its ass out on the front lawn," Max said with a smile.

Although cute, Shay was not amused with Max's display.

"Superheroes aren't supposed to knock the villains out and leave them behind. They're supposed to escort the bad guys to a real prison, not the basement of Ling Enterprises."

The grin on Max's lips dropped. He took a step back from Shay, pointing at the door. "I guess I should go check on that."

Alexie pushed past Max and headed for the door. "I'll go. Need to earn some good guy points back, apparently."

"My team will be here in five minutes." Evie clicked off Hetal's cell phone and tucked it into her own pocket. She stood tall despite her tattered clothes, scraped wrists, and horribly messy hair, and yelled, "Hetal."

Hetal jumped at the sound of her name. She dropped the armful of circuit boards she'd begun to ransack, jumping aside as they crashed to the floor at her feet.

"Are there any tranquilizers over there? I'd like to make sure these guys stay down until I get them secured."

"There's no need for that, Ms. Sinclair." A tall man in a black suit hurried into the room. He knelt beside Cyrus, flipped open his briefcase, and Shay smirked. It was so Evie. The guy just needed some shades and a little alien to chase and he'd be set.

"The team's right behind me," he said, jabbing a needle into Cyrus's neck. "I was right down the street when the message came through. We've been tearing the city apart looking for you."

After the man in black hit Lucius with a dose of whatever drug was in his case, he hurried to Evie's side. "Do you need medical attention, Ms. Sinclair?"

"No. Thank you, Trey."

Before Shay could demand answers, a line of men and women—all dressed in black—filed into the room. Within seconds, the bodies of knocked-out supervillains were carted away. Evie's people started to pack everything they could lift into crates, working around Shay and the two superheroes who stood stunned in the center of the room.

"I want that machine disassembled, carefully," Evie said while typing on Hetal's cell phone. "As well as all the large equipment in here. Everything gets inventoried, twice, before it leaves this room."

Shay grabbed Evie by the arm and pulled her to the other side of the lab, far from the platoon of SPU agents. "What's going on?"

Alexie pushed her way into the room, grumbling at every person who stumbled across her path. "What the f—"

"Where did you take them?" Simon bumped Shay aside to stand in front of Evie. "Lucius and Cyrus are extremely dangerous. They need to be contained properly."

"And they will be." Evie delivered Simon one of her signature *I mean business* smiles. "Incident scene cleanup is what I do. Trust me."

Evie turned toward Alexie, yet kept her gaze on the floor. "The shifter?"

"Gone. I circled the perimeter twice. I'm sorry, Evie."

"We'll find it."

"Not about that." Alexie tried to catch Evie's stare, but Evie was a pro when it came to evasiveness. "About everything that happened here, to you. I should have helped you escape when I found out Cyrus had you in the holding cell, but I really thought I could sway them back to our side."

"That's what you've all been up to?"

"Not me." Max held up his hands, as if to plead innocence.

Evie took a deep breath as she massaged her temples. "I've got a scene to sweep. Why don't you guys head home? We can regroup and you can all debrief me, properly, once I've wrapped this up."

Simon raised his finger. He opened his mouth, probably to complain, and Evie took Shay by the arm and walked away from him.

"I want you to go with them," Evie said to Shay, gesturing at the three superheroes who stood in a tight circle across the room.

"But, I always hang out at incident scenes with you."

"I don't want you knowing where I take Antiserum and Dr. Mayhem. It's safer this way."

The urge to protest came on strong, but Shay held back. It was no big deal, really. She'd only risked her life to save Evie, and her sister didn't even want to hang. That was just fine. She had important things to do anyway, things she didn't want Evie to know about.

"Whatever. I'll see you later." A heaviness took Shay's head down. It must have affected her boots too, because they thumped as she headed for the door.

"Hey, wait."

When Shay looked back at Evie, Evie hugged her tight.

"Thanks for saving me." Evie kissed Shay on the cheek. "I love you."

"How sweet," Alexie said on her way to the door.

Simon followed Alexie into the hallway and Max leaned against the wall beside the door.

"Love you too." Shay took one last look at Evie, just in case, then trailed Hetal and Max out of the room.

Reporters flanked the front of Ling Enterprises. Shay could see their cameras flash as she clung to Max, high above the skyline. They landed on the roof of Ling Enterprises and Shay hurried out of Max's grasp. She hadn't forgotten about the no flirting rule, which she'd imposed on herself. Having her arms wrapped around Max's neck was acceptable when flying, but she was on solid ground now.

Bolts of lightning struck the rooftop as Alexie set down beside Shay.

"We need to talk," she said, grabbing onto Shay's hand.

"Hey." Max took a firm hold on Shay's other arm and yanked, but Alexie held tight.

A hint of panic spawned in Shay's chest. She'd just become the chew toy for two superheroes, and they were both pulling on her arms pretty hard.

"Let her go," Simon barked. He set down beside Shay with a thump that vibrated throughout the rooftop.

Hetal staggered from Simon's arms, dropped to her knees, and actually kissed the ground. "I love you, and I'll never leave you again," she said to the rooftop.

"What's going on?" Simon swatted Alexie and Max away from Shay.

"I was trying to find out what she remembers," Alexie said. "About the thing that happened at the asylum."

"Umm, guys."

"You were there," Max said in a shout. "You saw what happened."

"I saw a superhero's power. Don't you wanna know where it is now?"

"Hello." Shay raised her hand, but just like in school nobody noticed her.

Simon pushed Shay's arm down. "Shay said she didn't remember anything, and Jenna's power is back inside Jenna where it belongs."

"You don't have to be so rough," Max said to Alexie in a sneer, which caused her to gasp.

"Rough?" Alexie's voice echoed on the breeze, circling around the building to pipe a second time. "I was just trying to get a second with Shay before you pulled her into a corner to make out."

The deepest shade of red colored Max's cheeks and he poked Alexie on the shoulder. "I don't do that."

"Hey," Shay shouted.

She stepped between Max and Alexie, smack-dab in the superpower line of fire. "I really don't remember anything. I go somewhere else when I'm unconscious, like … an inter-dimensional holding plain. Jenna told me it would be a wild card. I knew there'd be risks, but I had to do something. Don't worry. I won't let it happen again."

"You can talk to Jenna?" Hetal asked, tapping her chin. "Interesting. I wish I would have known Evie was gonna steal my cell phone. I would have emailed myself that vid. She'll probably erase it to keep it from going viral."

Shay nudged Hetal with her elbow. "Come on. We have stuff to do."

"We do?" Hetal squealed, gluing herself to Shay's side.

Shay got maybe five steps before she realized a pack of superheroes shadowed her every move. She turned toward them, and they stopped short.

"It's girl stuff."

Alexie shrugged, stepping forward, and Shay strong-armed her back.

"Scientist girl stuff." Shay took Hetal by the hand, pulled her close, and made a beeline for the roof's door.

"The lab," Hetal said in a chuckle. "It smells so clean and safe."

"You can't smell safe." Shay wiggled out of her heavy tactical vest and dropped it on a workbench.

"I hope Evie lets us have Dr. Mayhem's equipment. He was building some pretty wicked things and we're running low on parts."

"This might be our last day in the lab," Shay said softly, sadly. She looked around the room at the magnificent equipment, most of which she'd dismantled and repurposed. This wide-open space of metal tables, shining machines, and unfinished projects gave off more of a homely vibe than any other place she'd ever stepped foot. It would be hard for her to leave this lab behind.

"Why would you say that?" Hetal asked, her voice trembling in fright.

"We kinda put ourselves out of business tonight. The villains are captured. There's really no need for us to make fighting safer. The fighting's over."

"Are we here to give the lab an amazing send-off?" Hetal asked slyly. "Pull an all-nighter, do something incredible to earn our place in the history books?"

"Actually. Yes, we are."

Hetal smiled as she lightly bounced in place. Shay strained to keep from chuckling at Hetal's happy dance. She had to look strong, commanding. This would most likely be her last night as anyone's boss, and she'd need to use the full authority her fake title bestowed to get Hetal onboard with her next scheme.

"We're going to inject nanobots into my body."

"What?" Hetal tried to sit on the stool behind her, but she was too busy gawking at Shay and her butt missed the seat twice. "Why are we preforming this very experimental and incredibly dangerous procedure on you?"

"I've programmed the nanobots to collect Jenna's energy signature. They can absorb her soul."

Hetal slumped on her stool, letting out a little huff. "You've already spawned them?"

"Yeah. It took six hours for the machine to cook them up."

"I can't believe you made nanobots without me."

A pang of guilt shot through Shay's stomach as Hetal's pout hit maximum capacity.

"Sorry. I got bored waiting for Simon to fall asleep so I could sneak out and rescue you and Evie."

The deep crease anger created on Hetal's brow smoothed, and a hint of her smile returned. "Right. Thank you."

"You can thank me by helping me." Shay walked to the closet, pulling out a heart monitor and portable defibrillator. "I have no idea what type of state I'll be in when the nanobots hit my brainstem, so I probably won't be able to short 'em out. That's where you come in. Eight minutes after I inject myself, I need you to fry the little suckers with the defibrillator."

Hetal's jaw dropped and her body locked stiff, as if stunned solid. She didn't even flinch when Shay shoved the defibrillator in her arms.

"There's a magnet on my workbench," Shay said, careful to avoid Hetal's stare. "I'm sure you know how to harvest nanobots, right?"

"Shay." Hetal placed the defibrillator on the table beside her. "Nobody's ever done anything like this before. There's no way to predict what'll happen to you, what you'll be like afterward."

"I'll be fine. The bots will only absorb Jenna's essence, not mine." Shay walked to the nanobot chamber, and Hetal followed on her heels.

"It's a foreign object," Hetal said, on the verge of a tantrum. "Your body could reject the nanobots, go into shock."

"Duh. That's why I got a bunch of epinephrine and atropine."

A long gasp burst from Hetal's mouth. "I'm not that kind of doctor. My PhD is in physics."

"You're smart. And we have the internet." Shay pulled on thick rubber gloves then opened the small door to the nanobot chamber. "What more do you need?"

Huffs and puffs rang out behind Shay, but she barely heard them. Her ears belonged to the machine's gentle hum, her eyes stuck on the green glow of creation. Hetal was missing it. History was being made in this room and instead of marveling, Hetal grumbled. It kind of ruined the moment.

After collecting every bot into a syringe, Shay stepped back from the machine. A stillness had swept through the lab. Hetal must've finally grasped the gravity of this situation, since her eyes now shined with awe.

"If your heart stops, I'm resuscitating you immediately," Hetal said.

Shay handed the needle full of microscopic molecular-based computers to Hetal and shook off her gloves. "I need eight minutes overall."

"Three minutes with no oxygen and you'll likely suffer serious brain damage."

"Five minutes then?" Shay batted her eyes, clasping her hands together to plead.

"I'll give you two minutes if your heart stops, regardless of overall time." Hetal held her hand out firm. "That's it."

"Deal."

A flock of reporters crowded the sidewalk outside Ling Enterprises. They bombarded Evie the moment she stepped from the passenger seat of her sedan. Key words from their questions stuck in her head. *Shay, asylum, battle.* It baffled her how the media always knew so much.

At least she had the smarts to shower and change. She'd look cold and shrill on the news tonight—pushing past reporters as she ignored them—but she'd look stylish and fresh while doing it.

The brand-new doors of Ling Enterprises closed behind Evie and blocked out the shouts, camera clicks … even the standard drone of city life. Silence surrounded her, and it was pure bliss. She only got about two seconds to enjoy the silence. Three superheroes hurried across the lobby, toward her. They had just as many questions as the reporters outside, maybe more.

"No." Evie swatted her hand, and like flies, the super-people moved back from her face. "I need an hour of chill time with my sister before I can deal with all this."

"Shay's busy," Alexie said, crossing her arms. "Something about girly scientist stuff."

"I'm crashing that party." Evie turned on her heels. She walked toward the elevator and Max followed her.

"What?" She jabbed the down button, again, and again.

"Where's Lucius and Cyrus?"

Finally, the elevator door opened. Evie hurried inside and of course, since the universe hated her, Max tagged along.

"Why?" she asked, unable to curb her snippy tone. "You hoping to score some visitation time with your old pals?"

"You're one to talk. I know all about you and Cyrus."

The elevator rocked to a stop but Evie's stomach kept sinking. There was no her and Cyrus. She had fallen for Fitz, not a megalomaniacal super-jerk. Oh, but Max knew. Pretty soon, the entire city would think they knew as well.

Evie hurried off the elevator, squeezing out its door before it could fully open, but she couldn't shake Max. He followed her into the narrow hallway, keeping close to her side.

"Who's to say you're not a villain? You've been sneaking around with Cyrus for the last three months."

Evie slammed her hand against the wall, which stopped Max short in a wobble.

"There was no sneaking. I choose not to introduce the men in my life to Shay. When they leave, it crushes her. Like losing Dad all over again."

Evie's stare on Max turned venomous without her consent. "That's why I don't want you messing with her. Shay should have a normal life—go on dates, hold hands at the movies, make out by the lake—with someone her own age."

Hurt filled Max's gaze, which he lowered to his feet. It looked like he got the message. It also looked like his heart broke into a million jagged pieces.

Evie could be wrong. Shay and Max could be the only two people in the world who truly loved each other, and she was the thing standing between them. Parenting, if only it were as easy as clearing an incident scene. Children should come with an instruction manual.

"I'm sorry, Max, but—"

A long steady beep streamed down the hallway behind Evie. The sound ignited a whirl of panic in her mind. It was a screech that accompanied all her nightmares. She'd never forget the wail of death that stole her parents, the scream of a heart monitor as it flat-lined. The loud beep didn't belong here, not in the corridor that led to her sister's lab.

Evie ran down the hall that seemed to spin, toward Shay ... toward the sound of her worst memories.

Gray puffs of smoke gathered around Shay, rising in front of her like a wall. She reached for the barrier of clouds. It wasn't solid like she expected. Her arm went right through, but the smoke didn't part. This place was different than the realm she usually slipped into when unconscious. It had the same stupid clouds, but the air was colder ... emptier.

"Great," Shay said, her voice echoing off unseen walls. "I must be dead."

This was it, home. Her own dimensional holding plain of boredom. This had to be a punishment for playing God with souls that weren't hers to control.

"Shay?"

A soft voice, barely a peep, called out in the distance. It could've been Jenna. Shay would really like to know. If only these damn clouds would part, she could find out.

Anger surged within her, and brought a tingle that coursed

through her veins. It prickled every stitch of her flesh. When the sensation hit her fingertips, the wall of smoke in front of her peeled back. Pillars of gray mist towered at her sides, leaving a clear path straight ahead.

"Shay."

The shout was louder now, definitely Jenna. Shay hurried along the swells of smog, which rolled over each other as an invisible force held them back. An icy breeze blew against her chest, forcing her backward. Her hair whipped her face, and the roaring gusts of wind fought her every step.

"Jenna," Shay cried out, unable to hear her own call above the wind's howl. Fingers wrapped around her wrist, and someone pulled her to the side.

Into the wall of clouds Shay went; blind, except for the shimmer in the air. There was no cold here, no heat. It was strange, to exist yet feel absolutely nothing at all.

Just when Shay thought she might cry or giggle, the haze shrank back and Jenna stood before her. They both smiled, at almost the same time. When Shay moved in for a hug, Jenna leaned back.

"No time for your mushy shit," Jenna said. "We gotta move." She pointed over her shoulder then latched onto Shay's arm, pulling her forward.

In between running and swatting smoke, Shay glimpsed a giant metal sphere hovering overhead. Two red lasers beamed from its shiny surface, like evil crimson eyes. It scanned the ground below, racing through the fog after them.

"Left," Jenna yelled.

Before Shay could think, Jenna yanked her to the left. She almost ate clouds, but her feet found traction and cut to the side.

"Wait." Shay jerked her arm but Jenna held tight, only slowing the mad-dash to a crazy sprint. "That's the thing. Your way out."

That stopped Jenna in her tracks and Shay collided with her back.

"You did it?" Jenna asked, her voice quavering.

Dread. That what Shay saw in Jenna's stare, sheer dread.

"You wanted me to, right?" Shay took Jenna by the hand. "Please tell me you wanted me to."

"No. I do. I just thought I'd have more—"

A creak cut off Jenna's words as an oversized nanobot burst through the clouds. Its red laser struck the ground. The glow bathed the fog in a scarlet glimmer, growing brighter as the huge silver ball zigzagged closer.

Shay flinched when Jenna's arms wrapped around her body. She wasn't expecting a hug but sure could use one right now, so she hugged Jenna back.

"Things got away from me," Jenna whispered. "I'll have to leave them behind. Forgive me."

"I don't understand."

"Me neither." Jenna kissed Shay on the cheek then shoved her back. "Run, that way."

Jenna pointed at the clouds beside Shay, which floated in front of more clouds.

"I don't see anything," Shay said.

"There's a portal. It'll take you back, but you have to go now."

"Go where?"

A nanobot whirled to a stop midair just behind Jenna. The enlarged sphere, which had been microscopic when Shay injected it into her body, crept closer to Jenna. Its hum vibrated the air, and more nanobots glinted as they cut through the clouds in the distance.

Jenna smiled as she backed away from Shay. "It's been real."

There was a hardness in Jenna's expression. It was a brave front; Shay could tell by the tremble in Jenna's fingertips. The nanobot's bright red laser beam flooded over Jenna. She waved goodbye to Shay as the laser pulsed around her.

Shay shielded her eyes, backing away from the flashes of crimson light. A portal hid somewhere out there in the fog, a gateway to her awaiting body. She should be sprinting through the clouds, but she couldn't leave Jenna to face this alone.

Two more nanobots zoomed in from one side, three more floating in from the rear. A cascade of lasers fell over Jenna. Her body was lifted into the air toward the massive bots floating overhead.

Time seemed to slow as Jenna rose off the ground, farther away from Shay. A hint of hope shined in Jenna's eyes, clouded by the mounds of terror.

The lasers around Jenna surged. Its flash brought tears to Shay's eyes, but she didn't look away. Though she could no longer see Jenna beyond the light's glare, she wanted to hold a confident stare, just in case Jenna could see her.

In the brief moments when the pulsing red light dimmed, Shay glimpsed a whirlwind of sparkles drift up the wide laser beams. Those glittery flecks were Jenna. They glistened and spiraled toward monstrous silver orbs in a graceful dance.

A true superhero was ripped to atomic particles and sucked into nanobots. Then, she was gone. Every speck of Jenna Reagan had been swept from this hellish world of gray clouds within Shay's mind.

Jenna had done more in her seventeen years than most people could experience during an entire lifetime. Knowing that didn't soothe the ache in Shay's chest. Jenna had been taken too soon.

"I'll miss you," Shay whispered as a warm tear streaked along her cheek.

The red laser beams shifted, right to Shay's chest. She jogged backward, and a pack of giant nanobots floated after her.

"Crap." In a squeal of sneakers, Shay turned from the flock of soul-thirsty bio-computers and ran into the clouds.

Evie stepped inside the lab and her legs locked in place. She refused to believe what she saw. Her body had known, her mind had been expecting, but her eyes wouldn't process the sight of her sister lying dead on a cold steel table.

Hetal zapped Shay with a defibrillator. Shay's body flopped against the table it lay still upon and Evie turned away. She didn't have to look. The relentless shriek of a flat-line reminded her that Shay was dead, that her reason for living was over.

"What happened?" Max yelled as he ran past Evie. He bent over Shay, breathing into her mouth.

"She's dead," Evie sputtered. She was caught in the middle of the room, forced to stare at Shay's pale skin, limp fingers … empty eyes.

"No!" Evie ran to Hetal's side. She grabbed Hetal by the shirt and shook. "Bring her back."

"I'm trying." Hetal dropped the defibrillator's paddles and jammed a wide needle into Shay's chest.

"What is that?" Max asked between the breaths of air he breathed into Shay's lungs.

"Pure adrenaline." Hetal tossed the empty syringe aside and fumbled for the paddles, their wires tangling. "I just need one good jolt to her heart."

Max pushed Hetal aside and slammed his fist against Shay's chest, directly over her heart.

A violent quake knocked Shay to her knees. She tried to push herself back to her feet, and another tremor dropped her face down in the clouds. Lightning struck the ground beside her, so close its heat singed her skin.

Shay climbed to her feet. The six giant nanobots that chased her now swerved wildly through the air. They crashed against each other, bouncing off the cloud-strewn floor. Hetal must have hit her body with the defibrillator, because the nanobots were shorting out and they were on an uncontrollable rampage toward her.

"Double crap." Shay ran. Hard jolts rocked the ground, knocking her off balance, yet she kept going.

Two nanobots slammed together right above her head. Metal grinded and sparks showered onto her shoulders. A loud crash shook the ground, which split beneath Shay's running feet. She peeked behind her and all the oxygen swept from her lungs.

It took her a few seconds to grasp. See, it wasn't every day a person watched giant fiery nanobots roll toward them, but that happened today and it was happening to her.

Shay pushed her muscles until they scorched, sprinting faster across the ground that disintegrated below her feet. Gusts of blistery wind nipped at her back. She could smell her hair burning, which totally pissed her off and drove her to run faster.

Behind Shay, nanobots bounced into each other like pinballs. Every collision shuddered her body, and widened the fissures spreading along the ground.

A fire-laced breeze parted the clouds in front of Shay. Amid the gray plumes, a hint of color shined. It had to be the portal.

The smog cleared the closer she got to the shimmer. It was a portal. A small circle of white light tore through dimensional walls, growing smaller by the seconds. It sat midair, like a mirror attached to clouds. Its surface rippled, yet it showed an image of herself lying dead on a table clearly.

An explosion blasted, ringing in Shay's ears. Six flaming nanobots raced toward her, on all sides. They groaned, growled, reflected her fear off their dented curves.

Shay dove headfirst for the portal. Nanobots smashed against one another, lightning splintered out in thick bolts, and a burst of flames propelled Shay into a glass-like image of herself.

Silence clung to the lab. It had only lasted seconds, but in that time Evie couldn't breathe, think, or even move. Then, high-pitched beeps rang out from the heart monitor beside Shay. They were strong, quick, a symbol of her sister's heart beating.

Evie waited for Shay to sit up and say something quirky, but the body on the table still looked dead. Her sister didn't move, except for the tiny rise and fall of her chest.

"What's wrong with her?" Evie looked at Hetal. The woman was supposed to be a genius, but all Evie saw was a frightened girl in a lab coat.

"I don't know," Hetal said, her voice wavering. Metal clanked as Hetal pushed instruments around on a small tray. She lifted a large magnet in one hand and a giant needle in the other. "I have to complete the procedure."

"The hell you do." Evie pushed Hetal back from Shay, but Hetal returned for seconds.

"I have to," Hetal yelled.

Evie shrank down. She was a bit shocked to hear that fierce tone rumble from such a mousey girl.

"If I don't finish, Shay will kill me and then try this again." Hetal held the magnet to the back of Shay's neck and inserted the needle beside it.

"What did she do to herself?"

Hetal glanced at Evie. In the seconds their eyes connected, Evie glimpsed a deep sorrow.

"Shay injected herself with nanobots." Hetal removed the needle from Shay and held it up to the light, peering into the syringe's glass tube. "To collect Jenna's soul. There's six here. I got them all."

"Did it work?" Max asked, staring at the needle in Hetal's hand.

"Did she know?" Evie almost choked on her words but she forced them out of her lumpy throat. "Did Shay know she could die?"

Hetal placed the magnet and syringe on a tray, her stare caught on the floor. "Yes. We also anticipated the possibility of permanent brain damage."

"How could she be this selfish?" Evie slapped her hand over her own mouth. Damn these words, which just kept flying at liberty from her loose lips.

"She's not—" Hetal took one look at Evie's harsh glare, and the temporary courage she displayed fizzled out.

"She did it for Jenna," Hetal mumbled, softly.

"Jenna? Shay doesn't even know Jenna. I'm her sister. I need her."

Evie closed her eyes in attempts to stop her tears, but they gushed out anyway. She couldn't do this. The person in charge couldn't lose it, not in front of the team. She had to get out of this room, then she could sob uncontrollably somewhere in private.

By some miracle, her wobbly legs carried her backward toward the lab's door. She turned to run and crashed against Simon's chest.

"Evie?" Simon placed his hand on Evie's shoulder. "What's wrong?"

Both Simon and Alexie stared at Evie in confusion, which she could handle. It was the sympathetic gazes to come that would cripple her.

She shrugged out of Simon's grasp and ran down the hallway. The elevator door came and went, yet she kept going. She didn't know where this narrow corridor led, and she didn't care. She just had to get away.

"Wait," Simon called out but Evie didn't stop. She couldn't, not while tears flowed down her cheeks.

"Evie." Simon grabbed onto Evie's arm and yanked. The force of his super-strength lifted her feet off the ground and she crashed against the wall.

"I'm sorry," he said with a shaky voice. He looked more stunned to have thrown Evie across a hallway than she felt to have been thrown across it.

Evie wiped her eyes then straightened her top. She was actually thankful to Simon. If he hadn't flung her against a wall, rage would've never rushed in to mask her misery.

"I'm used to being manhandled by your kind."

"Oh." Simon took a step back from Evie. "I'm sorry about that, too. I guess."

Simon placed his hand on Evie's shoulder, slow and gentle. "What happened to Shay? Hetal rambled some nonsense about nanobots."

"Your adversaries are gone," Evie said, in the strongest voice she could muster up. "They'll never see the light of day again. There's no reason for the SPU anymore. I'm going to pack our stuff and have Shay transported to a hospital."

Every muscle in Evie's body shook as she attempted a firm stance. Her raised chin and confident stare had been executed rather well in her opinion, considering the last forty-eight hours. She headed back toward the elevator and Simon blocked her path.

"No. Stay." Simon grabbed onto Evie's hand, his fingers trembling. "I can have any medical equipment you need brought in. Specialists too. You want a neurosurgeon, a cardiologist? I'll fly them in on my corporate jet."

Evie pulled her hand from Simon's clutch. It was an amazing offer, from Mr. Amazing himself. Once he found out what Shay had done, that she wasn't harboring their fallen friend's soul any longer, he wouldn't need them and the amazing offer would go away. She'd rather speed up the process. It'd be best to part ways now, before she grew any more attached to the trio than she'd already become.

"Jenna's soul isn't inside Shay anymore. You don't need us here."

Evie weaved to step around Simon and Simon bobbed, barring her escape.

"I don't care about that. I care about you and Shay. You guys are like family."

Family. It sent chills through Evie. She couldn't remember the last time she heard that word used in relation to herself and Shay.

"Really?"

Simon took both of Evie's hands into his own. "Really," he said, and the faucets behind her eyes turned on again.

Beside Shay, Evie had no one. There was no one for her to turn to when she needed advice, not a person other than Shay she could trust. She missed comfort, missed having a family.

"I'd be lost without you guys," Simon said. He pulled Evie into a hug, and she fell against his chest. "I feel like I could tell you anything."

Simon's body grew stiff, his breath ceasing to flow for a moment. "I'm gay."

The declaration came out of Simon's mouth in a puff, one that rustled Evie's hair. She drew back from his embrace, finding a wide grin on his lips.

"Woo," Simon belted out, chuckling. "I never told anybody that before. It felt great."

"Umm." Evie searched for the right words, but her mind was thoroughly blown. "Good for you. I'm honored you told me first."

"Yeah." Simon nodded. His smile faded and he leaned close to Evie. "Don't tell anyone, okay?"

Simon, the strongest man in the world, had become a bundle of nerves. His dread was uncalled for. She'd take his secret to the grave—not because he called her family, but because it wasn't her secret to share.

"I'll never tell. I swear."

"Come on." Simon took Evie by the arm, ushering her toward the lab. "Let's go find out what we need to bring Shay back."

32

For three days, Max sat at Shay's bedside. She hadn't woken up, or moved a muscle since they revived her. Doctors had come and gone, tests were run inside their specially designed hospital room within the lab.

The many specialists Simon had flown in were useless. They spouted out crap like: *There's nothing medically wrong with her. It's unexplainable.* His top pick for a most ridiculous prognosis had been: *Her mind will awaken when it's ready.*

He'd finally convinced Evie to take a break from hovering at Shay's bedside. The woman hadn't showered in days, and with no windows in the lab it was in everyone's best interest she left for a bit.

Max leaned his elbows onto the bed in front of him, staring down at Shay. "How you doing today?"

As expected, the soft beep of a heart monitor answered his question. He felt stupid, like he was talking to himself. That's why he only did this when Evie slept, or the seconds he could score alone with Shay. This was a rare treat, one he'd take full advantage of.

"I have something for you." Max pulled a worn copy of Dante's *Inferno* from his pocket, which he had "borrowed" from Shay's desk.

"Evie said this is your favorite book. I was gonna read it to you but I can't figure out if it's happy or sad, and I want you to have happy thoughts right now so—"

Max sat up straight. He could've sworn he just heard a murmur flow from Shay's mouth. Over the steady beep of a heart monitor, and with Hetal yelling at her second batch of failed stem cells, it was hard to tell.

"Evie …" It was low, horse, and choppy, but Shay's voice slurred from her chapped lips.

The legs of Max's chair scraped the floor as he jumped to his feet. He bumbled in a circle for a good few seconds, unable to decide whether to step toward Shay, Hetal, or the phone. He'd spent hours imagining this moment, and now that it was here he didn't know what to do.

"Hetal!" Max's own shout startled him, shuttering his bones. "Call Evie."

Metal clanked to the floor across the room. As Hetal ran for the phone on the wall, Max dropped to his knees beside Shay's bed. "Evie's on her way. Can you hear me?"

Shay's head rolled toward Max. Her arm flopped against the mattress, which sent a burst of joy running through his body. He grabbed Shay's hand, pulling it to his chest.

"Can you open your eyes? Open your eyes, Shay."

"Max?"

"Yes. It's me." He might have squeezed Shay's hand a little too tight, but her eyes fluttered open so he counted it as a win.

He'd feared he'd never stare into Shay's soft brown eyes again. When he did, his smile spread wider than he thought possible.

"There you are." He brushed a strand of hair from Shay's forehead. "You had us worried."

"Why? What happened?" Shay's voice grated with each drawn out word. Max reached for the pitcher of water on the workbench behind him, but she tugged him back to her side. "Where am I?"

"In your lab. Evie wanted you in the suite, but Simon insisted we set everything up in here." Max gestured at the makeshift hospital room, surrounded by a thin blue curtain. "Since you love this place."

"The nanobots." Shay sat up, looking over her shoulder. "They're not there."

"No. Hetal got them all. I think. Hetal," Max yelled. "Get over here."

"I'm coming." Hetal slid the curtain back and walked straight to the EKG machine on the workbench.

"Did her finger twitch again?" she asked, scanning the printout of spiked lines.

"No," Shay said and Hetal jumped with a start. "My whole body twitched."

"Shay." Hetal bumped Max aside to dive into Shay's arms. "You suck." She hugged Shay tight then drew back and slapped Shay on the arm. "I thought you broke your brain."

"I might have." Shay rubbed her head, groaning. "The jury's still out on that one."

Hetal tossed the blanket off Shay, which fluttered Shay's short hospital gown. "Are you paralyzed? Wiggle your toes."

"My toes are good." Shay covered her bare legs, glancing at Max. "It worked. I got Jenna's soul."

"*I* got Jenna's soul," Max said. He pulled a small vial from his pocket. Tiny specks of metal clinked against the glass as he held it out for Shay to see.

"Wow." Shay took the vial, holding it front of her eyes. "They were so much bigger when they were inside me. I can't believe Jenna's in there. It seems highly insignificant for a person so ..."

"Loud-mouthed," Max said through a snicker.

"I was gonna go with extraordinary, but yeah. We have to set her free." Shay put the vial in Max's hand and closed his fingers around its cool surface. "How many hours have I been out?"

"Hours?" Max said. He shoved the container back into his pocket, keeping his hand wrapped around the thin glass that held the remnants of his first love. "It's been days."

"Days? Where's Evie?"

"I'm here." Evie sat on the bed, hugging Shay. "I knew I shouldn't have left, but stupid Max insisted."

"Good thing too," he said. "Your stink would've thrown her into another coma."

Evie ran her hand along Shay's cheek. "Are you all right?"

"It was incredible," Shay said, and Hetal shook her head while mouthing the word *no*. "The nanobots were ginormous, and I watched Jenna break away into sparkles."

Hetal waved her hands, lightly jumping behind Evie.

"What?" Shay looked at Hetal, who shrunk down.

"I think she's trying to warn you," Evie said, glowering at Hetal over her shoulder. "Because I ... am furious."

Shay leaned back against her pillows, her eyes wide. "Oh?"

"You're grounded," Evie yelled, standing so she could cross her arms.

"What?"

"For, like, ever."

Shay sat up straight in her hospital bed, narrowing her stare on Evie. "For what?"

"For being reckless. For preforming experimental procedures on yourself without permission."

"But. I freed the tormented soul of a superhero, using nanobots."

"I don't care." Evie walked to the workbench of medical equipment and picked up a keycard. "Your lab access is going to be restricted, and it's back to school with you, miss thing."

First Shay's fingers clenched, then her teeth. Max knew the indicators for an enraged outburst, and Shay exhibited them all. It was a clear sign for him to inch away from her bedside.

"That's not fair." Shay slammed her fists against the mattress and a gust of orange wind blew out from beneath her hands. The fiery breeze rippled as it shot out in a circle around the bed, and knocked everyone who surrounded Shay flat on their backs.

"Whoa," Hetal cried out. She sat up on the floor, smoothing down her hair.

"What was that?" Evie asked, climbing off the floor.

When Max rose to his feet, he found all eyes on him. Even Shay looked at him for answers and she was supposed to be the expert scientist, who did this to herself.

"That was Jenna's solar slap," Max said. "But I don't know why Shay has it. Jenna's supposed to be in the nanobots, in my pocket."

"It got away from her," Shay mumbled, more to herself than anyone in the room.

"What?" Evie placed her hand on Shay's forehead then neck. "I think we should get a doctor in here, have you examined."

Hetal stepped beside Shay's bed, nodding. "She has been disoriented."

"No, I have not." Shay glared at everyone, even Max whose only crime was standing back to gawk. "Jenna is in the nanobots. She told me she had to leave some things behind, it must have been her powers."

"How?" Evie sputtered.

"Their powers are just a super-charged form of energy," Hetal said, eyeing Shay like a shiny, new invention. "The first law of thermodynamics is conservation of energy. The powers themselves would have bonded with the most suitable host, for preservation."

Max tried to process all that, but Hetal might have been speaking French for all he knew. He needed someone on his level.

"I'm calling Simon." Max pulled out his cell phone and tapped the picture of Simon's smug face.

"I have superpowers," Shay said, staring at her palms. "Oh no. I have superpowers." Her brow scrunched as she looked at Evie.

33

Shay was in the same packed courthouse where her life took a turn for the strange, looking at the same stern-faced judge. Only, this time, she stood at the front table beside three superheroes, getting star-struck grins from the judge as *she* spoke.

"That's quite a tale," said the judge, closing his file. "And how are you adjusting to your new powers, Shay?"

Shay just stared at the bald, round man, who practically swam in his oversized black robe. This question. The lawyers, Evie, even her new publicist had prepped her for this question, and it stumped her every time.

To say having superpowers was freaking awesome would only be true on some days. Mostly, she blasted holes in walls when she sneezed then threw crybaby fits about it, only to have the curtains in her bedroom burst into orange flames.

"I think I'm adjusting well," Shay said with a firm nod. "I've been working with Simon on power control, Alexie taught me basic self-defense techniques, and Max …"

She looked at Max, the guy who took off two weeks ago without so much as a goodbye. The no phone call, text, or email guy who she thought fell off the Earth. Same one who still hadn't spoken to her since his reappearance on the courthouse steps this morning.

"Everyone has been very patient with me."

"Your honor," Simon said, pausing to smile for the cameras. "Shay Sinclair is a bright, honorable young woman. With a little more training, I have no doubt she'll become an exceptional superhero."

The judge smiled until his gaze landed on Evie, then he glowered. "And how is your guardian treating you? I know Ms. Evie Sinclair can be unrealistic and a bit of a grandstander. If you're unhappy with her parental role, we can reevaluate your custody order."

That question Shay didn't need to think twice about. "No sir. I love my sister; she's the best guardian I could hope for."

"I see." The judge opened the file in front of him, jotting a quick note. "And the people, with this energy signature?"

Evie opened her own file. "We administered thorough examinations to forty-five-percent of them. None have exhibited unusual abilities so far. We're hoping they're all just regular people with a harmless genetic abnormality. Of course, we'll need to continue interviewing the remaining fifty-five-percent."

"Indeed," said the judge as he wrote in his file. "Okay. I hereby grant the requested authority to the Superhero Policing Unit, under the command of Evie Sinclair. You're required to send me a monthly report, including details on Shay's progress."

The judge lifted his hard stare to Shay. "I expect you back at school once your powers are under control. If you take one step out of line, young lady, there will be consequences. Understand?"

"Yes sir."

"Just one more thing." The judge's chair creaked as he sat back and clasped his fingers together. "The supervillains, Antiserum and Dr. Mayhem, where are they now?"

Heads turned in a line, ending on Evie.

"Gone," Evie said, her chin high. "Forever."

Once the paparazzi got their shots and everyone settled back at Ling Enterprises, Evie snuck out the front lobby and into an awaiting sedan. A quick drive across town and she was in her warehouse, riding the elevator down to her forgotten underground base. Hope had driven the creation of this facility, strange how it ended as a dwelling place of despair. At least it wasn't her misery trapped thirty-foot underground. That privilege was reserved for the man who betrayed her and his maniacal brother.

Evie stepped off the elevator. She walked through the ghostly command center of her nearly abandoned SPU headquarters. The lone agent on guard duty nodded at her. They always nodded at her when she came here, which happen more and more these days. It'd be crazy for her to miss Cyrus, even crazier to want him back, which was why she constantly told herself she didn't.

Lights flickered on, gleaming off white walls as Evie walked down the narrow hallway. When she turned the corner, her feet skid to a stop. She still couldn't get used to the sight of Cyrus and Lucius suspended in blue liquid, asleep inside tall glass cryotubes.

It took a little mental scolding, but Evie finally got her legs moving forward. The wide-open room stretched out before her, dark and empty except for the blue glow of cryotubes.

She pressed her palm against the cool glass of Cyrus's containment tube. He had a gentle face, her doctor of mayhem. It was a quality that made him all the more dangerous.

"I found out today that you're conscious in there," Evie said, staring at the wisps of black hair that floated in front of Cyrus's still face.

"You can imagine how surprised I was. We had to dump you two in here before the trials were complete but when the test subjects emerged, they said they experienced it all. That it was torturous not being able to see or move, only listen as time slowly whittled by."

Evie's shoes clanked, their tap circling the spacious room as she strolled around the cryotube. The awkwardness that used to come from looking at these two naked men had long passed. She'd spent far too much time staring at the cuts of muscles rippling on every inch of Cyrus's body to be squeamish around people in the buff.

"I'm sure you've realized by now that I would *never* have said all that crap about still loving you if I'd known you could hear me. You can disregard that while you're stewing on your mistakes for an eternity. Because I also found out you don't age when you're in that goo."

Evie walked from the eerie glow of two lone cryotubes amid an empty room. A pang nicked her heart every time she spoke cruel words, even to supervillains, but she'd overlook the ache for Cyrus. As long as his betrayal weighted on her heart, kept her from trusting another man, she'd lash out on him.

"Enjoy your stay," she said, strolling into the hallway.

Shay pushed open the door to the roof of Ling Enterprises and poked her head outside. There he was, Firestorm, in his favorite spot—leaning over the edge of a building.

"Hey," Max said, without moving a muscle or glancing at Shay. "How you been, really?"

"Good." Shay walked onto the roof and the door slammed shut

behind her, which sent a flinch to jolt her bones. She stepped beside Max, but his gaze remained stuck to the vial in his hand. "How about you?"

"I was gonna set her free, but I didn't know how."

"You could've called." Shay looked at Max, finding his stare on her. Those deep eyes, she'd almost forgotten the sway they held in real life.

Heat rose in her chest, sizzling. If she didn't chillax, solar rays could shoot from her fingertips and pulverize half the city. Typical teenage girl problems.

"I'm sorry I took off on you guys like that." Pieces of broken rock crunched under Max's elbows as he shifted against the stone wall that bordered the rooftop. "I needed some time alone, to figure stuff out."

"I get that," Shay said, even though she didn't. It sounded nice. She'd like some time alone to figure stuff out. Hell, it took two lies just to shake Alexie and get on the roof.

"It was, just, kinda weird how you ran out of the room and left town the second you found out I had Jenna's power."

"I didn't leave because of that." Max stayed slumped on the roof's thick wall, rolling the vial in his hands. "There were things I needed to … learn about myself. I wouldn't have been able to do that here, with people buzzing in my ear."

That Shay did get. The shower and bed, those were the only times of peace she got since her and Evie moved into Ling Enterprises.

"It's cool. You don't have to explain yourself to me." Shay pointed at the vial in Max's tight grip. The glass looked worn, scratched. He must have spent a lot of time holding that thing, staring at it.

"You sure you're ready to let her go?"

"Yeah." Max handed Shay the vial, without hesitation. "I want Jenna to be free."

Shay unscrewed the lid and poured the tiny nanobots into her palm. She called upon the power Jenna left behind inside her, and focused it on the nanobots that held Jenna's soul.

Strands of orange wind swirled above Shay's hand. The light gusts swept the bits of metal off her skin. She flicked her finger and the bots shattered to dust.

An orange-tinged breeze carried the specks away. Sunlight hit the broken pieces of nanobots, and cast a rainbow of glistening light over the city as the sparkles whirled toward puffy clouds.

In Shay's mind, and inside her body, Jenna had left a while ago. But to Max, the ache must be fresh. The look on his face screamed to the world, letting everyone know agony lived in his heart.

"I have to tell you something." Max looked away from the sparkly dust that glided across the sky and gazed into Shay's eyes. "I've thought about this a lot. I want you to live a normal life, with normal experiences. Go to parties, date boys your own age. All that stuff."

"Have you been talking to Evie?"

Max grinned, even though sadness gripped his expression. "Evie did say some things to me that made a lot of sense."

"And this is what you want me to know?"

"No." Max took a step closer to Shay then shuffled two full paces back. "I want you to know when you're done doing all that stuff, I'll be waiting for you."

He smiled at Shay as he backed toward the roof's door. "Even if it takes ten years, I'll be waiting for you."

Shay tried to speak but her throat clamped shut. Max opened the door and walked away, leaving her alone with his words. That dude sure knew how to make an exit. Too much, it was way too much for Shay to take in.

She tilted to the side and let herself fall over the roof's edge. An icy breeze ran through her hair, clearing her mind as she plummeted past the many windows of Ling Enterprises. No thoughts, no Evie, no Max, just the rush of falling free and the heat inside her chest.

The street raced closer as she plunged downward, but she wasn't afraid. An unnatural energy surged beneath her skin, and every fiber of her being told her it'd protect her no matter what came her way.

A sensation of bliss overcame Shay's mind, just as a bright orange orb flared out to surround her body. She launched toward the sky, leaving a trail of rippling light in her wake. Her giggle echoed off the tall buildings she soared past. Never had she felt this free, clear-headed, and connected to the pulse of the Earth.

Shay dropped straight down in a spiral roll as she buzzed the front of Ling Enterprises. *This* she could get used to.

Her fist shot out, body stiff as she flew full-speed above Liberty Street. The downdrafts between each building swayed her from side to side, and the force of flying bunched her clothes. She could see the logistics behind a skin-tight suit and a cape now.

In a burst of solar winds, Shay rocketed through Gemini City. The orange-laced cyclone around her kicked up the bits of trash strewn along the crowded streets below, and her laugh bounced off the gleaming skyscrapers above.

The End

Acknowledgements

I'd like to acknowledge the everyday heroes: the police officers, firefighters, and first responders. These brave men and women run headfirst into danger to save others and keep their communities safe. They are real-deal heroes and I'd like to thank them for their service.

As always, I'd like to thank my awesome family (including my farm family). Their support and encouragement is what keeps me going.

Big thanks to Georgia McBride and everybody at Month9Books for continuing to have faith in my writing. She, the editors, cover designers, and marketing team have worked tirelessly to get my words out into the world.

I only have one critique partner, but she's worth a million. Thank you, Kaelan Rhywiol. You are an amazing author, an irreplaceable friend, and a beautiful person. It's an honor and a pleasure to be riding shotgun with you down this bumpy road of publishing.

Last but definitely not least, I'm sending many thanks to my friends in the #amwriting community. The interactions we have on Twitter brighten my days and remind me I'm not alone in this wild writer's life.

−xoxo

Jamie Zakian

Jamie Zakian lives in South Jersey with a rowdy bunch of dudes, also known as family. A YA/NA writer, her head is often in the clouds while her ears are covered in headphones. On the rare occasions when not writing, she enjoys blazing new trails on her 4wd quad or honing her archery skills. She's a card-carrying member of the Word Nerd Association, which means she's probably stalking every Twitter writing competition and offering query critiques so keep an eye out.

OTHER MONTH9BOOKS TITLES YOU MIGHT LIKE

THE SPONSORED
YELLOW LOCUST
STANLEY AND HAZEL

Find more books like this at http://www.Month9Books.com

Connect with Month9Books online:
Facebook: www.Facebook.com/Month9Books
Twitter: https://twitter.com/Month9Books
You Tube: www.youtube.com/user/Month9Books
Blog: www.month9booksblog.com

THE
SPONSORED

DON'T BREAK THE RULES.
DON'T FOLLOW YOUR HEART.
DON'T GET CAUGHT.

CAROLINE T. PATTI

Neither quick fists nor nimble feet can save Selena Flood, a fighter of preternatural talent, from the forces of New Canaan, the most ruthless and powerful of the despotic kingdoms around.

YELLOW LOCUST

JUSTIN JOSCHKO

STANLEY & HAZEL

BY JO SCHAFFER

A dark discovery.
A forbidden relationship.
A dangerous path.

A great depression has gripped the city of St. Louis in 1934. Stanley, an orphaned newsy and son of a police detective lives in a poor part of town hit especially hard by the economic downturn. One night, Stanley runs into Hazel, a restless debutante in waiting who has begun to question her posh lifestyle in the midst of the suffering she sees. She's out and about without an escort and against her wishes. ... body of a girl with her head ... very different—and ... from their ...

But getting involved with each other and digging into the secrets behind this murder alerts them to some powerful enemies, including a secret group seeking to rid society of all those they deem "undesirable." They've put into motion The Winnowing, a plan sealing to take over the city and enforce their will.

As Stanley and Hazel's forbidden feelings for one another grow, their lives depend on ... Now it is up to Stanley and his gang ... to keep her before it's too ...

CPSIA information can be obtained
at www.ICGtesting.com
Printed in the USA
FSHW01n1804080718
49991FS